SAMUEL LYLE
CRIMINOLOGIST

"There it is just as we found it, mud and all!" he
exclaimed

SAMUEL LYLE
CRIMINOLOGIST

BY

ARTHUR CRABB

ILLUSTRATED BY
S. C. COLL

Fredonia Books
Amsterdam, The Netherlands

Samuel Lyle:
Criminologist

by
Arthur Crabb

ISBN: 1-4101-0764-7

Reprinted from the 1920 edition

Fredonia Books
Amsterdam, The Netherlands
http://www.fredoniabooks.com

CONTENTS

LIST OF ILLUSTRATIONS

SAMUEL LYLE
CRIMINOLOGIST

SAMUEL LYLE
CRIMINOLOGIST

A PLEASANT EVENING

ONE Saturday in October Hugh Ladd, Norman Dean, James Norris, and Frederick Scott had finished a lunch at the Lanning Golf-Club in Hopedale. Jimmy Norris stood at the window. "It's raining harder than ever," he said. "It's auction for us."

They played steadily until five o'clock, when John Harden came in and joined them. Within an hour Andrew, a waiter, said that Mrs. Norris was outside. Frederick Scott said good-by and went out by way of the locker-room, and Jimmy drove away with Mrs. Norris, followed by Hugh Ladd and Norman Dean in Hugh's car. They saw Harden walking down the drive toward Lanning Road.

Sunday afternoon at two o'clock Sam Walker and Arthur Smith, with Sam's dog, went into the wood which begins about a quarter of a mile from the golf-club. They were wandering about

3

when the dog began barking furiously near a large pile of brush. Scenting sport, they investigated. An instant later they were running to Arthur Smith's house. They had discovered the body of John Harden.

Arthur's father telephoned to the police in Hopedale, and the chief made his plans promptly; he told Mr. Smith to stay where he was and keep the boys with him, telephoned Inspector Gibb of the " Murder Squad " in Alden, and ordered one of his men to take to the woods every available man. The chief knew that the murder of John Harden would shock the whole country, for John Harden was a great financier, and the chief wanted to be sure that no act of his should be open to criticism later on.

Inspector Gibb, too, with four of his men, was there within an hour and found the woods surrounded by men who allowed no one to pass who had no business there. There was good reason for this, for footprints might be a most important clue. Inspector Gibb's men found footprints before they had been there ten minutes, and they were measured and photographed and their peculiarities noted in the most elaborate detail.

Harden's body lay in a small clearing, fifty feet to the right of a path which ran from Lanning Road to almost exactly opposite the drive to Harden's house. Harden always took that short cut to and from the club. Only two evergreen boughs had been thrown over the body. Death had been caused by a blow with a blunt instrument having a knob on the end. The knob had struck just over Harden's right ear, and the shaft of the instrument had crushed the skull across the temple to the eyebrow; the police surgeon said that Harden had been dead about twenty-four hours.

One of Inspector Gibb's men went to the Harden house and learned that Mrs. Harden was away and that Harden himself had told the servants he would not be home for dinner Saturday night. They said that it was not unusual for him to come home and dress and go out again. No one ever sat up for him, and thus his absence Saturday night had not been noticed. Neither was his failure to return unusual, for he sometimes stayed away all night without warning, playing bridge very late and going to bed wherever he might be.

By the time Gibb's men returned a crowd had gathered on Lanning Road and the news had reached Hugh Ladd in Stockton. Hugh telephoned Norman Dean and Jimmy Norris, went for them, and drove to the woods. Within ten minutes they had told Inspector Gibb of Harden's leaving the golf-club for his house at about six o'clock the night before.

"He never got there," the inspector said.

Then a man rushed up, holding in his hand an engineer's single-head wrench, about a foot long, found near the path. A quick examination proved that the wrench, a terrible weapon, fitted exactly the wound in John Harden's skull.

Norman Dean felt a trembling hand on his arm. "What's the matter, Jimmy?" he asked.

"Matter? It's terrible!"

And hardly had he spoken when another man came up and whispered to the inspector. Suddenly the inspector wheeled about.

"Was any one else with you at the club yesterday afternoon?" he asked.

"Yes, Fred Scott."

The inspector motioned to them and, removing the covering from a footprint, said:

"Isn't that the print of a golf-shoe?" They nodded, and the inspector said: "I thought so. Look at the name on this." And there, staring up at them, were the letters "F. Scott," stamped into the white paint of a golf-ball.

"That was found just the other side of the path," the inspector said.

For a moment there was utter silence, then Norman Dean laughed.

"Nonsense!" he exclaimed; "that doesn't mean anything. A caddy dropped it here. Scott left before we did and went in the other direction; he could n't have had anything to do with it."

"Perhaps not; we 'll see. Where did he go? Where is he?"

"He went to the Grants', in Pitcoe. He told me he was going away to-day for a day or two." Jimmy Norris's voice was husky.

"Where does he live?"

"At the Alden Club."

"Will you come with me to the golf-club?" They nodded. The inspector gave orders to his men, and the four sped to the Lanning Golf-Club. There the inspector called Orchard 20, and gave orders as to Scott's rooms at the Alden Club. Then he went to Scott's locker, and found in it a pair of golf-shoes covered with dried mud; and every one of them knew that those shoes had made the prints around the brush pile in the woods, for not only did the shoes have nails of the same number and arrangement, but the corner of one rubber heel had broken off and that missing corner was distinctive in the prints.

"Do you polish shoes here?" the inspector asked a locker-boy. The boy nodded.

"Have you cleaned these lately?" The boy said he had cleaned them on Wednesday or Thursday.

"Has he used them since?" the inspector asked.

The boy thought not, and Jimmy Norris muttered that Scott had not played golf since the previous Tuesday.   Then the inspector examined the contents of the locker carefully, but apparently he found nothing that interested him.

They went to a card-room and the inspector asked: "What time did you leave here Saturday night?"

They talked it over, and in the end they were sure that they had left the club at almost exactly five minutes after six and that Fred Scott had left five minutes earlier. Hugh Ladd remembered that he had reached home just as the clock in his hall was striking six-fifteen. The clock was five minutes slow and he had noted the fact because he was regulating it. It took him fifteen minutes to drive from the club to his house.

Jimmy Norris, when he had reached home, had noted the time because of some reason connected with dressing for dinner. Norman Dean was sure that it had been just six o'clock when word came that Mrs. Norris was outside; it would undoubtedly take about five minutes to settle accounts, get their hats and coats, and go out to the cars. There was no question that it had been five minutes after six when they left.

"And where did you say Mr. Scott went from here?" the inspector asked.

"To Pitcoe," Jimmy said, "to the Grants'. He is engaged to Miss Grant."

"You said he was going away. Has he gone?"

"I don't know. My recollection is that he said he was going to-day."

"Will you call up and find out?"

Jimmy's eyes flew to Hugh's and then to Norman's. Poor Jimmy! He was younger than the others and had no such ability as they to hide the agony that was in their hearts. Inspector Gibb was closing Freddie in a net — Freddie, who was pretty nearly his best friend — and there were things he knew that the inspector had n't found out, and when the inspector did: *when he did* — Suddenly something snapped in Jimmy's brain, and the big fact was as clear as crystal.

"Look, here, Inspector," he cried, "Fred did n't do this; he could n't do it. It 's all a mistake; he 'll come back and explain about the shoes and the golf-ball and all the rest."

The inspector's gray head nodded slowly. "I hope so, I hope so, but we 've got to follow things up. Call up the Grants' and see if he 's there, and if he 's not, find out when he left and where he went. You can do it better than I can."

Jimmy went to the telephone and called the Grants'. Frances Grant answered and said that she had taken Frederick to the three-o'clock train for Chicago that afternoon.

"Ask her what time he reached her house last night," the inspector whispered. "Ask if he was late or something, so as not to make her think anything is wrong."

Jimmy asked the question as best he could.

"He got there at ten minutes of seven, she says. He promised to be there at half-past six, but she had to forgive him because he had a puncture on the way."

"How far is it from here to the Grants' house?"

"Ten miles," Jimmy said.

"And there's a good straight road all the way, is n't there?"

"Yes."

"What kind of car has Scott?"

Jimmy named the car, which was large and high-powered.

"And he drives fast, does n't he?"

"Sometimes," Jimmy admitted.

The inspector stood with his mouth tight shut and his eyes half closed. Suddenly he said:

"I guess that's all, here, to-night. But tell me, what sort of walker was Harden — fast or slow?"

"Rather fast than slow, I should say," Hugh answered.

The inspector walked to the front door, looked at his watch, said good-by, and walked steadily till he came to the clearing. It took him just eight minutes.

Back in the Lanning Golf-Club the three men sat overwhelmed by the terrible thing that had happened and the awful revelations that had followed. They sat in silence for a long time, till Norman Dean almost shouted: "It's all damn nonsense. Fred never did it; he *could n't* do it."

Hugh Ladd smiled. "Did that brilliant idea just occur to you, old top?" he asked, and Norman laughed.

"What fools we've all been!" he said.

But Jimmy Norris did n't laugh. There was agony in the boy's face.

"Will you stick by him," he said, "no matter what happens? He's pretty nearly alone in the world and he may need friends."

"I'll stick to him till hell freezes over," Norman said. "It's absolutely impossible that he should have done it."

"We three'll see it through if trouble comes," Hugh said.

"You mean that *whatever happens* you won't go back on him?" Jimmy's voice was uncertain.

Both men nodded to him.

"Then," Jimmy muttered, "the wrench that Harden was killed with, or its exact duplicate,

was on the floor of Fred's car when he brought
me out here yesterday, and on the way he said
he believed that Harden had been trying to break
him."

For an instant there was a deathly silence, a
silence that Norman Dean broke.

"I imagine a lot of men in Alden won't shed
any tears when they hear about it. Harden was
a powerful and merciless man. He tried to
monkey with my business once; he and I settled
that alone in a little room." Norman smiled
grimly. The others could guess what had happened in the little room. "So," Norman con-
tinued, "when it comes to a motive, the same one
would fit fifty men in Alden. I suppose they'll
dig into Fred's affairs to find something definite,
but it's a wonderfully fine thing to have such
absolute faith in a man that, no matter how black
the evidence against him is, you know he's lily-
white."

"Which means that we tell Gibb it was Fred's
wrench that killed Harden?" Jimmy Norris
asked.

"Of course," Hugh Ladd said. "The truth
can do no harm, and hiding facts may. There's
some explanation of it all, but, just to be on the
safe side, we'll get Sam Lyle to look after Fred's
interests."

"And we'll get him this very minute," Norman exclaimed. He went to the telephone and called Mr. Lyle's house and Mr. Lyle's man said that his master was out of town, but where he did not know. Norman damned the luck.

"I'll find out from his office to-morrow," he said. "He'll come at once if he possibly can. There's nothing more we can do now."

They went home, and when Jimmy Norris had been left at his house, Hugh said: "Bad business, Norman."

"Very bad, but I can't believe it."

"No, of course you can't, nor can I, and there's one thing that looks hopeful. Fred could n't very well have left the club at six o'clock, gone to the woods, waited for Harden, killed him, gone back to the club, changed his shoes and changed tires when he had a puncture and gotten to the Grants', in Pitcoe, all in fifty minutes. Why did n't we think of that before?"

Inspector Gibb had thought of that point. When he found that it took him eight minutes to reach the clearing he knew that Harden had died at about six-thirteen. Allowing five minutes for hiding the body and eight minutes to return to the club, Scott would have reached there at six-twenty-six. Four minutes for changing his shoes would leave him twenty minutes in which to drive ten miles, which would be a simple matter in Scott's car on that road.

But the puncture? Inspector Gibb thought the puncture needed looking into.

The inspector learned that Harden had been robbed, for his watch and money were gone. For an instant he was in doubt as to what that meant, for it was inconceivable that Scott would steal. Then he understood.

"A blind," he muttered.

The inspector gave his orders, went back to Alden, and telephoned the police in Pittsburgh to take Frederick Scott into custody when his train arrived there.

On Monday at two o'clock the three friends of Frederick Scott walked into Inspector Gibb's office. The inspector wasted no time on formalities.

"I'm going to be frank with you, gentlemen," he said. "I take it that what you want is the straight of this business, just as I do. It looks bad for Scott, everything's against him, but I'll give you all the chance in the world to help him if you'll do the same by me. We've tried to find him and have n't done it. Do you know where he is?"

They said that they knew only that he had gone to Chicago.

"He did n't even get to Pittsburgh," the inspector said. "I had the train searched, and he was n't on it."

Jimmy Norris interrupted and told the inspector about the wrench.

"I know all about that," the inspector said. "He bought it, or one exactly like it, Saturday morning, for your green-keeper, and did n't give it to him, and it was n't in the car at Pitcoe."

Then Norman Dean said that it was impossible for Scott to have done it, for there had not been time.

"He left the club at six and got to the Grants' at ten minutes of seven; it would take him fifteen minutes to change the tire that was punctured and —"

"He did n't have a puncture," the inspector interrupted. "He punched a hole in one of the spare tires and let the air out through the valve. Miss Grant took Scott to the station in his car and on the way back stopped at the garage and left the tire. It had been repaired before my man saw it. He had the tube taken out and examined the hole that had been patched. There was n't a nail in the shoe when it got to the garage; Miss Grant says she pulled it out Sunday morning. Perhaps she did; he could have driven in a nail easily enough. She said, too, that he had rolled up the curtains, to explain taking so much time to reach Pitcoe." The inspector shook his head. "I tell you, it looks bad."

"If Fred would only come back!" Jimmy Norris was pretty nearly all in. "He could explain it all; there's some terrible mistake somewhere."

The other men glanced at one another sadly. They were nearly as sorry for Jimmy as they were for Scott.

"Is that all, Inspector?"

"Yes, except one thing. Do any of you know how much money Harden had on him Saturday night? I know that he probably had as much as a thousand dollars. Did he have more than that?"

They did not know; he carried a great deal.

"There's nothing more," the inspector said, "except to find Scott. We'll have him before long."

"Don't worry, he'll come back without being asked to," Jimmy exclaimed.

Hugh Ladd patted Jimmy's shoulder. "Don't worry, son; lots sicker cats than this one have gotten well." Hugh wished he was sure of that.

They talked for a few moments and then Norman Dean telephoned his office.

"Lyle will be here to-night," he said.

"So," muttered the inspector, "you've got *him*, have you? If any man in the world can get Scott off, he's the one."

"Except Fred himself," Jimmy Norris said.

That night at half-past eight the three arrived
at the Lanning Golf-Club. As they entered the
house, Andrew, a club servant, took their coats
and hats, a matter of dull routine for him ordi-
narily, but to-night a ceremony. The steward
came and asked in whispers if there was any
news; the servant hovered round, wide-eyed and
intent.

They went to one of the card-rooms, where
there was a fire. Jimmy Norris picked up a pack
of cards, subconsciously thinking of solitaire, but
he started suddenly and put them back in the
drawer and closed it. Hugh and Norman sat in
big chairs, slumped down, their heads dropped
forward, biting hard on their cigars and glancing
at the clock on the mantelpiece. There was not
a sound in the room but its tick-tock, tick-tock.

Lyle came at nine.

Samuel Lyle — a simple, kind-hearted elderly
bachelor — was Alden's ablest criminal lawyer.
He was a huge man, awkward as a man could
well be, and so homely that he was fascinating.
His hair was thin and gray. His nose was large
and bent downward toward his lips. His mouth
was very large and his lips were almost always
moving, as though they were never able to find
a comfortable position. His jaw was heavy, his
chin projected well forward, with just enough
tilt to suggest that it was pointing toward his

nose. Yet, however homely of feature he might be, his face was remarkably attractive; for the lips that always moved seemed always ready to smile, and his eyes, small and far apart under their shaggy brows, twinkled kindness and good nature. His normal voice was very low and wonderfully modulated and except on rare occasions he was very slow and methodical of movement. There was about him a subtle suggestion of force, of keenness of mind, and of honor.

Sometimes, when there was apparently no reason for it, Mr. Lyle seemed to be nearly asleep, his eyelids dropped, his hands hung limp, his head was bowed, and his lips became quiet and drooped a little. I think that it was an unconscious pose and that it came when he was thinking hard, oblivious to his surroundings.

As he entered the room the three stood facing him, and he smiled and nodded to each. He took a cigar from the table and turned a chair so that it faced the three other chairs.

"Pretty serious business, this," he said.

"Very," Norman muttered, "very, indeed. We want your help. Do you know the facts?"

"Only what I have read. Suppose you tell me the whole story."

Lyle sat down, his clothes wrinkling all over

him as he slouched in the chair. Norman Dean told the story, and during the long recital Lyle showed not the slightest emotion. He smoked as though his cigar were his only care in the world, his eyes were half closed as though he dozed, his huge hand lay motionless on the arm of his chair. When the story was finished he seemed almost to be asleep.

"That all?" he asked, very softly.

"Yes, I think that's all," Norman said.

"Very complete strand — I don't like 'chain' — of circumstantial evidence, isn't it, if Scott actually did drive a nail into one of his spare tires? Very clever to think of that, wasn't he?" Lyle turned to Jimmy Norris. "You can't tell whether or not two of the tires were actually interchanged, can you?"

Jimmy shook his head. "No, they're all cord tires, and all nearly new. All I know is that he had two spares."

Lyle stood up and shook his clothes into place.

"I'll take another cigar, if I may," he said, and turning to Norman: "Might I have a glass of water, say Apollinaris or something of the sort?"

Norman rang a bell. Andrew the waiter came, and the Apollinaris was ordered. Lyle lighted his cigar and, walking to the fire, pushed the logs together with the toe of his boot. Then he turned to the three who sat dejected in their chairs.

"And what motive has been discovered?"

They were explaining the possible motives when the door was opened by the waiter, bringing Apollinaris. He filled the glasses and passed them to the four. Then he wrote the check and Lyle reached for it and was about to sign it when he laughed.

"I almost forgot," he said, "that my name is n't good here." He handed the check to Hugh Ladd, who signed it.

The waiter was at the door when Lyle spoke to him. "Just a moment," he said, and then to Norman: "Might I see Scott's golf-clubs, do you think?"

Norman turned to the waiter. "Bring Mr. Scott's clubs here, Andrew, won't you, please?"

Jimmy Norris got up and banged a fresh log on the fire. What on earth did any one want to look at golf-clubs for now?

"If something does n't happen pretty soon," he said, "I 'm going clean raving mad. I 've known Fred Scott for years, he 's one of the best friends I 've got, and I know damn well he did n't kill Harden or anybody else. All this circumstantial-evidence stuff is rot; it can't be true. Some —"

Again the door opened and the waiter came in, this time with a bag of golf-clubs. Mr. Lyle took them and, without more than glancing at them, rested them against the table. The waiter went out.

"We were speaking of motives, I think," Lyle said. "You say Scott hated Harden thoroughly. I imagine he had good reason to, but I know nothing definite. I suppose if there was anything specific, it will be discovered, and in the meantime you want me to think up some way of getting this precious friend of yours off. Naturally he did it: the evidence you have given me is conclusive in your own minds, is n't it?"

"There's some explanation of it all. Fred could n't do it; it 's utterly impossible!" Jimmy Norris exclaimed.

"And you think the same way, Hugh; and you, Norman, don't you?"

"Yes," Hugh said. "Scott could n't kill a man."

Lyle raised himself up and down on his toes before the fire.

"I think I understand the circumstances clearly," he said, "but there are one or two questions I want to ask. You know the path through the woods well. Are there bushes along it?"

Norman answered: "There is a clearing in the woods where Harden's body was found; it is on the right of the path, walking away from here."

"Exactly. The path is on the extreme left of this clearing. Are there large trees or bushes on the left of the *path* at that point?"

"There is a large oak, but no bushes," Norman said.

"And you say Scott left at six o'clock. Did you see him go?"

"We saw him go to the locker-room, which is the shortest way to the sheds."

"But you did n't actually see or hear him leave?"

"No, we would n't. He would go out the back road; it is more direct and easier driving."

"Nobody else saw him leave in his car, I suppose?"

"No, no one saw him."

"And no one saw him come back?"

"No. There was no one in the locker-room after about quarter of six. The two locker-boys had gone home and Andrew was in this part of the house. Andrew is the waiter that came in here. He has charge of the locker-room on busy days; at other times he 's a waiter."

Mr. Lyle turned to Jimmy Norris. "You say Scott's car was equipped with new cord tires. They do not puncture easily, do they?"

"No. But one of them *did*. Fred says so."

" Did he say where he changed the shoe? Did
any one see him, or anybody, changing a shoe
along the road? "

" No one has been found who did."

" All the curtains of his car were down when
you reached here from town, and up when he
reached the Grants'? How long do you suppose
it would take to put them up? "

" Two or three minutes, perhaps."

" And how long does it take to change a shoe? "

" Fifteen minutes, probably."

" So if things happened as Scott said, it took
him fifty minutes, less fifteen, less three — that
is, thirty-two minutes to drive the ten miles to
her house.   Actually I don't believe that he could
put up the curtains and change the tire in
eighteen minutes.   I think it would take nearer
twenty-five. But that is not important. What
is important is that there was a nail in the tire.
If it got there naturally, Scott certainly did n't
have time to kill Harden, return here and change
his shoes, change tires, and get to Pitcoe, all in
fifty minutes. If the nail was not picked up,
Scott must have driven it into the tire. He was
very clever if he did that; very clever indeed.
Did the punctured tire show signs of having been
driven through mud? "

" The car was washed, tires and all, early Sunday morning, by the Grants' man. He does n't

remember anything about the tires, except that one was flat."

"That's too bad, if Scott is innocent," Lyle said.

"He is innocent, don't worry about that," Jimmy Norris said, as though he were giving the lie to every man in the room.

"He's got to be innocent," Norman Dean said. "Anything else is beyond belief."

"What are we going to do?" Hugh asked. "There is something wrong somewhere. We want you to tell us what we should do."

"That's a nice mid-iron." Lyle had walked to Scott's bag and taken a club from it. "You're sure these are Scott's clubs?"

"Yes, those are Fred's, right enough," Jimmy cried; "but what has that got to do with it? If something does n't happen pretty soon, I 'll kill somebody myself." The strain was tearing his nerves to pieces.

Lyle paid no attention to him, but took the clubs from the bag, one by one, looking at them with apparent indifference.

"Nice clubs," he said, "but about twice as many as I use." Then he brightened up a little, as though he had suddenly remembered the important matter.

"Is there a telephone near?" he asked.

There was a telephone in a dark corner of the

"Nice clubs," he said, "but about twice as many as I use"

room. Mr. Lyle called his number, and in a
moment said, " Miss Grant! " and explained who
he was and who were with him. " Have you the
nail you took from the tire on Mr. Scott's car? "
Apparently Miss Grant had not.

" But you did take it out with pliers, did n't
you, while you were waiting for him? You
meant to show it to him, but something distracted
you and you forgot it. What did you do with
it? "

Miss Grant had thrown it away, for Mr. Lyle
said :

" Are you sure you threw it away? Are you
sure you did n't save it, unconsciously perhaps,
to show Mr. Scott? Is it in your pocket, or if
you are sure you threw it away, do you think you
could find it? "

Lyle waited with the receiver at his ear. " It
would be most remarkably good luck if that nail
should be found," he said, " provided, of course,
Scott did n't kill Harden. She has gone to look
for it. I rather think she had a sudden inspiration."

Hugh Ladd threw the end of his cigar viciously
at the burning logs.

" I have a first-hand knowledge of what hell
is," he said. " If that boy has done this thing,
I shall never trust —"

" Yes, yes, Good! " Lyle spoke into the telephone. "Found it in the pocket of your sweater. What sort of nail is it?"

The nail was described, for Lyle repeated: "A rusty wire nail, badly bent. Is it rusty all over?" There was a pause. "Just the nail part, the head is quite bright. Is the head smooth or scratched?" He listened a moment. "I understand, it is both smooth and finely scratched. Good! Look at it again and tell me whether there is any sign of a little ridge across the top of the head, or any breaks in the edge. None, you say? Good, again. Keep that nail safe, and dry."

Then Lyle listened, saying "Yes" and "No" over and over into the telephone. He was just about to hang up when he heard an exclamation over the wire. He put the receiver to his ear again, listened, and then said: "All right, I'll wait." Then he spoke to the others: "There's something going on over there."

The room was as still as the grave. They waited and waited. A log fell in the fire and Hugh Ladd jumped. Suddenly Lyle snapped the instrument upward; his eyes sparkled and his teeth clicked together. There was news coming over the wire.

"Come here as quickly as you can, both of you, and bring the nail. Don't lose a minute," he said.

He hung up the receiver and turned back to the room.

" Scott and Miss Grant will be here in less than half an hour," he said. " He has just reached there, undisturbed."

Mr. Lyle took up the telephone again. "Orchard twenty," he said, and the others started as though they had been struck. Ladd leaned forward in his chair.

"Good God!" Jimmy Norris groaned.

Poor Jimmy sat with his arms stretched out before him on the table and his head on his arms. He was breathing like a blown horse; his hair was wet on his forehead.

Orchard 20 answered. " Inspector Gibb, please." There was a moment's wait and then: "This is Samuel Lyle. I am at the Lanning club-house. Can you come at once? " Lyle listened. " All right, in half an hour. Leave your men in the car outside the grounds and get on to the side piazza without being seen. We will leave the shades up in the room we 're in. Tap on the window and come in when we open it." A pause. " Yes, yes, I 'll explain when you get here."

Again Lyle put down the telephone, and again Norman Dean cried: " What does this mean? If you know anything, for God's sake tell us ! "

" You 've told me all I know. We shall have

to wait nearly half an hour before we know anything more, unless —"

"Unless what? Unless what?" Jimmy Norris's voice cracked.

"Unless the wildest guess man ever made
should be the right one. Call your waiter friend
and the steward — they are the only employees
here?"

"Yes."

"Call them here and keep them here, on any
pretext you like, until I come back. I won't be
more than a minute or two."

Andrew was summoned and he in turn brought
the steward. Mr. Lyle stepped out as they came
into the room. He returned quickly.

"I broke into the cigar-case," he said. "I
don't like to sponge, Hugh, but I came away in
such a hurry I forgot cigars."

Andrew wrote the check, Hugh Ladd signed it,
and the two employees went out.

"You know, I have often thought that I should
go into the market," Lyle said. Then he kept
them in suspense while he carefully cut the end
from a cigar, lighted it, and watched the smoke
clouds. "Fine cigars," he said, "much better
than I usually smoke, but it's an occasion; we
are entitled to fifty-cent cigars. As I was saying, I should undoubtedly go into the market.
I have the most wonderful luck guessing." He

put his hand into his pocket, drew something from it, and held it under the lamp.

"Ever seen that before?" he asked. It was a gold watch and a slender gold chain. Harden's initials were on the back of the case.

"Where did you get it?" Poor Jimmy Norris hissed the words at Lyle. Jimmy was getting pretty near the end of his rope, and Samuel Lyle knew it.

"I'm not going to tell you now," he said. "I'm not going to tell you anything. I don't know anything, but if it will soothe you any, I'll bet you ten to one Scott did n't commit murder for that watch."

"I'll bet you a hundred to one he did n't!" Jimmy snapped back.

Mr. Lyle shook his head. "No, but I'll give you three to one that somebody confesses within, say, twelve hours.

"And I'll make a confession to you all, two confessions, on your vow of secrecy. I have a love of melodrama. I cannot resist the lure of the dramatic; my greatest regret is that I am not an actor; I am fascinated by the thrill of a theatrical situation. That is the first confession. The other is that when I make up my mind that I am right, I go ahead, but I never give my reasons. Often I am right; my reasons seldom are. That is as near the quotation as I can remember it. I found the watch; my reasons for believing that I should find it where I did are, more than likely, entirely wrong. It is pretty nearly time our friends arrived; they will drive fast."

Samuel Lyle walked to the card-table in the corner of the room and, taking the cards from the drawer where earlier in the evening Jimmy Norris had put them, he began to play solitaire. Jimmy Norris sat at the table, bending a book backward and forward till the covers cracked.

The minutes they waited seemed as eternity. The clock sang its everlasting song over and over again. Jimmy Norris drank from a pitcher of ice water and then wiped his face with his wet handkerchief. Lyle played his cards without a sound. Hugh and Norman chewed their burned-out cigars to rags.

It was fifteen minutes before they heard a car come flying up the drive. Lyle, without stopping his playing, told Norman if it was Miss Grant and Scott to bring them into the room.

They came in, and Jimmy Norris put one of his hands in Scott's and the other on his shoulder.

"Don't worry, don't worry, Freddy," he cried, "it will come out all right; we're fixing it all up here; all of us. We're having an awfully pleasant evening, old man, awfully pleasant."

Scott smiled: "Lord, but you're a sad-looking crowd! Don't worry! I'm not."

Lyle, still holding his unplayed cards, had
risen and bowed to the girl.

" Did you bring the nail? " Lyle smiled when
he saw it. " It is very precious," he said, and
sat down again at his table, laying the nail before him. He finished a game, shuffled the cards,
and began to arrange them again. " Norris,"
he said, " won't you ask Mr. Scott what he did
with the wrench that you saw in his car? "

Scott did not wait for any repetition of the
question.

" I don't know what I did with it. I remember taking it from the car and going into the
locker-room with it, and that 's all I remember
about it."

" Exactly. I thought that would be about
it." Mr. Lyle moved the cards about. " Don't
tell me where you 've been, Mr. Scott — it is not
important — but how did you ever get back without being arrested? "

" I came just as I always do. I did n't know
Harden was dead till I read to-night's papers on
the train. I met on the train the man whom I
was going to Chicago to see. I left the train at
Pittsburgh, went to a hotel, slept till noon, and
took the first train back."

Samuel Lyle chuckled. " Gibb will be pleased
about that," he said.

There was a tap on the window. Lyle walked

to it and opened one of the French sashes. Inspector Gibb came in.

" I think you know every one here, Inspector, except Mr. Scott. You are undoubtedly very glad to see him. Hugh, I hate to trouble you, but I *am* thirsty again."

Hugh rang, and Andrew came into the room.

" Won't you bring some more Apollinaris? " Lyle said. " Inspector, will you have anything stronger than that? "

Inspector Gibb shook his head.

Andrew went toward the door, and his hand was on the knob when Lyle spoke again.

" Just a minute, Andrew. Before you go won't you tell us who killed Mr. Harden? "

There was a heavy silence. Quick glances were shot at Samuel Lyle, standing before the fire. From him the eyes flew to Andrew the waiter, standing with his hand on the knob of the door, and on him they remained fixed.

He was as if stunned, powerless to move or speak. His long, sad face was of a ghastly pallor. His eyes were motionless, staring at nothing in far, dim space. It was as though an electric current had passed through his body and paralyzed it. The men and the girl waited, waited till suddenly a tremor passed through the man's body and his head turned so slowly that it took a time interminable for his eyes to reach

Samuel Lyle. Then, like the twitching of dying muscles, his arm began to move in sharp jerks, his lips moved as though he were trying to speak and could not, and then his jaw fell and his head dropped forward. For a moment he stood swaying, holding with all his last remaining strength to the knob of the door. Then his knees gave way, and he sank slowly to the floor, his arms spread apart and trembling, his eyes closed, as a sinner sinking to despairing prayer.

They caught him and placed the limp form on a couch. Within a half hour he was taken away.

Within the half-hour, too, Scott and Frances Grant were gone, and the three who had first been there were left with Inspector Gibb and Samuel Lyle.

Lyle took Harden's watch from his pocket and handed it to Gibb.

"It's your job, Gibb, not mine. What has happened here to-night need not be known," he said.

"I don't know what happened," the inspector said, "but it's one on me, that's sure."

"If it were, you could stand it, but it is n't; it was plain guesswork, mostly. There was only one thing that was n't guesswork, and I think perhaps that *is* one on you, Inspector. Harden was struck while he was walking toward home; he was struck above the right ear and across the right temple with the free end of the weapon striking over the ear. For a right-handed man to strike such a blow he must have struck backhand. That was unlikely. The thing that was likely was that the murderer stood on the left-hand side of the path and struck with his left hand. There are plenty of places on the right of the path where a man could conceal himself, but this man chose a spot where there was protection on the left, and as it happened, on the left only. When I saw Andrew write, I knew he was left-handed; when I saw Scott's golf clubs I knew he wasn't, and Andrew had as good an opportunity to do the deed as Scott.

"With that much to start on, the rest was easy. Scott had left the club-house. Andrew had on his waiter's coat, thin shoes, and no hat. Scott was fresh in his mind, and he innocently borrowed Scott's hat, coat, and shoes. The golf-ball later on fell from the pocket of the coat. He saw — probably on top of Scott's locker, but possibly on the shelf inside it — the wrench which Scott had brought in from his car, left there and forgotten. We've all done that sort of thing dozens of times.

"Andrew cut across the lawn and ran on ahead of Harden and was back within a half-hour. He wasn't missed; there was no one to miss him.

"Thus there was a better case against Andrew

than there was against Scott, for everything was
equal except the left- and right-hand part of it.
Andrew probably could produce no positive alibi;
Scott had the basis of one. If he drove ten miles,
changed a punctured tire, and put up the curtains
in the car, he did n't kill Harden — there was n't
time.

"Therefore, did Scott really have a puncture
or did he drive the nail into the spare tire on
the rack? The nail was bent — one does n't
choose a bent nail to drive into a large cord tire;
the nail was rusty — which would prove nothing
were it not for the fact that the head was bright
and scratched and the edges worn smooth. That
a man would prepare such a nail for the occasion is inconceivable.

"As to motive, how quickly a good motive becomes a poor weak thing when the one whom it
accuses is proved innocent! Not one of you
thinks now that Scott had any more reason for
killing Harden than you yourselves had. A
while ago you certainly did; at least your condition conveyed that to me."

Jimmy Norris sighed as a man sighs when all
the troubles in the world are lifted from him.

"Oh, no," he said, " he did n't have any motive,
but coming out in the car he told me that some
day he 'd get that crook if the crook lived long
enough, and would get him good if he had to

knock him over the head with a club. Oh, no,
with that staring me in the face, I could n't think
of any motive at all."

Lyle laughed. " I suspected all evening that
you had something on your mind," he said.
" Have you seen your collar lately? "

" I don't have to see it," Jimmy said, " I can
feel it; it 's just as comfortable as a piece of nice
wet chamois."

" Where did you get Harden's watch? " Hugh
Ladd asked.

" In Harden's locker, in the pocket of a
sweater. Can you imagine a simpler way of disposing of it? Andrew knew he could n't keep it,
and he was afraid to throw it away, and his disarranged brain had an inspiration. Put it in
Harden's locker, and the natural supposition
would be that Harden had left it there. Of
course there is another side to that, but Andrew
was a one-sided man."

" Crazy? " Norman Dean asked.

Lyle nodded.

" And the motive? Imaginary, of course."

Samuel Lyle shrugged his shoulders. " That
would be too much guesswork, and there 's been
enough guessing for one night." He spoke as
though it would not be guesswork at all. " But
I 'll venture this much: Andrew saw Harden take
a thousand or more dollars in bills from his

pocket when you settled for your auction. My
impression is that it was not so much that he
wanted the money himself as that he did n't
want Harden to have it. Let me know if you
find it, won't you? But I 'm afraid that it has
been destroyed or given to some society or charity
before this. I 'll take you along, Inspector, if
you like. Did you ever see a more vivid por-
trayal of a tortured conscience than when
Andrew broke down? It 's been a very pleasant
evening, has n't it? "

"By the way," Jimmy exclaimed, " I owe you
a hundred dollars."

Samuel Lyle shook his head. "No, son," he
said, " it 's been, as I said, a very pleasant evening. To profit by it would spoil it. Good
night." And he stepped into his car.

The three stood staring after him.

"I suppose it has been a pleasant evening, in
a way, after what went before, but one is enough
for me," Norman Dean said.

"One is plenty," said Jimmy Norris.

AMONG GENTLEMEN

HAVE you ever in all your life read a love story, a short modern love story, that did n't turn out happily, at least so far as the story takes you in the life of the hero and heroine? You have n't, unless you 're an editor or a reader for an editor and therefore, in either case, don't count, for I 'm talking about love stories that see the light of day and are blessed with a large circulation.

Therefore, Friend Reader, and Mr. Enemy Editor, know that this is not a love story, and don't take it for granted that, no matter how dark things look along the way, at the end the sun will come out by hook or crook; maybe it will and maybe it won't, there 's no guaranty either way, and with that made plain, we 'll explain about Virginia and Richard Morgan.

Have you ever wondered how a girl like Virginia ever crosses the great divide, the gulf that lies between her youth and innocence and independence, her reserve, her clean-cut dignity, her modesty, and her confession to a mere man that thereafter, forever and ever, he is her whole life, that she is his, body and soul? In other and less frilly words, how does a girl like Virginia finally fall in love and then admit it to the party of the second part?

With many girls falling in love is, of course, an everyday affair; if the said party of the second part reciprocates, the matter is concluded; if he does n't, she mends her heart overnight and looks about for another p. o. t. s. But Virginia was not that sort of girl.

Do you remember the light haired boy who played tackle for Yale six or eight years ago; the one with the jaw that shot out a little on the bias and was square at the end, and who had all the courage that could be crammed into one boy; whose voice was low and who was as modest as a boy can be; whose blue eyes twinkled and whose smile was a thing of joy, and whose heart was as big as a barrel? Of all her four brothers Virginia looked most like this one, freckles and all. She had shoulders like his, and she was as like him, from beginning to end, as a girl may be like a boy. She was tall and strong, straight as a string every way, sweet as honey, and a good, lively, happy, and lovely young woman generally.

Virginia, being the fifth child with four Yale brothers coming before, had a fancy for things Yalesian. She yelled for Yale, danced at Yale, teaed at Yale, was saturated with Yale. Droves of Yales, men and boys, paid her homage and remembered her with pleasure, regret, or broken hearts, as the case may have been, but not one of all that horde, passing before her from her short-dresses days even until she was twenty-six, stuck. Not one of them quite suited Virginia, and she loved not — she did n't, honest — not a single, solitary one of 'em, even for a day. Virginia was saving all her love for the final man and not wasting any of it along the way.

Yale was n't to blame; things like that happen, and there 's no explaining it — there undoubtedly are, and undoubtedly have been, very decent fellows in Yale. My being from Harvard does not prejudice me in the least. But you can't get around the fact that Richard Morgan was a Harvard A.B., and that when one evening in July — when she was twenty-six — Virginia went out to dinner and saw him, she had then and there, on the spot, a sensation that she had never experienced in her life before.

During the evening she saw Richard looking at her once or twice in a most peculiar manner, and she felt his eyes on her all the time. At the end of the evening he told her that it was very easy for him to run down to Naylor's Point for the week-end and put up at the hotel, and that he 'd like to do it, if, being there, he might see something of her.

It was no idle business, that, and Virginia

knew it. Something had happened, something serious; she knew it by that queer feeling inside her and by the way Richard spoke and by his eyes. She told him that of course he could see her if he came to the Point, and when she reached home and was alone in her room she stood before her open window a long time looking out into the darkness where she could n't see a blessed thing.

Three weeks from that evening Richard proposed marriage to Virginia, and she refused him, absolutely, emphatically, and with no equivocation whatever.

Richard grinned, which displeased Virginia greatly. "Just the same," he said, "I'll stay round, if you don't mind. If I'm very respectful and do exactly what I'm told, can we keep on being friends, even if I'm impossible as a husband?"

"Of course, if you want to," Virginia said, and Richard stayed round, and for the life of her Virginia could n't evade him nearly as much as she wanted to.

By the first of September Virginia's father, mother, and four brothers had investigated Richard's past life, his family, his prospects, his character, reputation, and various and sundry other details, for Virginia was very precious and must be guarded with infinite care. Not one of the six could find a thing against him except that he was a graduate of Harvard and all that that implied.

I, Sam Hicks, am no reader of maidens' hearts, but if I had to guess I'd say that Virginia knew perfectly well that first of July evening what was going to happen to her, and I'd give long odds, maybe a hundred to one, that if on the evening Richard proposed marriage to her, she was n't perfectly sure that Richard would make the same suggestion to her again and again and again, if necessary, she would have said "yes" then and there, or at least given him much cause to hope.

But the fact is that well along in September Virginia had not said "yes," and Heaven knows she had had plenty of opportunity to say it if she'd wanted to. Why she did n't say it, if she was ever going to, I don't know for sure, but I have a hunch that Virginia looked upon marriage seriously and was not going to rush into it without full consideration; likewise she was a woman of fine spirit and had no intention of admitting that any man could sweep her off her feet in an instant, and again it is quite possible that she was well aware that she would lose nothing in Richard's eyes by being a little difficult. Furthermore, and I may be wrong, perhaps Virginia did n't love Richard.

Be that as it may, that was the status quo when the story, *which is not a love story*, began.

On a Saturday morning, late in September, I

arose at an unearthly hour, dressed quietly,
kissed Mrs. Hicks good-by, stole two bananas and
a glass of milk from the refrigerator, and drove
away from our humble cottage by the sea. It
was foggy, so foggy that driving was difficult, not
to say dangerous, but the hour was early and I
had faith that the day would be fine.

I drove forty miles to the cottage of Harold
Child, my brother-in-law, and there breakfasted
with him and his good wife Hope. Thence
Harold and I went on to the Indian Island
Country Club, which lies not far from Naylor's
Point. Waiting for us were a cousin of mine,
one James Norris, and a cousin of Harold's,
yclept Frederick Child. The occasion was one
of magnitude, being an annual event; to wit,
thirty-six holes of golf to decide the family championship. There was only one drawback, a
minor item, that detracted from my interest in
said family championship, and that was that
Harold and James played normally below eighty-
five, whereas when I achieved a score below
ninety I was greatly pleased. But that has
nothing to do with the story. What has to do
with the story is that when we reached the club
it was drizzling and it took all our optimism to
convince ourselves that it was going to clear and
not get worse. Notwithstanding the drizzle, we
found Richard Morgan and Virginia there, but

considering the advisability of playing. With them were Virginia's brother, Arthur Morse, and Mrs. Arthur.

We dressed and set forth, meeting as we went down the steps Mr. John Bowers, Mr. Samuel Lyle, Mr. George Ballin, and Mr. Grosvenor Hewitt. They made twelve golfers at the club that morning and all of them but one are, or are to become, characters in this tale, and eleven are too many for any well-conducted story. But there they are, and it is n't my fault, so the best I can do is to ask you to try to keep them straight as we go along.

It had stopped raining. We played two holes, and then it began to drizzle again, two more and it began to rain, two more and it poured without restraint, and at the tenth hole we quit in disgust and, soaked to the skin, beat our way back to the club-house. Incidentally, the storm kept up all day with not a moment's let-up.

We were sad as well as bedraggled. The day was gone, and that day came but once a year. We changed into dry clothes and spread out our wet ones to dry. Some one said that we could play after lunch, but our optimism had gone up in smoke; 't was a sad world, very, very sad indeed, and it proceeded at that moment to get sadder.

The Child — we call Harold that, more or less

— had been digging through his black bag. He stood up and searched through all his pockets and then examined the pockets of the coat and knickerbockers he had just taken off; likewise he looked through the locker he had used. "My pocket-book is gone," he said finally and stood there with that utterly foolish expression a man has when he is confronted by a most unpleasant fact and does n't know what to do about it.

"I left it in the pocket of my bag," he explained.

"Which is a blamed silly place to leave it," the precious Frederick said. "How much was in it?"

"Sixty dollars and a lot of papers that I 'd hate like thunder to lose," the Child answered.

"Finder may keep the money if he will return the papers," Freddy suggested lightly, and then, feeling a bit sorry for Harold, he added: "Are you sure you put it there?"

Harold was, and gave us a few details. He had got sixty dollars the afternoon before, three tens and six fives, nice new ones, and had n't spent a cent of it. He remembered distinctly taking the pocket-book and some loose papers from his coat pocket and putting them on the bureau when he went to bed the night before. He remembered distinctly putting the pocket-book in his pocket that morning and leaving the

loose papers behind, and he was absolutely sure
that he had put the pocket-book in the side pocket
of his black bag when he dressed for golf.

We suggested to the Child that he call Hope
and see if the pocket-book was n't on the bureau
at home.   He did.   It was n't.   Of the four of us
only Jimmy Norris was a member of the club,
therefore Jimmy was troubled.   Technically we
were Jimmy's guests, and it 's not the thing in
the best clubs to permit one's guests to be robbed.
Jimmy was very sure that it was up to him to
do something about it, even if Harold had not
used the best judgment in the world when he left
so much money in his bag.

Jimmy decided that the only thing to do was
to report the matter to the steward.   The
steward heard the story and, being up to date,
passed the buck; he went straight to the table
where four gentlemen were playing auction,
spoke to George Ballin, and in a moment Mr.
Ballin arose and joined us.   Mr. Ballin was
chairman of the house committee, and the buck
was undoubtedly where it belonged.

I told you that this was n't a love story, and it
is, of course, perfectly clear by this time that this
is a detective story.   George Ballin knew that it
was his duty to do all he could to discover the
thief.   Sixty dollars is not a matter of great
moment, but the harboring of a thief is, and Mr.

Ballin knew that he must do all he could to discover the thief. This meant that he must for
the time being become a detective, a profession in
which he had had no experience whatever, and in
which, therefore, it is reasonable to suppose he
had no skill. He was quite aware of the difficulty of the task which confronted him and perhaps that is why he asked Grosvenor Hewitt for
help. Mr. Hewitt was a close friend, an able
man, and an influential member of the club.

Thus we all went to the locker-room and looked
over the ground. There was n't much to see. It
was a long room with double tiers of lockers with
benches between, bath-rooms, lavatories, and the
typical appurtenances of an up-to-date club.
There were two entrances to it, one by the stairs
from the first floor and the other a door at the
end which, with the aid of some stone steps, led
out of doors in the general direction of the home
green. It was a rule that no club servants except
the locker-room attendants should enter the
locker-room, for the possibility of valuables being
taken from lockers when players were on the
course had been considered, and as a result
waiters, caddies, and other employees were
strictly forbidden to enter that part of the house.

Thomas, whose last name had long since been
forgotten, had been in charge of the room for
years. During the season he had several assist-

ants, but then, with the summer gone, he had but
one boy under him.   When we reached the room
it was just twelve o'clock and Thomas and the
boy were both there.   The boy was young, possibly fifteen, and he was sitting in a corner clean-
ing and oiling shoes when we arrived; also he was
whistling happily as though he had n't a care in
the world.   His blue eyes were frank, and I am
sure that every one of us was absolutely sure that
Eddie — that was his name — would cut off his
right hand before he would steal a cent.

Perhaps George Ballin did not go about his investigation skilfully, but he certainly went about
it directly.   He asked Thomas whether he had
seen any one in the locker-room that morning
except the members.   Thomas was sure that he
had not, and further that no one else had been
there except himself and Eddie.   Then Mr.
Ballin told him that some one had taken Mr.
Child's pocket-book.   Thomas's surprise was
written clear as day on his face, and he said, with
all the respect he could, that he did n't believe it.
He said that the back door had been locked all
morning, except when he let us in, that he and
Eddie had not been out of the room after we
arrived, and that not a soul but members and
their guests had been there.

"And," Thomas added, " I 'd trust the boy as
I 'd trust myself."   He called Eddie, and Eddie

confirmed everything that Thomas had said, and his manner proved beyond all shadow of doubt that he knew nothing of the affair.

It is quite evident that I, Sam Hicks, know as little of telling detective stories as George Ballin knew of playing detective — a fact which I shall immediately prove by saying that Thomas and Eddie were correct in their statement that none but the members, guests, and themselves had been in the locker-room that morning.

You can easily imagine that George Ballin had run head first into a stone wall. Either one of the members or one of the guests had stolen Harold's pocket-book, or it had n't been stolen at all, his memory had played a trick on him, and he had left his pocket-book somewhere else than in his black bag.

It was utterly inconceivable that any one of those ten members and guests had stolen or ever would steal sixty dollars or any other sum of money. Incidentally, there were only eight of them, for Harold would n't rob himself, and I was dead sure I had n't robbed him.

On the other hand, Harold was absolutely sure, would gamble his last cent, that he had left the pocket-book in his bag. Jimmy Norris, struggling with the problem, saw a chance for a gamble.

"What will you take for your rights to the

sixty?" he asked the Child, by which he meant
— what sum would the Child accept on the spot
for his right, title, and interest in the sixty
dollars. If it were never found, the Child would
be so much in; if it were found, Jimmy would
get it for the price agreed upon.

The Child was in no frame of mind to trifle,
but he couldn't resist the conventional answer.

"What am I offered?" he asked.

"Ten dollars," said Jimmy.

"Make it fifteen," said Freddy.

George Ballin was annoyed at this talk and
suggested that we go upstairs. We went and sat
down about a table, and the Child begged Ballin
to drop the whole thing.

"I was a fool to leave it there," he said.

"It should be perfectly safe anywhere in the
club," Ballin answered. "Nothing of the sort
has happened here for years — and it mustn't
happen again."

They did a lot more talking; the Child described the papers that were in the pocket-book
as consisting of valuable memoranda, automobile
license cards, and the like. He said also that the
bills had been taken from packages of new money
just received from the bank and that it was quite
possible that their numbers could be discovered.

During the discussion I sat quiet, as was becoming, and my eyes wandered about the room.

In one corner of it were Virginia and her brother, chatting. At a table were John Bowers and Samuel Lyle, forced into solitaire by the desertion of their companions. I knew both of these gentlemen well; they both practised law in Alden, where I live. I waited my chance and then I said: "Why don't you get Sam Lyle to help you?"

George Ballin looked at me in surprise.

"You know Mr. Lyle, don't you?" I asked.

"I just met him this morning. I know John Bowers very well, and he came with him. Mr. Lyle, I believe, knows every one here very well indeed, except Hewitt and me."

"He is our leading criminal lawyer," I said, "and, in a way, he's a sort of superdetective. I'm told he's the leading criminologist in America, and I know he's a great genius at cross-examination. At least he would give good advice if you want to get to the bottom of this business."

George Ballin looked dubious for a moment and then said: "Do you know him well enough to ask him?" I said I did, and I went over to him. He came back with me readily enough, and Ballin told him, rather apologetically, the facts as we had them.

Among his friends Samuel Lyle was a charming man, kind-hearted, jolly, and simple as a

child.   In court or when he was putting together
the evidence in a case he was a holy terror.   His
fame as a criminal lawyer extended far and wide,
and his ability to read the minds and hearts of
men was almost superhuman.   He had undoubtedly won more cases that he should have lost and
lost fewer that he should have won than any
lawyer in America.

And there he was, because he was a genial soul
and a friend of mine, dragged into a case involv-
ing sixty dollars.   He heard the evidence, and
when it had all been presented he looked at
George Ballin hard, with an expression that I for
one could n't read.   Then he turned to John
Bowers, who was a substantial and brilliant
lawyer in our civil courts.

"Heard the evidence, Judge?"   Mr. Lyle
asked.

Mr. Bowers nooded.   "Not guilty," he said.

"Who's not guilty?" asked Mr. Lyle.

"I 'm not," said Mr. Bowers.

"As to that, we shall see.   One of us is guilty,
surely, unless the witnesses are mistaken or per-
juring themselves.   The only question is to decide which of us it is.   It seems to me that that
would be simple, were it not for the fact that the
criminal has probably hidden the pocket-book
somewhere, with the idea of escaping with it
later.   Now that the alarm has been sounded, he

may make no effort to regain it. Does any one of us suspect any other one of us? "

The company was not quite sure whether Mr. Lyle was making a joke of the whole thing or not. We could not get away from the bald fact that the money was gone and that one of twelve men must have taken it. At that minute Thomas came into the room, and at that moment Thomas was all man and not at all a servant.

" It is n't in the locker-room," he said, addressing Mr. Ballin directly but including us all. " I 've been from one end of it to the other, and through every locker that was n't locked, and it 's not there."

" Could it have been thrown through a window? " Mr. Lyle asked.

" No, sir. Every window has a heavy wire screen over it, and the screens are made fast with strong staples."

" You 're sure of the boy who is there with you? "

" Yes, sir, sure. I 've known him since he was born, and I 'd trust him anywhere."

" So would I," said Mr. Lyle. " I talked with him for a minute this morning. He 's out of the question."

There was silence for a moment, and then Ballin said: " All right, Thomas. Thank you," and Thomas went back to his locker-room.

"Of course there can be no question of Thomas? " Mr. Lyle asked.

" No, no, no," Ballin said. " He 's been here for years and we 've had proof of his absolute honesty over and over again."

" I think Thomas can be eliminated," Mr. Lyle said, " and that leaves — us, ten of us. Crossing off Harold leaves nine of us, including the two gentlemen who were playing with the ladies."

" Morgan and Arthur Morse," Ballin said.

Then the Child broke loose. " Look here," he said, " this has gone far enough. If it 's a joke, well and good, but I 'm not going to have my sixty dollars kick up all this fuss. Naturally, none of us took it — there 's some mistake some-where. Somebody — some caddie or servant — slipped in and took it."

" That has been proved impossible," Mr. Lyle said, " and it makes a most interesting situation. Which of us nine men, previously of good reputa-tion, has descended so low as to steal a pocket-book from a man's bag? Again, does any one suspect any one, or has any one evidence that will prove any one else innocent? "

For a moment no one spoke, and then Child Harold, with an attempt at a smile, said: " None of my crowd could have taken it; they went out to the course before I did; they all went to the shower-room before I did and came back after I did. I was the last to finish dressing. I would have seen it if any of them had opened my bag."

" Good! " exclaimed Mr. Lyle. " Very good! Now we 're getting somewhere. We 're down to six. Has any one else any ideas? "

We waited a moment for some one to speak.

" Were you in the locker-room, George, " Hewitt asked finally.

" No, I dressed in my room upstairs, and you dressed with me."

" You see how simple it is if you go at it methodically," Mr. Lyle exclaimed. " That leaves Bowers, the two gentlemen who played with the ladies, and me. I will take my oath, on general principles, that Mr. Bowers did n't take it, and I know that he could n't have taken it for much the same reason that Harold knows his friends could n't have done it. Now we 're down to three. Suppose we ask the gentleman in the corner what he has to say for himself."

Some one called Arthur Morse, and he came across the room. Ballin explained matters to him, and we knew from Arthur's expression that he did n't know whether the whole thing was a huge joke for a rainy day or whether it was very serious.

" Every one has been proved innocent, beyond a reasonable doubt, Arthur, except you, Richard and me," said Mr. Lyle. " Can you give us any information? "

Arthur Morse still suspected an elaborate joke, but decided that if it were a joke he would not spoil it. " I dressed downstairs," he said, " and came directly to this room. You may search me if you like. Unless you suspect me of having a confederate, I could hardly have hidden it. Have you searched thoroughly? "

Mr. Lyle walked toward Arthur Morse, and Arthur, suddenly convinced that it was not all a rainy-day farce, shut his mouth tight and flushed. He was not quite sure that he liked being searched, but in an instant he laughed and held his arms away from his body. Mr. Lyle touched him lightly with his fingers and found nothing till he came to his pocket-book. He held it up so that Harold could see it.

" Not yours, of course," he said, and Harold shook his head.

Mr. Lyle shrugged his shoulders. " I was afraid not. He looks honest. Is there, judge, sufficient evidence to let him join the innocent? "

Mr. Bowers's face was judicial, being severe with a touch of incredulity. " I think that all your evidence is flimsy at best," he said.

" I 'll be obliged if your Honor will answer the question and not edify us with irrelevant comment, and I might say that seldom, if ever, have

I had so good an opportunity of telling the court exactly what I thought of it."

" I believe the term to apply is ' contempt of court,' " Mr. Bowers said. " A repetition of the offense will carry with it a fine of a box of golf-balls."

I did n't know what was going on. Mr. Lyle and Mr. Bowers had seemed serious enough until they began their banter, and then I wondered whether Mr. Lyle was n't making fools of us all, aided and abetted by Mr. Bowers. My thoughts were interrupted by Mr. Lyle. " Ruling, please," he asked.

" I think Mr. Morse may be considered inno-cent," Mr. Bowers said.

" Which leaves 'me and one other," Mr. Lyle said. " Where is he? "

" Richard Morgan? " Ballin asked.

" Yes."

" He went to the Point — took Mrs. Morse home — he 'll be back any minute," Morse said.

" And have had ample time to dispose of the stolen goods — if he, and not I, took them," Mr. Lyle commented. " It 's too late; it can't be pre-vented now. There is nothing for us to do but to wait till he comes back. Then he and I can settle it between us. I suggest that no one leaves the room and that no one be allowed to enter it in the meantime."

There was a scraping of chairs; half of us rose, half of us stayed at the table till one by one that half of us got up and wandered about. I went over and spoke to Virginia — I don't know what fool impulse made me do it. I knew what was going on between her and Richard Morgan, and I knew Richard. I knew Samuel Lyle, too, and I knew that beyond all question he was playing some game. Heaven only knew whether it was serious or whether it was all a rainy-day joke. Somehow I felt that it must be a joke, and yet the facts stared me in the face — some one *had* taken Harold's pocket-book, and I could not conceive of Samuel Lyle, a comparative stranger at the club, making a joke of it when he was asked seriously to advise the officials of the club what they should do about it.

He had, on what was certainly flimsy evidence, eliminated every one but himself and Richard Morgan. I knew that Samuel Lyle was no thief, and naturally, granting for the sake of argument that he was a thief, he would not convict himself. Was it possible that he had some knowledge of the theft that we did not have? If he had, how had he got it? I could make only one guess: it was said that Samuel Lyle could detect guilty consciences and guilt itself by watching a man, by watching his eyes, his mouth, his hands. How much truth there was in it I did n't know:

perhaps there was a great deal. And that brought me face to face with the awful thought that one of those eight men, of irreproachable character, of high standing in the community, might have stolen sixty dollars.

It was impossible! But what was Samuel Lyle driving at?

"What's going on?" Virginia asked me. "You look terribly serious."

"I don't know whether it's serious or not. I hope it isn't. Ask Mr. Lyle — he's the boss." Mr. Lyle happened to be close to us, and Virginia turned to him. Never was I more surprised than when Mr. Lyle, in answer to her question, told her that a pocket-book had disappeared and that it was perfectly clear that either he or Richard Morgan had taken it. For an instant Virginia looked as though she had been struck, and then she laughed.

"Nonsense," she cried. "Tell that to the marines."

"Why nonsense?" Mr. Lyle asked.

"Imagine Richard taking any one's pocket-book!" she cried.

"Then *I* am guilty," Mr. Lyle said, and at that minute Richard Morgan came into the room, and he must have felt the tenseness of the atmosphere, for he stopped near the door and looked about questioningly.

Mr. Lyle greeted Richard Morgan, and then he spoke to us.

"We are all here now," he said. "Suppose we get down to business and settle things, once and for all." And when we were seated around the table he told Richard of the loss of Harold's pocket-book and what had been done since the discovery of the theft.

"It has been sifted down to you and me, Richard," he said. "If you can prove yourself innocent, or if any one can do it for you, I will assume the guilt. I had the opportunity of taking the pocket-book."

"Did any one see me take it?" Richard asked. No one answered, and he said: "I presume some one did n't see me take it. Is that good evidence?"

"Referred to the court," said Mr. Lyle.

"It would be negative evidence only, and in this case, I think, valueless," the court ruled.

"Have you anything further to say in your defense?" Mr. Lyle asked.

"Can I plead previous good character?"

"Not now — save it for later on, if you need it," Mr. Lyle said. "Now, gentlemen, I propose that we play a little game. We will all close our eyes and at a given signal toss our pocket-books on the center of the table. At another signal we will open our eyes and see what we shall see.

Miss Morse will give the signals and see that we keep our eyes closed. Are you ready? My eyes are closed."

I closed my eyes and put my hand on my pocket-book. I heard Virginia Morse move, and then I heard her say: "Now." My pocket-book fell with the others on the table, and Virginia said: "All right."

I opened my eyes and saw a pile of pocket-books on the table. I looked at Mr. Lyle and saw that he was looking at Harold.

"Is your pocket-book, the one that was stolen, among those on the table?" he asked. The blood rushed to Harold's face and his jaw set hard. "From your expression I take it that it is," Mr. Lyle said. "Which one is it?"

Harold picked up one of the pocket-books — it was brown and almost square. "This is mine," he said.

You could have heard a pin drop. It was perfectly evident that one of the men around that table had had Harold's pocket-book in his possession and had got rid of it when every one's eyes were closed.

"Will you examine it?" Mr. Lyle said. Harold opened his pocket-book and took from it three ten and six five-dollar bills and laid them on the table. They were all new and clean, as he had described them.

"So," muttered Mr. Lyle. "I am not surprised; I expected something of the sort. Does any one wish to confess to having had Mr. Child's pocket-book in his possession?"

Never in all my life had I been in such an awful silence. Mr. Lyle had slumped down in his chair until his clothes lay in rolls all over him; his chin was on his breast, his eyes half closed, his lips still and drooping, his hands flat on the table.

Finally he said: "As apparently no one wishes to confess, does any one object to having his own pocket-book identified?" Again no one spoke. "Then suppose we ask Miss Morse to do it." He made room for her between himself and Richard. Virginia laughed.

"It's as good as a circus," she cried, and if her gayety was assumed she was a clever actress indeed.

Of course it was apparent then what Mr. Lyle had in mind. Each of us had, when all our eyes were shut, thrown one pocket-book on the table, except Harold, who had had none. Now, if each pocket-book was returned to its owner from the pile, one of those men would find no pocket-book waiting for him and that man must be the one who had thrown Harold's on the table. In his anxiety to rid himself of that stolen pocket-book he had not realized that he would identify himself beyond all doubt.

Virginia drew all the pocket-books toward her and opened one. As luck would have it, it was mine.

"Samuel Hicks," she said and looked at Mr. Lyle.

"Give it to him," he said, and Virginia handed it to me across the table. I put it on the table before me.

"G. Hewitt," Virginia said, and went through the same performance. Then followed the names of George Ballin, Arthur Morse, Frederick Child, James Norris, and John Bowers. One pocket-book remained before Virginia and Richard Morgan, and Samuel Lyle had received none. The lone pocket-book was black and long and narrow.

"It comes down to Richard Morgan and me, again," Mr. Lyle said. "One of us put this pocket-book on the table, the other put Harold Child's there. Is this your pocket-book, Richard?"

Richard picked it up, looked at it, turned it in his fingers slowly. Finally he shook his head, a very little. "No," he said, "it is not mine — it must be yours." And he handed it to Mr. Lyle.

I told you that this was not a love story, and it is n't, but at that moment I saw Virginia's hand grasp Richard's under the table as plainly as though the table had not been there, and I saw an expression of unutterable happiness flash over Richard's face, on the face of the boy who, on the evidence, stood convicted of having stolen another man's pocket-book.

Mr. Lyle laid the black pocket-book on the table before him and spoke to George Ballin. "Will you ask Thomas to come here?" he said. Ballin went to the door and sent for Thomas. "I hope to explain to you," Lyle said to us, "exactly how this happened."

Thomas came, and Mr. Lyle spoke to him so that none of us heard what he said. Thomas went out and returned with a black traveling bag, which Mr. Lyle placed on the table.

"Is that your bag, Harold?" he asked. Harold said that it was.

Mr. Lyle whispered to Thomas again, and again Thomas departed and returned with a black bag.

"Is that your bag, too?" Mr. Lyle asked Harold.

Harold was already examining the two black bags and promptly came to the conclusion that he had been mistaken — the second bag and not the first was his. They were almost exactly alike; originally they had been exactly alike, now a

slight difference in wear was all that distinguished them.

"Suppose you open the first bag — that is the
one that is not yours — and see what you find in
the compartment on the side," Mr. Lyle said.

Harold opened the bag and brought forth a
pocket-book, brown and almost square.

"So," said Mr. Lyle. "Will you compare it
with yours, the one that was stolen?" Harold
put the two side by side and they were as alike
as two peas; they were exactly the same size, of
the same thickness, of pigskin, and they had both
seen about the same years of service.

"Now, gentlemen," said Mr. Lyle, "everything
should be perfectly clear. You have a long room
with rows of lockers in it, every row like every
other row. Harold put his pocket-book in a
black bag and left it there; some one else put
his exactly similar pocket-book in an exactly
similar black bag, went upstairs and decided
that, after all, it was n't wise to leave his money
behind. He went down, saw a black bag at the
end of an aisle, presumed the bag was his, opened
it hurriedly and, finding a pocket-book exactly
like his own and exactly where he expected to
find it, put it in his pocket and went his way
with never a thought of anything wrong. He
paid his caddie with change from another pocket;
his host paid for everything else. He did not

discover that he had taken another man's pocket-book until we played our little game. Don't you think that that is a plausible and charitable explanation of the whole affair? I do, and I hope you agree with me. Will those who agree please raise their hands?" We all raised our hands.

"Good!" exclaimed Mr. Lyle. "I was sure that you would agree with me. Harold has his pocket-book and all that it contained, intact." Mr. Lyle turned to Harold. "Will you please give me the pocket-book you took from the black bag — be careful not to give me yours." Harold handed Mr. Lyle the square brown pocket-book, and Mr. Lyle put it in his pocket. Then he picked up the long narrow black pocket-book, that was still lying on the table before him, the pocket-book that Richard had said was Mr. Lyle's.

"This happens to be Richard Morgan's," he said, "notwithstanding the fact that not many minutes ago he said it was mine. Mine is now safely in my pocket, and I think I have gotten out of this mess pretty well. Thomas, will you take Mr. Child's bag and mine downstairs again?"

For a moment there was silence. Then Mr. Lyle himself chuckled, and in an instant all the others laughed till the tears rolled down their cheeks. Mr. Bowers, being a lawyer and well versed in the art of letting his face lie for him, sat solemn as a judge.

George Ballin spoke up. " I suppose," said he, " that if players are going to bring in half a dozen black bags all alike, the only solution will be a check-room."

Mr. Bowers nodded. Then he said : " Sam, when did the truth penetrate your —"

" Now, now, John, remember it 's a rainy day and that you were my partner at bridge: you play a most painful game — I was bored to death. Can you blame me for taking advantage of the chance for a little excitement when it turned up? "

Surely you never can tell what Sammy Lyle is thinking.

As for Richard and Virginia, maybe the little incident of his handing Mr. Lyle the last pocket-book and saying that it was Mr. Lyle's, when he, and Virginia herself, knew perfectly well it was n't, but was Richard's own, had something to do with their love story. It has n't with ours, for ours is n't a love story, but I have reason to suppose that Virginia fessed up to Richard — about ten seconds after Richard got her where no one was looking — that perhaps it took a very smart woman to discover all his good qualities, but that she believed she had been equal to the mental strain. This must have been before lunch. Anyway, they were late, and they surely did look self-conscious and very happy when they finally appeared.

Richard, for his part, refused to be a hero when we suggested that he had tried to accept the guilt to save Mr. Lyle.

"I did like thunder!" he said. "I knew I had n't swiped the pocket-book, and I knew he had n't, or any of us. I knew he was up to some game, and I tried to queer the works; that 's all."

Perhaps that was all — I 'm not quite sure.

THE GREATEST DAY

IT was a glorious day of autumn sunshine, and Paul Waters should have rejoiced thereat. Instead, the morning's mail on Paul's office desk was crying for attention and not getting it and Paul himself was as glum as though he were going to be hanged at ten o'clock sharp.

Paul was thinking of a dinner that he had gone to the night before at Mrs. George Farson's. Mrs. Farson was a widow and the dinner had been an affair. There was a note of it in the morning papers: there always were notes of Mrs. Farson's dinners in the papers. But notwithstanding the large number of male and female servants, the glittering company, the glistening gold, silver, and glass, the great quantity and delicacy of the food, wines, liquors, and cigars and all the rest of it, Paul did n't like to go to Mrs. Farson's dinners, and would n't have gone to that one if Miss Polly Wesson had not been going.

Mrs. Farson was undoubtedly beautiful, a woman of the world, chic and ambitious. Taking her by herself, Paul would have smiled and been indifferent; taken with her son George, Jr., he disliked her and compared her with other middle-aged women he knew who had the charm of sweet simplicity and were governed by their hearts rather than by their heads. The real trouble of course was the son, George.

George Farson, Jr., was a stock-broker. He lived with the market, had profound economic views, knew many men in high places intimately — a little bit too intimately when they were not about, Paul thought — smoked many cigarettes in fancy holders and drank many cocktails. He dressed with great care, had a weakness for flashy automobiles, and was handsome as the devil. He played auction and golf for high stakes and considered it so entirely the thing to do that it was worthy of no remark; he made large bets with a flippancy that was most impressive, if one were the sort to be impressed by that kind of thing.

He was a member of the Alden and one or two other clubs, but he did not belong to the Orchard Club or to the Lanning Golf-Club, of which Paul was a member, and Paul was very sure that Farson did not dare take the chance of having his name put up for them.

But, whatever he was, he was n't Paul Waters's sort, and Paul disliked him and his type profoundly. He had n't liked him to begin with, and when George had suddenly begun to make fast and furious love to Polly Wesson, that moderate and unenthusiastic dislike had become a good, substantial hatred.

The trouble was that Polly Wesson not only seemed to like George Farson, but seemed to like him much better than she liked Paul, which was, of course, all wrong. Paul and Polly had been playmates, then they had been, unofficially, sweethearts till Polly came out, and after that Paul had been a suitor. He had asked Polly to marry him, and Polly had said no — which meant nothing at all, for she gave him plenty of chances to ask her again and seemed to enjoy the occasions. Paul was just beginning to see the rose-pink of a beautiful dawn after a long dark night when George Farson appeared on the scene and the whole world went black again. Polly, who Paul was sure was weakening fast, became as cold as ice. She preferred George Farson to him, and that in itself was a calamity. If he lost Polly to one of a dozen men he knew, Paul would have died of a broken heart, but he would have died knowing that Polly would be happy with a man worthy of her. To have her marry George Farson would be a horrible tragedy.

He had considered the matter of money. He was junior member of a firm of insurance brokers and earned an honest living, but no such living as George Farson indulged in. For one short instant he had, within himself, accused Polly of

thinking of the money and not of the man, and
had immediately blushed furiously and been
ashamed of himself.

" No," he muttered, " Polly 'd never do that.
She thinks he 's a better man than I am, that 's
all, and — and he 's a bounder! "

And that is why Paul, sitting in his office on
that beautiful autumn morning, did n't care
whether school kept or not.

Paul's telephone rang and roused him from his
melancholy reverie. Mrs. George Farson was
speaking, and the moment Paul heard her voice
he suspected something was wrong. There was,
and Mrs. Farson was so excited that she found
difficulty in explaining it clearly.

Paul finally got the facts straight. The Farson house had been entered and all of Mrs. Farson's rings, pins, necklaces, tiaras, and so on, had
been taken in the stilly night. She herself was
at the moment prostrated in her silken negligée,
the loss having just been discovered by her maid,
who had come in to remove Mrs. Farson's breakfast tray. It was, perhaps, mere luck that she
called Paul Waters instead of the police on the
telephone. For some reason or other she looked
upon Paul as a dear friend, and undoubtedly forgot completely that he had taken out for her fifty
thousand dollars' burglary insurance, and that
when she got over the first shock she would

expect Paul to see that she was reimbursed for the value of her jewelry, if it was not recovered.

Paul sympathized greatly with Mrs. Farson, said nothing of his or his company's need of sympathy, and promised prompt action, thus recalling the matter of the insurance to her mind.

He telephoned the home office of the company which had issued the burglary policy and then telephoned Mr. Thomas Higgins, head of the detective agency which handled all of the company's business in Alden.

The investigations made by Thomas Higgins and by Inspector Gibb of the Alden police revealed but one important fact: the sash of the bath-room window, which room adjoined Mrs. Farson's bedroom, bore the unmistakable marks of a jimmy. This had not been noticed by Mrs. Farson or her maid, or any of the household. The maid was, however, sure that the window was not latched Thursday morning. Questioned further, she said that that window, like all the other second-story windows, was often not fastened. No one could remember whether or not it was fastened Wednesday night, as it was quite natural they should not.

Access to this window from the outside was easily possible to an agile man. The Farson house ran from Orchard Street through to a narrow alley in the rear, used by delivery wagons

and servants. A path from the alley ran to a
one-story brick extension of the house, which, by
the aid of a board fence, could be climbed easily.
This low roof led to the window of Mrs. Farson's bathroom, the sill being about three feet
above it. Nothing could have been simpler than
to gain a surreptitious entrance in this fashion.

Mrs. Farson explained about the jewels. They
were kept in a safe, not a particularly elaborate
or strong contrivance, built into the wall. It
was locked by a key and not with bolts and a
combination, as many of them are. Mrs. Farson
said that she had taken three or four rings, a
string of pearls, and a diamond pin from the safe
and worn them at dinner, and had, on returning
to her room, placed them on her dressing-table;
after being comfortably undressed she sent her
maid away, saying that she would not forget to
put away the ornaments, and lay down on a
couch to read for a few minutes. She admitted,
with tears in her eyes, that she had later started
to open the safe, having gotten the key from its
hiding-place for that purpose, but something had
distracted her and she had gone to bed and to
sleep, leaving the jewelry and the key on the
table. The next morning all of the jewelry was
gone, and the key was in the closed door of the
safe. Her maid noticed this and spoke of it, and
Mrs. Farson immediately remembered that she

had left the rings, necklace, and pin with the key on the dressing-table. The loss of everything, in and out of the safe, was immediately discovered.

The maid was questioned closely and told a perfectly straightforward story. The other servants denied the slightest knowledge of the affair, and not a suspicious thing could be found against them. A servant would have no reason for forcing an entrance through a window when access could be had through an open door. It was evident that the job had been done from the outside.

A microscopic examination made on the morning of the discovery of the robbery revealed no finger-prints nor footprints. There had been no similar crimes in Alden for some time, and no specialists in that science were known to be about. The routine of such cases was followed, a description of the stolen jewels was sent to every pawnshop and jeweler, and then there was nothing to do but wait. The robbery had appeared in the news of the day, and that had been followed by notes in the society news.

Mrs. Farson made out her claim against the insurance company for the full amount of her insurance, and swore to the loss, the value of the jewels, and divers other facts, before a notary, and asked Paul Waters to get her the money just as soon as he could, for she simply had to have some trinkets to wear and needed the money with which to buy them.

Again Paul Waters sat at his desk, this time staring at Mrs. Farson's affidavit. Everything was in order; it was the sort of loss that his company must expect; if there were no losses, there would be no business, and the business was profitable. But fifty thousand dollars was a pile of money. Paul sent for his stenographer and dictated a letter to the insurance company, suggesting that there was nothing to do but send Mrs. Farson a check promptly. Later he signed the letter, attached the proof of loss, sent it to the mail, put on his hat and coat, and went out. It was nearly quitting time, anyway, and he 'd walk up-town to the Orchard Club for a rubber before dinner. At the corner of Orchard and Main streets he saw walking ahead of him a tall man with very broad shoulders and an unmistakable gait. Paul caught up with him and spoke to him. Samuel Lyle smiled and put his free arm across Paul's shoulders. His right hand was engaged with his ever-present walking stick.

"Well, Paul, my boy," he said, "how are things with you?"

Paul made the stereotyped reply that everything was right as could be.

They talked unimportant pleasantries for a

block and were nearing the parting of their ways when Mr. Lyle said:

"Has that pretty widow friend of yours got her diamonds and pearls back yet?"

"No, she has n't, and I don't believe she ever will. It 's costing us a pretty penny, too."

"Is it? That 's too bad, but I suppose those things will happen. I don't know a thing about it except what I 've read in the papers."

"The papers had it pretty nearly right. I 'll tell you the whole thing if you 'll tell me how I can get our fifty thousand back."

"Hum-m," muttered Mr. Lyle. "As much as that, was it? That 's a lot of money. I 'll tell you what I 'll do — I 'll bribe you. You stop at my office with me just a minute and then we 'll go over to the club. You tell me the story, and I 'll buy you a very fine cigar to smoke while you 're doing it." Samuel Lyle chuckled.

"I 'm bribed," said Paul. Samuel Lyle knew every one who was any one in the city, and he knew more of human nature, its strength and weakness, more of the working of men's minds and more about the way of criminals than all the rest of the members of the Alden bar put together. To talk crime with him was a treat, and Paul jumped at his offer.

It was dark when they left Mr. Lyle's office.

"Where does Mrs. Farson live?" he asked

Paul, and Paul told him. Then he said : " Suppose we walk round that way; it's not far."
Accordingly they went north a few blocks and, turning into Orchard Street, came back past the Farson house and stopped opposite it, across the street. Paul pointed out the window through which the thief had made his entrance. An arc-light shone against that side of the Farson house. Paul described the old-fashioned sash-fastener and told Mr. Lyle how the jimmy had pried the sash apart so that a bit of wire could be thrust between them and the latch pulled back.

They went on to the Orchard Club, and Paul told him the whole story. Mr. Lyle, when he had heard the end of it, said simply :

" An ordinary job, and the only way that the stolen articles can be found will be by unlimited patience, a search of infinite detail, and a lot of good luck."

" If you 'll tell me how to find them, I 'll see that you get a big fee as a lawyer, and darn good pay as a sleuth."

" It 's no job for me, son; I'm no de-tec-a-tif."

" No?" said Paul. " Seems to me you 've done a job or two de-tec-a-tiffing."

Mr. Lyle smiled. " Perhaps, perhaps I have, but they 've been cases where there was some interesting psychological condition. It was not sleuthing; it was study of human beings. It 's very evident that there's nothing of the sort here. I'll break my rule and offer you a cocktail if you insist, though I'm agin licker, as you've heard me say before. No? Then I must be going, I'm having dinner with a friend of yours to-night, at her special request."

Paul had been blowing smoke into the still air, but Mr. Lyle's tone made him glance up. He immediately returned to his smoke. There was a moment's silence.

" I said that I am dining with a friend of yours to-night, Paul, at her special request. Her parents honor me quite often, but I think this is the first time Polly ever invited me. She says she wants to see me about something." Samuel Lyle rose and put his hand on Paul's head. " Be brave, boy," he said, " and stick at it. It will come out all right." And he went away, leaving Paul staring blankly before him.

Paul sat in the Orchard Club alone for half an hour, forlorn and unhappy. Then he went home, dined with his father and mother, went to his room, and tried to read. He read very little, for Polly Wesson's face danced across the page before him till he went to bed and dreamed of her as Mrs. George Farson, Jr.

Samuel Lyle went from the Orchard Club to his house, where he dressed. From there he walked to the Wessons' and was ushered into the

family circle. It was not until after dinner
that he saw Polly alone and then only by virtue
of her taking his arm and leading him to her
father's study, where she shut the door, having
shooed various members of the family away.

Miss Polly Wesson was a young lady of decided beauty and great charm; she was blessed
with a fine brain and had a streak of deviltry in
her which she concealed under a most demure
exterior. She had also a very decided will of
her own.

She placed Mr. Lyle comfortably in a chair and
arranged the light so that it shone on him and
not on her. Then she said:

" Promise that you 'll never breathe a word of
what I 'm going to tell you."

They argued at some length the propriety of
making such a promise, and finally Polly won.
She watched Mr. Lyle very closely as she told
him what she had to say, but not a sign of surprise or even interest could she detect. Mr. Lyle
smoked on as calmly as though he were alone and
listening to distant music. Long training had
made it second nature for him to conceal his
thoughts and emotions.

When Polly had finished he smiled and shook
his head.

" No, my dear," he said, " there is trouble

enough in this world without you and me hunting for it."

Polly sighed as though he had taken a great
load from her mind, and when Mr. Lyle asked
her the most innocent question imaginable she
answered him without an instant's hesitation,
and when he kept on asking her question after
question, mixing up amusing little remarks in
between, she kept on answering him without a
suspicion, until suddenly he shot a sharp statement at her.

She sprang from her chair as though she had
been struck, and glared at him. He too had
risen and stood twirling an ornament on his
watch chain and looking at her as though she
were a naughty child discovered in a criminal
act.

"You 're a brute! You 're horrid to make me
say that!" she cried.

"But, Polly, you will trust an old man, won't
you?"

Her eyes were blazing, and she was blushing
furiously.

"Promise on your word of honor that —" All
the fight went out of her and she walked straight
into Mr. Lyle's arms, where she had been many
and many a time before, and they did n't say a
word till a little while later Mr. Lyle said:

"It's time we were playing bridge with the parents," and he offered her his arm and with mock ceremony they marched out of the room.

They played bridge with the parents, and later, when the parents were alone, Mrs. Wesson said:

"What do you suppose was going on between those two to-night?"

Mr. Wesson had n't noticed anything special.

"They're up to something," Mrs. Wesson said, and was entirely sure that it was some silly joke of theirs.

The next morning Mr. Lyle went down-town a little later than usual and dropped in at the People's Trust Company. He nodded to the at-tendant outside the president's office and, receiv-ing a satisfactory signal in return, he walked in and said, "Good morning, Gus," to the very dig-nified and important president, Mr. Augustus A. Warren. They chatted for a few minutes, and then Mr. Lyle asked Mr. Warren for two bits of information, and these being forthcoming after investigation, Mr. Lyle departed. Mr. Warren followed him almost to the street, but the best he could get was a promise of a story later on, *per-haps*.

Reaching his office, Mr. Lyle called a firm of real-estate brokers on the telephone and asked for certain unimportant information, which he got. He then called Paul Waters.

" Paul," he said, " I 've been thinking over the little matter you and I were talking about yesterday. Business has n't been good, and I need a little money. I wish you 'd talk with your people and ask them what they 'll pay me, on a contingent basis, if through my efforts you don't have to pay any of that Farson claim."

Paul exploded and yelled for details, but nothing came of it, for Mr. Lyle would say nothing except to repeat the question.

A few minutes later Paul, having telephoned in the meantime, called Mr. Lyle.

" My people want to know if ten thousand dollars will be satisfactory, and if not, what will; and will you please tell them and me what's going on? "

" Tell your people that ten thousand dollars will not be satisfactory, that I will listen to nothing except sixteen thousand three hundred and seventy-five dollars and thirty-two cents, spot cash, no more, no less, and the privilege of expending and charging to them not exceeding one thousand dollars additional. They must say yes or no within an hour, and what is going on is none of their business, or yours, for the time being."

" Yes," Paul shouted the word into the telephone, " the company and I accept."

" Very well, young man; just drop me a line

confirming that agreement and authorizing me
to act for you. Send it by messenger, and send
along a copy of the policy blank, and send me
a copy of the proof of loss, filled out as the original is, as soon as you can have it made. I'll
send for you when I want to see you, and in the
meantime mum's the word, absolutely."

Paul rushed the letter of confirmation and
authority to Mr. Lyle and then walked round his
office, trying to look unconcerned, but it was no
go. He went back to his room, drummed with
his fingers on the window-pane, and then exclaimed:

"Does n't that old boy beat H! He's dug up
something sure as shootin'. I wonder what
it is."

In the meantime Mr. Lyle had hung up the
receiver, leaned back in his chair, and worked his
face and his lips into all sorts of curious shapes,
till, seemingly against his will, they broke into a
broad smile, which certainly was not Mr. Lyle's
smile of professional joy or triumph.

Finally he managed to drive the smile away,
and when he was sure it was gone he pressed a
button and told the responding young woman to
send for Mr. Higgins at once.

Then Mr. Lyle called up another friend of his
in the real-estate business and asked for information which was promised as quickly as it could

be obtained. Then Mr. Higgins came in and Mr. Lyle gave him some very simple instructions, as a result of which an operative of Mr. Higgins's set about finding a room, the window of which offered a view of the alley entrance of the Farson house. The room found, Mr. Higgins's man sat himself down at the window with a note-book handy and a couple of newspapers with which to while away idle moments.

Mr. Lyle, having nothing further to do with the Farson jewels for the time being, made a note on his calendar pad and gave his attention to other business. All this happened on a Tuesday morning.

Tuesday afternoon Paul had tea with Polly Wesson. He was very glum, but Polly did not seem to notice it, for she was very bright and laughed merrily, her eyes snapped, and she seemed entirely content with life. Paul thought he had never seen her so beautiful and so desirable. Something in Polly brought his courage back, and George Farson became nothing more than a memory of a hideous nightmare.

"Seen old Sammy Lyle lately?" Paul asked, and then with a sudden rush of righteousness he hastened to add: "I know you have; he told me yesterday that he was going to dinner with you last night."

"Yes, he came and we played bridge afterward." Polly was watching Paul out of the corner of her eye. She discovered nothing alarming and breathed easier. " Is n't he a perfect dear? " she said.

" Yes, he 's all of that," Paul said slowly. " I had a long talk with him about business and then "— Paul looked Polly squarely in the eyes —" he told me that he was going to see you, and out of a clear sky he told me to stick to it — that everything would come out all right."

" You mean your business? "

" I mean your business and mine; he meant that some day you would marry me. He 's a wonderful de-tec-a-tif."

" It 's a wise shoemaker that sticks to his last." There was banter and the old-time merriment in Polly's voice. Paul put down his cup and walked to her side.

" Polly," he said, " will you marry me? "

Polly, her head a little on one side and her lips squeezed tight together, arranged things on the tea tray with great care before she answered.

" You 've asked me that a great many times, Paul."

" Yes, and I shall ask you a great many more times if it is necessary. I shall keep on asking you till you are promised to another man."

" But I have told you so many times "— Polly hesitated and looked up from the tea things to

Paul, and Paul's heart began to beat as though —
" Mr. Farson."

The maid stood in the doorway, and George
Farson was close behind her. Fifteen minutes
later Paul cursed under his breath as he went
down the Wesson steps. To add to his unhappiness, Polly had told him that she could not see
him on either Wednesday or Thursday. His
only consolation was that he might telephone to
her Friday morning.

On Thursday morning Higgins reported to Mr.
Lyle, and again Mr. Lyle gave him instructions.
On Friday morning Mr. Lyle telephoned Paul
Waters to come to his office and to bring some
letterheads with him. Paul, before he went,
telephoned Polly Wesson and found that she had
gone out and would not be home till late that
afternoon. He took his way sadly to Samuel
Lyle's office.

" Paul," said Mr. Lyle, " your policy restrains
the insured from bringing suit for ninety days
after the loss. That clause does not prevent the
insured from bringing suit the day of the loss,
but in that case we could plead the contract and
make no other answer until the three months
have expired. I want you to notify Mrs. Farson
that you refuse payment of the claim pending
further investigation, and call her attention to
the ninety-day clause. Don't suggest that we

are looking for a suit; just tell her that she can't start it for a while, and say also that, if she wants to talk things over, you await her commands.   Suppose we write the letter now."

The letter was written, and down at the bottom of it was a line saying that the bearer would take an answer if Mrs. Farson so wished. It was a very pleasant and friendly letter, and Mr. Waters trusted that Mrs. Farson would understand the company's position and that she would be in no way inconvenienced by the delay. The letter was despatched, and Mr. Lyle settled back in his chair to await developments as though he did n't have a care in the world.

Paul had no such equanimity. "What's going on?" he asked. "You don't have to keep me on pins and needles if you don't want to."

"Young man, am I managing this little affair or am I not?"

"You are, but that does n't prevent your satisfying an interested and burning curiosity, does it?"

"Have I your confidence, sir?"

"You have my confidence, sir, but —"

"Then you stop badgering me. If you'll tell me how to make a seventy-five around the Lanning golf course, I'll tell you anything I know."

"Make every hole in four but three, and make those in five apiece."

"A quibble, and you know it! Tell me how to make fifteen fours and I'll manage the fives myself. How well do you know the Farsons, mother and son?"

"They're acquaintances."

"Proud of them?"

"Hardly proud —"

"Exactly, but too proud yourself to admit, in the circumstances — in all the circumstances, I say — that you have no use for them and that if things were otherwise than they are you would leave them politely alone. Don't answer, I quite understand — a very pretty compliment to some one else — a bit of fine feeling. Now, to go back to those fifteen fours, to say nothing of a few threes on the short holes —" And Mr. Lyle refused to be serious till the messenger returned, bringing with him a note from Mrs. Farson.

Mrs. Farson was terribly disappointed and did not understand matters at all, as she had been led to believe that the insurance company would pay the claim at once. Would n't Mr. Waters please come to see her and tell her what the trouble was, just as soon as he could?

Mr. Lyle read the note and tossed it on the desk.

"Call her up," he said, "and ask her if you and three other representatives of the company can see her this afternoon at four o'clock."

Paul telephoned and Mrs. Farson was so glad that they could come at four o'clock, and she did hope that things could be arranged.

Paul looked at Mr. Lyle hopefully. "Come on, loosen up. Tell a feller something."

"Have you an engagement for dinner tonight?"

"Yes, I have."

"Break it and dine with me."

"But I'd like to, of course — but —"

"Break it! Break it! Do you hear me? Business comes before pleasure."

"Very well, sir, very well. I'll be good, I'll break it."

"Meet me here at quarter before four."

"How about the other representatives of the company?"

"Never you mind about them — I'll provide the other fellows."

Paul went outdoors a sadly befuddled young man.

"If I did n't know otherwise," he thought, "I'd believe old Sammy was just a good-natured, irresponsible old kidder, and he can make juries and criminals and lawyers and judges lie down and roll over. I never saw him act like this before."

As a matter of fact, Mr. Lyle never had acted exactly like that before, but then he had never felt exactly as he had felt for the previous two days. He had done good jobs, but if all went well to-day would see completed the best job of his life, and it would not be his fault if all did not go well, for he had planned carefully.

Walking from his office to the Farson house that afternoon, he said as much to Paul.

" Young man, I have a feeling in my old bones that this is to be one of the greatest days of my life. The thought of it makes me feel young again. I am sure that I should have made a good actor, for I love the thrill of a dramatic situation, but more than that I crave the thrill of bringing it about. I 'm not proud of it; it 's a weakness, I 'm afraid, like a craving for drink or drugs, though I suppose not so harmful. For years I have lived on those thrills; they are necessary in my life. I need the excitement of them once in so often, just as most men need a vacation occasionally, just as all men need food and sleep. I think — I 'm not sure, but I think — we're going to have one of those little thrills this afternoon, though somehow or other I 'm not looking forward to it with any pleasure; in fact, I almost regret it — and yet — and yet "— the tall, awkward man threw his shoulders back and brandished his walking stick and laughed —" these old bones of mine tell me that to-day is going to be a great day. Here are the other representatives of the company. Mr. Higgins you know; let me introduce Mr. Worthington, a notary from my office."

They went up the Farsons' steps and were admitted by the Farson butler, who ushered them into Mrs. Farson's library, and Mrs. Farson did not keep them waiting, for she appeared almost immediately with her son. She was all smiles and greeted Paul effusively.

"What *is* the trouble?" she cried. "You don't mean to tell me that there is some hope of getting all my playthings back?" The prospect of getting them back was very exciting.

Coming from the brisk outdoor air into the dim light of the library had wrought a remarkable change in Mr. Lyle. His enthusiasm, the light in his eyes, his smile, had flown, and there was a sad expression on his face; he was a little bored, a little tired, his shoulders dragged downward and his clothes fitted him not at all, but lay in wrinkles all over him.

"Oh, do tell me!" Mrs. Farson cried.

"Madam," Mr. Lyle spoke slowly, drawing Mrs. Farson's attention from Paul to himself, "there is some possibility, perhaps a remote possibility, of returning your jewels to you. It is the policy of the company to pay claims immediately on receipt of proof of loss, but in this case it would much prefer to return to you the jewels themselves. Undoubtedly you yourself would much prefer that."

" Oh, of course."

" And you are, then, willing to do without them for a short time, rather than accept their value in cash now, and have them become the property of the company when, and if, they are recovered? "

" Oh, yes, of course."

" Then I think there is nothing more to be said. The company appreciates your feelings and your kindness to it." Mr. Lyle bowed a very little, but enough to suggest that the interview was at an end.

" But you are *sure* you will find them? " Mrs. Farson's question was a demand for a positive statement.

" I am quite sure that most of them at least will be found."

" How — how are you — how do you expect to find them? "

Mr. Lyle turned slowly and examined the room. He moved a chair a little nearer the lamp on the table.

" It is a long story, Mrs. Farson. Perhaps you would like to hear it. Will you sit down? "

Mrs. Farson walked rapidly to the chair, sat down, and turned quickly back to Mr. Lyle. He nodded to the others and sank into a chair himself. His eyes, peering from under his heavy brows, fixed themselves on Mrs. Farson's.

"Well, Mr. Lyle?"

"Mrs. Farson, jewels are seldom lost; they do not disappear into thin air. The thief who takes them does not destroy them; to reap the profit of his crime he must sell them, and the man who buys them knows that they are stolen. He in turn must offer them for sale. So, Mrs. Farson, at least two men know where your jewels are. Men of that class fortunately are known and are watched. Now, if one of these men was foolish enough to enter your rooms by a window which was in the bright light of an electric street lamp, a window which he must have reached by walking over a roof that was in the same bright light, on the most fashionable street in Alden, where passers-by might be expected all night long — if a man was foolish enough to do that, then he will do some other foolish thing that will result in his apprehension."

"But he was not seen."

"True, he was not seen, but that does not explain why he chose it when there were other windows far more sheltered."

"But it is all so indefinite. The window really means so little."

"It means a great deal, Mrs. Farson. It

means that the company thinks that a man did not enter."

For a moment there was a hush over the room and then came a cry: " What! What do you mean? "

" The company thinks, madam, that perhaps it would be best if we placed the question of the brightly lighted window before the court." Mr. Lyle spoke casually and waited, his eyes never leaving Mrs. Farson. Then when he saw her about to speak he said, very slowly: " That is, of course, unless you care to open, of your own free will and for the company's inspection, your safe-deposit box in the trust company."

" My box in the Alden Trust Company? " Mrs. Farson did not understand, was indignant, and snapped her answer at Mr. Lyle.

" I am speaking of your box in the *People's* Trust Company. If you do not care to open it for us, we shall have to place the matter before a magistrate."

" What is the meaning of this? " George Farson jumped to his feet, burning with rage. He had suddenly grasped what Mr. Lyle was driving at. " We did not ask you to come here to insult us."

" There, there," Mr. Lyle drawled the words as though the young man annoyed him greatly.

"Go and sit down, and when we want to talk with you, we will let you know." George Farson sank back in his chair. "Now, Mrs. Farson, out with it. Tell us the whole story — or would you rather have me tell it for you?"

Mrs. Farson had gone deathly white, her beauty had disappeared, leaving her face weak and drawn. Her breath came in short gasps; one hand clutched her chair, and the fingers of the other grasped at the edge of the table nervously and without purpose.

"We know, madam, that you have been living far beyond your means, we have a list of tradesmen who have been clamoring for money, and refusing you further credit; your landlord has threatened proceedings against you; your son is head over heels in debt — it is common knowledge that he does not pay even his debts of honor. You were at your wits' end for money. Tell us how you proposed to get it."

"It's a lie." Again George Farson jumped to his feet and rushed at Mr. Lyle. "So far as my mother is concerned, there is and never has been any question of money. I —"

"Stop, oh, stop! Your mother rented a box in the People's Trust Company and put her stuff into it; ask her, look at her."

"She did not: I took them and sold them, and be damned to you!"

"George!" The word was a long scream of anguish. "George, oh, George!"

"Such a pretty pickle; the son confesses and the mother is guilty. Won't you please agree on something that in turn agrees with the facts?"

"I tell you I took them and sold them. I made the marks on the window. I —"

"But your mother put them in the safe-deposit box. Don't be silly."

The mother was hardly able to utter the words that would save her son. "George — George — I did — they — they are — there — I did it. They know — they — they have — found — out."

Higgins had an inspiration. "I wonder maybe did n't he take the things off the bureau, and she the rest of 'em? And when he sneaked in and found the biggest part of them gone, what a disappointment it must have been, after him thinking how pleasantly the company would make things right with his mother, and both of them thought there 'd been a real robbery just in the nick of time to cover everything up."

"Good, good!" Mr. Lyle exclaimed. "A pretty family, each planning to make an honest penny!" Then to George Farson: "Get your mother brandy, or smelling-salts, or something."

Mrs. Farson was in dire need of assistance, certainly. The vivacious, smiling woman of the world was gone, and a poor, weak woman had taken her place, lying moaning against the table. Her son, with trembling fingers, gave her brandy. Samuel Lyle watched them, frowning. Finally Mrs. Farson regained sufficient composure to satisfy him.

"Madam," he said, "you confess without reservation?"

Mrs. Farson's lips moved, but if she spoke her words were inaudible. George Farson, a sorry spectacle, stood by the window, the perspiration rolling down his face. His hand gripped a curtain and his body swayed back and forth weakly.

"Do you confess, madam, that you have your jewels in your possession; that in making your affidavit in connection with your proof of loss you committed perjury?"

Mrs. Farson's body trembled as she comprehended the awful meaning of the word.

"Speak. Do not keep us waiting."

George Farson tottered across the room like a drunken man. His arms waved before him, his fingers opened and shut like a huge bird's claws, and he made his way toward Mr. Lyle with murder in his eyes. Samuel Lyle waited for him and motioned the others away, and when the time came his long arm shot out and his great hairy hand grasped Farson's coat where the V met over his chest, and shook him as though he were a rag, and threw him into a chair. Then, with a glance at the prostrate figure, he turned again to Mrs. Farson.

"Well, Mrs. Farson, have you committed perjury and sundry other crimes?"

They could just hear her hissing: "Yes."

"We have no interest in your crimes. The fact is the thing: read this carefully, please." He took a paper from his pocket. "It is a release of all claim against the insurance company. It states nothing of your attempted fraud. Mr. Worthington will attest your signature. Will you read it, or shall I read it to you?"

George Farson, in the chair, moved, and Mr. Lyle nodded to Higgins.

"Be still, you," said Higgins. The mother's eyes were on her son.

"Listen to me," said Mr. Lyle, and read. Then: "Will you sign?" Mr. Lyle took a book from the table and placed the paper on it. He took a pen from his pocket and stood beside the woman. She took the pen and signed, blindly, every bit of courage, pride, and hope gone from her. Then Worthington did his part.

"We are through, gentlemen," Mr. Lyle said. "I imagine, madam, that you and your son will not remain long in Alden. Good afternoon."

Samuel Lyle and Paul Waters went out into Orchard Street.

"Damn poorly done," Mr. Lyle muttered. "I am ashamed of myself. However, I shall expect your check to-morrow morning for sixteen thousand three hundred and seventy-five dollars and thirty-two cents exactly, and, remember, you are dining with me to-night at quarter after seven. Be prompt; I do not like to be kept waiting."

"I'll be there. Don't worry," Paul cried, "but please tell me how you found out about —"

Mr. Lyle made a gesture of disgust. "Bah! Any fool could have guessed the probability and then confirmed it easily enough. I'm ashamed of Higgins. Don't forget the check; business is rotten, and I need ready cash." And he strode away, leaving Paul staring after him. He did not suspect that Mr. Lyle was chuckling inside.

And then Paul too walked away, blindly, seeing only a man collapsed in a chair.

At quarter after seven, promptly, Paul took off his hat and coat and walked into Mr. Lyle's parlor. There was no one there, but he heard a voice and he went toward the door that led to the library. Samuel Lyle saw him, but paid no attention to him and kept on speaking to a great high-backed, deep leather chair the back of which was toward Paul. The huge man was making a speech, slowly and eloquently; his whole mind was intent upon it, his eyes bored into the chair. Paul heard the words:

"— capacity for inflicting torture has been cultivated in the highest of all animals, developed into a fine science. Man himself has no such power or skill. The hand that soothes, the eye that sends forth signs of purity and sweetness and gentleness, go arm in arm with a mind which takes fiendish delight in the writhing of the agonized victim of its machinations. The voice which is attuned for the production of the sweetest music the world has ever known hisses forth curses that shrivel the hearts of the innocent and the worthy. The noblest work of God, improved, perfected, and worshiped by man, turns upon him and stabs him with the dagger received from his hand, and laughs at his dying gasps, knowing not a moment's sadness for the hell created. Thus, and much more, which reminds me that I 've got to go and see that the dinner does n't burn on the kitchen stove. Bless my soul, if there is n't little Paul Waters! Where do you suppose he came from? I 'll leave him to take care of you. Dinner is at eight," and as he passed Paul he whispered: "She knows nothing of what happened this afternoon. I have n't breathed a word of it, on your account."

Paul stared at the high-backed leather chair.

"Miss Wesson — Mr. Paul Waters," and Samuel Lyle disappeared.

Paul walked around the high-backed leather

chair. Polly Wesson, who was no midget, was almost lost in it.

"Did you hear what Mr. Lyle was saying about me?" she asked.

Paul nodded.

"Am I like that?"

Paul nodded and then Paul smiled.

"Is n't he a funny old man?" said Polly.

"Polly, I can't talk to you way down there; come up." He offered her his hand to help her, and she took it.

"He told me dinner was at seven and not to keep him waiting," she said.

"He told me dinner was at quarter after seven and not to keep him waiting."

"I wonder what he meant."

"I wonder."

Polly, not quite realizing what she was doing, held out her other hand too, and Paul, drawing her upward, held them both.

"Polly!"

"All right, Paul, I 'll be good." She *was* very good, and during the half-hour that followed she admitted that she would have been good to Paul long before if he had n't made her furious by thinking that she could even like George Farson, when Paul ought to have been sure that she had loved him ever since she was a little girl. She said that she hoped the lesson would do him good, but Paul was n't worrying about lessons or anything else.

A little before eight a voice came from the doorway: "Well, well, well! Bless my soul!" They spun round and saw Mr. Lyle beaming upon them. There was great joy in his voice. "Hm — m," he muttered. "So! Now let me see, what did I do with it, what *did* I do with it? Oh, yes, I remember. Paul, will you please look in the dictionary, that large book on the table, and tell me the meaning of 'mastership'? Quickly, please!"

Paul, laughing and wondering what joke Samuel Lyle was playing now, reached for the book. It opened at a place marked by a folded paper. Paul read: "'Mastership, the state or office of a master; mastery; dominion; superior skill; superiority. An ironical title of respect.'"

"An ironical title of respect," Mr. Lyle mused. "A dangerous word, Miss Polly. Now, on the opposite page, what word catches your eye, Paul?"

"Match."

"Match, to be sure. Most appropriate. And between 'mastership' and 'match' what have you?"

"Mastiff — mastodon — mat —"

"Blind! There in your hand. Suppose you present that paper to Miss Wesson, and while she reads it tell me what word comes before ' mastership ' in the dictionary."

" Masterpiece."

" I take that word unto myself. Did n't I tell you that to-day would be the greatest day of my life? I 've never had such a thrill before. You 've been trying to do for years what I 've done for you in —" He stopped and laughed at Paul; he was as happy as a boy.

Polly interrupted them. She had been trying to decipher the document that had lain between the leaves of the dictionary.

" What is this? " she asked. " I don't understand."

" My dear young lady," Mr. Lyle said, " that is the deed of the very pretty little brick house in Stockton which you have admired for so long, the house in which you told me you could live happily with almost any man if he was n't too homely. The house is yours. Is the man too homely? "

Polly Wesson, bewildered, looked from Paul to Samuel Lyle.

" Oh, no ! " she cried. " I — I — it can't be — it —"

" The lease of the present tenant expires June first," Mr. Lyle said. " June is a good month for weddings."

" Paul, what shall I do? "

" ' Paul, what shall I do?' So soon, and in this day of the equality and independence of women! What can you do? Let me tell you something. When you are married and living in the little red house with vines and flowers all about, recall to-day to Paul and see if he remembers the little business transaction he and I had. I think he will, and then you whisper into his ear that your nest cost exactly sixteen thousand three hundred and seventy-five dollars and thirty-two cents, and then perhaps the truth will burst upon him. If it does n't, tell him how one day you were in the safe-deposit vaults of the People's Trust Company and saw a woman there who, when she saw you, flushed and behaved in a most embarrassed and guilty manner, though you could n't imagine any reason for it. And then tell him how, when you heard of a certain robbery, you had a sudden inspiration, and how finally you told me about it and asked me whether what you had seen could by any possible chance help Paul, and how I pooh-poohed the idea and then went and got all the credit for myself. I think he 'll understand everything then, except, of course, that after you had told what you had seen a certain old rascal brought out, by cross-examination, that —"

" Stop! " Polly rushed toward him.

"— that you were really very much in —"

"Stop! Stop! You promised."

"No, no, I did n't promise. I — but here are the others. That story will have to wait."

Mr. Lyle greeted Peggy Dean and Mary Ladd and their husbands. For a moment there was calm. Then suddenly Peggy Dean discovered something and exclaimed: "Polly!" and then she took Polly's two hands in hers. Her eyes flashed to Paul and then back to the blushing girl, whose eyes were shining bright. "Polly! Really?" she cried, and when Polly nodded she took her into her arms and kissed her.

"It 's perfectly wonderful," Peggy whispered.

For a moment Samuel Lyle was entirely neglected, but it was for only a moment.

"I 'm cupid," he said, "and blessed if I don't like the job. It 's a heap better and lots easier than uncovering criminal cupidity. Lor' me, what a pun!"

A STORY APROPOS

ON a Monday late in July Norman Dean, Hugh Ladd, and James Norris had lunch together at the round table in the Orchard Club, as was their custom. Norman and Hugh had returned that morning from the shore, but Jimmy, his wife being far northward, had stayed at home and played golf at the Lanning Golf-Club. During lunch Norman Dean suggested that they find a fourth and have dinner with him at Stockton that evening and play bridge afterward. Hardly had the other two agreed when the great figure of Samuel Lyle loomed close beside them, and within a moment he had accepted their invitation to complete the party.

Accordingly, late in the afternoon, the four drove to Norman Dean's house, played a rubber or two before dinner, and returned to their game after dinner.

Samuel Lyle was the eldest of the four. No one would ever have suspected, to see him then, that he was one of the greatest criminologists in the country and the most feared and respected practitioner in the criminal courts. He seemed to be a simple, kind-hearted, humorous man, and

yet, when occasion required, the lightning's flash
could be no more penetrating or illuminating
than the words which he hurled forth in court.

Norman Dean and Hugh Ladd were middle-
aged, prominent in the business world of Alden,
and rather quiet and serious men. Jimmy Norris was the youngest of the four; and no matter
what Jimmy's age may have been, he was a boy
and probably always would be. It was against
all the principles of Jimmy's life to be serious:
he always saw the funny side of every blessed
thing, and if in real life no funny side existed
Jimmy manufactured one out of his own fertile
imagination. Nothing ever dismayed him; every
human being had a good side to him, and although Jimmy undoubtedly admitted to himself
that on occasion a man's good side was hard to
find, and when found was hardly worth the
search, nevertheless that side was the side to
think about.

Jimmy Norris had brains and used them, but
mirth had been born in him and was so large a
part of him that very nearly every one of those
who knew him thought of him as a happy-go-
lucky youth and only on occasion gave heed to
the keenness of his mind and the depth of his
philosophy.

But on this Monday in July something was
wrong with Jimmy — so wrong that Jimmy

seemed not to be himself at all, but an entirely different man. Norman and Hugh noticed it at lunch, but did not give it much thought, being content with asking him whether he was feeling well. It might be possible that Jimmy's physical being was disarranged, but it never occurred to them that Jimmy could by any possible chance be suffering from mental depression not caused by physical ailment. But Jimmy ate his lunch and he ate a substantial dinner; there was not an indication that there was anything, serious or not, the matter with Jimmy's insides, and yet before dinner was over not only Norman and Hugh but Samuel Lyle knew that something very serious indeed was troubling Jimmy. They glanced at one another inquiringly and uneasily: they loved Jimmy from the bottom of their hearts. Even before dinner they set about discovering what was on Jimmy's mind.

"Missus all right?" Norman Dean wanted to know.

Jimmy said the missus was fine.

"And the kids?" Norman went on.

"Splendid," Jimmy said. "I had a letter this morning, and they are all having a grand time."

That eliminated family worries, and they tried business, veiling their inquiries as best they could, and they could discover nothing wrong there. As the evening went on evidence accu-

mulated that there was something very wrong
with Jimmy somewhere. He was silent as they
had never before known him to be. They saw
him staring fixedly into space, and they saw his
face first white and then suddenly flushed; two
or three times beads of perspiration were on his
forehead, and he mopped them away with a handkerchief. He played auction as though his mind
were a thousand miles from the game — he made
terrible blunders and showed not the slightest
mortification. Many times, when one of the
three spoke, Jimmy started nervously. It was so
bad that the three became almost as pathetic
figures as Jimmy himself, and late in the evening, when Norman went to the sideboard for a
glass of water, Hugh followed him and made a
quick suggestion to which Norman assented.

They went back to the table, and at the end
of the hand Hugh said: "Now, then, Jimmy,
tell us what's wrong. You can't go on this way,
and it will help if you get it off your chest.
Maybe we can do something to help."

Jimmy sank back in his chair and looked from
one to the other of the three and shook his head.
" There is nothing that you or anybody else can
do. I have been through more hell in the last
twenty-four hours than I ever went through in
my life, and the worst part of it is that the thing
is done and over with and no power on earth

can ever change it. There is no use even talking about it."

The others would not agree to this and shot question after question at Jimmy until he could n't stand the strain any longer.

" Do you know whom I was playing golf with yesterday? " he asked.

None of the three knew.

" Will you give me your word that you will make no attempt to find out, and, more than that, be sure that you don't let any one talk golf to you and tell you whom I was playing with? "

The three promised.

" It happened on the eighteenth hole, in the afternoon," Jimmy said. " We were playing a four-ball match at the Lanning Club, and two of the men made rotten drives. I had messed up my second and did n't reach the green. The fourth man hooked his second shot; I saw it go into the woods but I could n't follow it and did n't know just where it fell. I walked in that direction to help the man find it, but he told me not to bother; that he knew exactly where it was. I walked along a little way and saw him go into the edge of the woods to a place where the weeds came up perhaps to his knees. I asked him again if he was sure that he could find it and he said yes, and I turned and walked toward where my ball was.

" Then, for some reason or other, I knew that the ball might be hard to find, and as the match depended on it I turned to help him, and I saw him lean over and drop a ball. I saw the ball in his hand, and I saw him drop it; I saw him keep on walking around in a circle, and as he was walking his caddie called to him that his ball had n't gone as far as that; that it was ten or fifteen yards farther back. I saw him continue in a circle, and I saw him come back to where I had seen him drop the ball. He called to me that he had it, and if ever there was guilt in a man's voice it was in his then.

" I turned and went back to my ball. I heard him play out of the weeds and saw the ball go up to the edge of the green. I could n't see my ball — I made a wild stab at it and missed it almost completely and hit it again. It took me three or four shots to get anywhere near the hole, and he holed out in two and won the hole and the match. It was worth five dollars to him.

" That 's all that happened except that that man is a man that we 've all known for years, a man who was one of us, a man we trusted and believed in, a man whose good name we would have defended to the utmost of our ability, a man whose honor was bound up in our honor, a man prominent in the community, a man in whom

our faith was unbounded; and he did that for
five dollars and the sake of winning the match.
I 've tried to think up some excuse — it was the
end of a long, hard day, and he was tired; we
were all tired; he did n't want to bother looking
for the ball — but that excuse won't do. I can't
get any consolation out of it.

  " If I told you who the man was, you would n't
believe me; you would say that it was an utter
impossibility, and yet I saw him with the ball in
his hand; I saw him drop it; I saw him walk
round in a circle and come back to where he had
dropped it, and I heard his voice when he told me
that he had found his ball. If there are three
men in the world whom I would have trusted
more than I trusted him, you are those three.
That 's all."

  If in a match a ball be lost, then the player
loses the hole. That is one of the fundamental
and best-known rules of golf. If a man loses his
ball and pretends that he has not done so, but
to deceive his opponent drops another, unseen or
believing the act to be unseen, he cheats.

  If a man steals, he has broken the law of the
land and is punishable by imprisonment, yet he
has shown a certain mistaken courage in match-
ing his wits against the law: you may consider
him a victim of circumstances, greatly to be
pitied; you may bear him no malice; you may

forgive him and help him to become an honest man and reinstate himself in his community, but a cheat you abhor forever. When a man cheats at sports, as at cards, there is no law which may be invoked against him, no prison of stone and iron awaits him, and yet eternal punishment shall be his.

The game of golf, as no other game, is founded upon the honor of its players; day after day thousands of men go forth to play, and each man is the keeper of his own honor and the honor of the game, and he must hold men's faith in him inviolate if he would remain among them. There is but one degree of honor, and if a man cheat he has no honor and is false to a sacred trust. And when a man cheats, then he shall know prison indeed, for he shall become an outcast and may never again associate with honorable men. The word travels fast, making men sad, yet never so long as he lives may he be forgiven; always, wherever he may go, his sin shall follow close behind him, crying his shame. Earth is a living hell for him, for honorable men turn from him; he is ostracized, a moral leper.

A man, because of the accident of his birth and environment, may know little of honor and yet be accorded respect by honest men, but if a man assume honor and forsake it, then he shall forever be called vile and be despised. If your friend cheat, abandoning the honor which you have believed inviolate beween you, then it would have been better if he had died, with his name untarnished. And Jimmy Norris's friend had cheated.

There was a deathly silence in the room. What could any of them say; what could any of them do? All of those men had played golf for years and years and in all those years not more than once or twice had any of them known a man who cheated, and those few men had been despicable characters, little respected, and when their cheating had been discovered they had been quickly sent into oblivion. And now one of their own kind had committed the unforgivable crime. Who was it? Who could it be?

It was no small matter of curiosity that made that thought flash through their minds. Would it not have been better, now that the story was told, if Jimmy Norris had told them the man's name? Would not suspicion fall on every man they knew? Would not the whole fabric of their friendships and their regard for their fellow men be torn and tangled until the one was known and set apart? Suddenly Samuel Lyle spoke, and as he spoke there was a smile on his face and a kindly light in his eyes.

"Suppose," he said, " I tell you a story. It's a rather long story, but perhaps in the circum-

stances it will be worth the telling.   It seems to
me that it is apropos."

Samuel Lyle told the story and the story was
this:

Alden is a city with many aspects, as any city
of two million population must be, and one of
the most unpleasant aspects of Alden was the
condition which existed in its southeasterly sec-
tion, half a dozen blocks back from the Nesse
River.   Scott Street runs through that part of
the city, and it was on Scott Street that the thing
happened, between Madison and Grant, and it
happened late at night.

On the southwest corner of Grant and Scott
Streets was a saloon run by Theodore McManus,
and Theodore's saloon was a pretty tough joint.
In it on that February night were a dozen men,
among them Mike Higgins and Fred Cantry.
Cantry was a watchman in a store yard next door
on Scott Street where a builder kept a lot of
lumber and building equipment when it was n't
in use.   Cantry had a little office in the corner
of the store yard away from the saloon and he
had a room over it where he slept.

There was bad blood between Higgins and Cantry and had been for years — nobody knew for
sure how it had started, but however it had
started it had grown and each one had tried a

half dozen times to get the other into trouble. Cantry was a big man, but his bigness ran to fatness more than anything else, and as he had n't any education to speak of and was not at all active physically, jobs were hard for him to find. The job of watchman in the store yard suited him perfectly.

Higgins wrote anonymous letters to the building company, telling them that Cantry was n't paying attention to his job and was letting a few tools get away from the company for his own benefit. Cantry got hold of these letters, and it was easy enough for him to convince himself that Mike Higgins wrote them. There was always a chance for a fine fight at McManus's when Higgins and Cantry were there together, but the fights degenerated into vituperation, largely because Higgins was a small man and extremely active, whereas Cantry was powerful but very slow; neither one of them could see that much was to be gained by physical encounter. They came pretty near to blows that night, however, but the other men kept them apart and each of them took it out on the other by swearing he 'd get him some of these days.

McManus closed at twelve o'clock and Cantry went back to his office with his bed overhead, and Higgins went off alone somewhere. A half-hour later two plain-clothes men walking down Madison heard three revolver shots in quick succession and turned into Scott Street. There was a street lamp opposite 1721, which was next door to Cantry's office, and by the light of that lamp the plain-clothes men saw a figure on the sidewalk and a fat man leaning over it. They would never swear whether the fat man had a gun in his hand or not. They recognized the fat man as Cantry easily enough and they saw him go into his office. They ran along Scott Street and found Mike Higgins dead on the sidewalk. They found Cantry's office door locked and broke open the door and found Cantry upstairs half undressed. They arrested him and took him downstairs.

By that time two policemen had come in from Grant Street. They found a revolver with three empty chambers lying beside Higgins, and they found a revolver with all the chambers full in Higgins's back pocket. The revolver they found beside Higgins was afterward identified as being Cantry's or one exactly like a revolver that Cantry had had and which he could not produce. Cantry was indicted for the murder of Higgins and additional testimony was produced.

Mrs. King, who lived at 1720, diagonally across the street from Cantry's office, said that she had just gone to bed when she heard the shots. She jumped out of bed and ran to the window and could n't see anything for a minute, and then, as her eyes grew accustomed to the light, she saw Cantry with a revolver in his hand standing over Higgins's body. Mrs. King kept a lodging-house, and her only failing seemed to be loquacity; not a blot could be found on her character, nor could it be discovered that she was in any way prejudiced against Cantry. As a matter of fact, Cantry was a friend of hers, and she would be inclined to favor him in her testimony if she could.

Mrs. Cassidy, who lived next door to Cantry's office, gave even more damaging testimony than Mrs. King. She heard one shot just as she was going to bed, and it sounded as though it were right below her window. She rushed to the window and opened it, and as she did so she heard two other shots in quick succession. She looked out at the window and saw Cantry, whom she knew well, standing over Higgins with a gun in his hand. As was the case with Mrs. King, Mrs. Cassidy's statements could not be questioned. There was no doubt whatever that she was telling what she believed to be true, and while it would undoubtedly be possible to confuse her on cross-examination such procedure would result only in clouding the issue and hiding the real facts.

Other people of all sorts and descriptions had stories to tell of what they had seen and heard, but so far as truth could be distinguished from imagination, or purely emotional fabrication, what they said bore out the known facts of the case and the testimony of Mrs. King and Mrs. Cassidy.

It was easily proved that Cantry had been drinking, but that he was not actually drunk; it was also proved that when Cantry had had two or three drinks he got ugly — he was a man of violent temper, and up to a certain point the more he drank the worse his temper became. Cantry denied that he had shot Higgins. He said that he had been in his office when he heard the shots; that he had rushed out into the street and had seen Higgins lying there, and he went to him. He admitted that he had seen the revolver lying beside Higgins and he admitted that it was his revolver, but said that it had been stolen from him two or three weeks before. When he was looking at Higgins and the revolver beside him it never entered his head that it was his revolver; instead, he took it for granted that it was Higgins's revolver and that Higgins had fired at least one of the three shots. Cantry said he knew that if he were seen leaning over Higgins his position would be hard to explain, and he thought the best thing to do was to go to bed and deny the whole thing. He knew Higgins was dead and there was nothing he could do to help him.

He had looked up and down the street and had seen no one in either direction, and he admitted, as he must, that whoever had shot Higgins must have run to Grant Street to escape unless he could have got into one of the houses nearer Madison Street. No evidence could be found that any one had gone into one of the houses on Scott Street, nor had the plain-clothes men or the policemen seen any one on Scott Street or emerging from it, except Cantry. There was no escape between the place where Higgins lay and Grant Street on either side of Scott Street. There was a big warehouse with no doors in it on the north side; the store-yard gate and the door in it were closed and locked, and the saloon on the corner was closed.

That was the state of affairs when the court appointed Thomas Nash, a junior in Mr. Lyle's office, to defend Fred Cantry on a charge of murder. There wasn't a chance on earth for Cantry; he couldn't even plead self-defense, and naturally he made no attempt to do so, as he denied having committed the crime. He admitted the ownership of the revolver and insisted that it had been stolen from him, but he had told no one of the theft, as he did not want it known that he was unarmed and he did not want to pay for another revolver.

Tom Nash did his best to get Cantry to confess and plead guilty to murder in the second degree. He explained to him that the evidence was complete and overwhelmingly against him; no jury on earth would believe him innocent, and no defense was possible. Cantry insisted that he was innocent, but he offered no explanation whatever as to how the murder could have been done if he had not done it himself.

Nash went over everything with Mr. Lyle and Mr. Lyle threw up his hands. What could he or anybody else do in the face of the evidence which would be presented by the district attorney? Cantry's guilt was plain as day, and while it might be possible to confuse the issue, to entangle witnesses, possibly to bring about a retrial, none of those things would serve a useful purpose, as in the end truth must prevail. Nothing would be gained by postponing the inevitable. The district attorney stated that he would refuse to accept a plea of guilty of second-degree murder, and in due course Cantry stood trial, was convicted of murder, and sentenced to death.

Mr. Lyle, when he reached that part of his story, stopped and went back to the story Jimmy Norris had told.

" There," he said, " you have a strand of cir-

cumstantial evidence which proved beyond any
reasonable doubt that Cantry killed Higgins.
You have physical evidence; you have Cantry's
admission that Higgins had been shot with his,
Cantry's, revolver: he could offer no plausible
explanation of how his revolver had been stolen
or by whom it had been stolen.   The buildings
along the street made it impossible for the man
who killed Higgins to escape without being seen.
You have the positive testimony of two women
who, if they were prejudiced at all, were
prejudiced in Cantry's favor; one said that she
had seen Cantry leaning over Higgins's body; the
other said she had seen him standing there within
at most two seconds of the time the last shot was
fired.

"And yet, Jimmy, Cantry was n't guilty.
What evidence have you except your eyes and
your ears that your friend was guilty yesterday
afternoon?   How do you know that it was a golf-
ball that you saw in his hand and not some other
thing, perhaps a bit of paper or a flower — any·
thing that he had picked up or had had in his
pocket?   Perhaps it *was* a golf-ball which he had
taken innocently from his pocket to see, as we all
of us often do, what ball it was that he had been
playing with.   You know that we change balls
constantly in playing, and when one is lost we
don't remember just which one it was we had

been using. Suppose his having gone round in a circle and come back to where he had dropped the ball was simply a coincidence.

" Is it not more than probable that you were convinced of his guilt before you heard him speak and that the confession that you heard in his voice was nothing but your own imagination? Can you in a case like this trust your own eyes and ears as against a man's character? Are you, granting your superior intelligence, more to be trusted than the physical evidence against Cantry and the human evidence of the two women who saw him standing over Higgins's body with a revolver in his hand within not over two seconds in one case and four or five in the other of the time the shots were fired? You can't; you 're simply mistaken, just as we were all mistaken about Cantry; just as Mrs. King and Mrs. Cassidy told what they thought was the truth and told something that was entirely untrue.

" A man named Fleck, who lived at 1718 Scott Street, next door to Mrs. King's, was arrested for burglary and was guilty, and, further than that, he was about as low a character as can be well imagined. When he was caught with the goods and faced a long term in prison he tried to find a way out, and when Cantry was convicted of murder this man sent for me and told me that he had seen the whole thing. He told me

that he did n't like Cantry and that he did like
the man who had done it. That was why he
had n't said anything. Then he asked me what
I 'd do for him if he straightened everything out
and saved Cantry.

" You are not interested in that part of it, but
you are interested in the fact that a man named
Beggs was in Cantry's store yard stealing and
that Higgins, drunk, came down the street looking for Cantry or perhaps trying to find something on Cantry. Beggs had unlatched the small
door into the store yard, so that he could make a
quick getaway if he were discovered. Higgins
found this small opening in the large door unlocked and stuck his head in to see if anything
interesting was going on inside. He came face to
face with Beggs, and there was as little love between those two as there was between Higgins
and Cantry.

" Beggs knew well enough that Higgins suspected him of being in cahoots with Cantry in
the matter of stealing a few small tools from
time to time. Beggs was a dope fiend and a bad
actor generally; it was he who had stolen Cantry's revolver, with the intention of returning it,
perhaps, but he rather fancied it after a while
and decided to keep it. He drew that revolver
and shot Higgins, and Higgins started to run
and fell on the sidewalk, perhaps twenty feet

from the gate. Beggs took a quick look up and
down the street, saw that it was empty, and
finished Higgins with two more shots. Then he
went back through the gate and over the rear
wall, leaving Cantry's revolver behind him to do
a little dirty work for him.

"Fleck, the man who gave the whole thing
away to shorten his term in jail or to keep out
of jail entirely, had seen the whole thing from
the window of his room. He did n't like Cantry, and Beggs was a friend of his, so why inter-
fere? There was n't much question that Fleck
was telling the truth and no question at all that
he could distinguish the enormous Cantry from
the small, thin Beggs. In addition to all this
Fleck produced two other witnesses who had seen
the whole thing from beginning to end, and they
described every incident so accurately that there
could be no question that they were telling the
truth, and the bullet wounds in Higgins's body
corroborated their tale.

"Beggs was caught easily enough; they took
his dope away from him and drove him crazy, and
he confessed and went to prison for life.

"Mrs. Cassidy and Mrs. King retained their
reputation for probity, and when the final truth
was known experts in testimony understood perfectly well that the women had heard the shots,
had seen Cantry standing over Higgins, and had

jumped to the conclusion that Cantry had fired the shots into Higgins's body and had the revolver in his hand. They worked back from that, unconsciously, to make their own actions correspond in time with the thing which they believed they had witnessed."

Mr. Lyle smiled at Jimmy Norris. "What chance does your story stand, my boy, against the story of Fred Cantry? Forget what you thought you saw and heard and have faith in the honor of your friend."

Norman Dean rubbed his eyes with his fingers and then breathed sharply with a hissing sound between his teeth. It was a sort of sigh, an expression of relief. Hugh Ladd took a cigar from the box on the table and lighted it and blew great clouds of smoke into the air, as though he too could enjoy the comforts of life again. But Jimmy Norris sat slumped down in his chair with a frown on his forehead and his jaw closed tight, staring straight ahead of him. He sighed as Norman Dean had sighed, but with a different meaning. He rose and started toward the sideboard, as though he were looking for something to eat or drink. When he was half-way there he turned and faced them; he hesitated a moment and then said:

" On the fifteenth hole he drove out of bounds. The ball hit the hard tarred road, and there was a black mark on the ball as big as a ten-cent piece that he tried to rub off when the caddie brought it back to him, but it would n't come off. He played the sixteenth hole with that ball and the seventeenth, and on the seventeenth green I picked up his ball and tossed it to him and I saw that black mark on it. I did not notice whether he drove that ball on the eighteenth hole. When he reached the green after playing out of the woods there was no black mark on his ball. After dinner last night I went back to the woods and I went to the place in the woods where the caddie had said the ball was, and I found a ball with the black mark on it, and it had his initials stamped on it."

Jimmy Norris stopped and stood looking at them, waiting for them to speak. His eyes went to Mr. Lyle and stayed on him, but Mr. Lyle's head hung down till his chin rested on his breast; his eyes were half closed and his lips turned and twisted themselves into all sorts of curious shapes, but he did not speak.

Then Jimmy Norris, his voice husky, said: " I am much obliged for trying to straighten things out for me, but I guess there 's a black spot about as big as a ten-cent piece on my heart, or wherever those marks are put, and I 'm afraid it will have to stay there for a long, long time."

Mr. Lyle motioned Jimmy to come to the table, and when Jimmy was beside him he tore a sheet from a score pad and began to sketch on the back of it.

"Here is the green," he said, "with the hollow in front of it, and here's the top of the hill; here is the second hollow, with long grass in it, and here is the big oak-tree on the edge of the woods." Mr. Lyle made a cross on the paper. "As I understand it, it was about here that Stephen Lee lost his ball."

Stephen Lee! Mr. Lyle had spoken the word softly and casually, but Jimmy Norris took a step backward in horrified surprise and Norman and Hugh sat upright in their chairs, staring at him. Jimmy's face told them as plain as day that the man had been Stephen Lee.

"I thought you did n't know whom I played with yesterday," Jimmy stammered.

"I had n't the faintest idea," Mr. Lyle said. "I just guessed that it was he. You see, I played at Lanning Saturday, and on the tenth hole my ball struck the road and had a black mark on it as a result, about as big as a ten-cent piece. Those oily black marks stay on; water won't take them off. I lost that ball in the woods, on the eighteenth hole. It had my initials on it, S. L., and the only other man I know who has those

initials and might play golf with you is Stephen
Lee.   His ball was one of those new ' sixty-sixes,'
was n't it? "

"Yes, it was," Jimmy said.

"So was mine.   Suppose we settle this business, finally and forever."

Mr. Lyle rose, walked across the room to the
telephone, and called the steward at the Lanning
Club.   It took some time to rouse the steward,
but when he answered Mr. Lyle said:

"Won't you go to Mr. Stephen Lee's locker and
see whether, on the shelf or in one of the pockets
of his trousers, there is a quite new ' sixty-six '
golf-ball with a black spot on it, about as large as
a ten-cent piece? "

Mr. Lyle waited and finally he heard the
steward speak.

"Please say nothing whatever to any one about
this," Mr. Lyle said, and hung up the receiver.
Then he turned to the others.   " It was there, on
the front part of the shelf."   Mr. Lyle put his
arm around Jimmy Norris.   "How about it,
son? " he asked.

"Of course I 'm plain damn fool," Jimmy said,
"but I 've paid.   I hope you 'll all forgive me."

"Nonsense," Mr. Lyle exclaimed, "there 's
nothing to forgive, and you 're not the first man
whose eyes and ears have led him astray.   But
remember this: the mind seldom acknowledges

or thinks of the fallibility of its children, the senses, but those senses are far from infallible; they are often gay deceivers, whereas when we have known a man well for a long time and have faith in him, we may trust him in the face of all the adverse evidence in the world and be very sure that he will vindicate our faith."

PERCEPTION

FRANK MERRITT left the brokers' office where he worked, and went home. He opened the door and went upstairs without speaking to his mother, who was in the kitchen. He closed the door of his room, sat down in a chair, spread his arms on a none-too-firm table, put his head on them, and was just plain unhappy. Everything was wrong, so wrong that life was n't worth living, the world was no fit place to live in, and Frank did n't want to live. After a while he got up and started to spruce up a bit, decided not to, and then decided that he would, though he could n't have explained why it was worth while, considering how rotten a place the world was.

He went down to supper when his mother called him and sat through the meal without uttering two words together. It was nothing new; it had been going on for a month, only it was getting worse; even his sister had given up trying to tease him and was getting worried.

After supper he went out on the street and hesitated as though he did n't know which way to turn. Finally he decided to go west, and walked past house after house, each exactly like the one it was fastened to, two-story brown houses with more stamped metal cornice than they needed. He turned north, past two blocks of the same sort of houses in rows, and came to a corner, where he stopped. He stood there for half an hour, with woe on his face, calamity in his heart, and indecision all over him.

Frank was twenty-three, and Sarah Neely lived half a block down the street; Frank loved Sarah, and Sarah did n't love Frank. You could hardly blame Sarah, especially if her love was to have anything practical in it, for Frank was getting twenty dollars a week and not only had to support himself but, with his sister, he had to support his mother. Perhaps Sarah could n't see that loving Frank would get her anywhere. But that may not have been the reason; perhaps Sarah, who worked in a department store, was looking for pure romance, and Frank certainly was no romantic youth. No one would ever pick him out of a crowd to be a heroic lover or, for that matter, any other sort of hero. He was tall and thin, not handsome; his taste in clothes was not elegant, his manners were not polished, and he was not brilliant. But he had his good points: he worked steadily, he was n't fast, and he loved Sarah, thereby showing good sense, for she was quite worth loving.

But Sarah preferred Benny Scullin, who made thirty a week, had no one dependent on him, and was a man of the world, and Sarah was keeping steady company with him if she was n't actually engaged to him, all of which Frank knew only too well, and that was why, at the end of the half-hour, he turned away from Sarah's house and not toward it.

He jumped on a car and rode down-town, blew himself to a gallery seat at the Arena, saw the fights, went to the Palace Hotel, had a glass of beer with some friends, and went home. The next morning the dull life with no future to it began all over again worse than ever, for he saw Sarah Neely on the car going down-town, and what she said to him did n't help a bit.

Sometime after one o'clock that day Frank was eating lunch at a counter when a plain-clothes man came up behind him, spoke to him, and with no commotion whatever told him that he was under arrest, and led him away. Within an hour several men had identified him as the man who had stolen three thousand dollars in Liberty Bonds from the cashier's cage in the office of W. R. Fiske & Co., bankers and brokers. Frank refused to admit it, and he refused to discuss the matter in any way whatever, which was undoubtedly in keeping with his frame of mind. He did n't care what happened to him: anything

would be better than life as it had been, with
Sarah loving Ben Scullin.

The next morning Mrs. Green walked into
Samuel Lyle's office. Mrs. Green was a widow,
the aunt of Frank Merritt, and had been for
many years a servant in the house of Mr. Lyle's
mother. Mr. Lyle could have received her with
no greater courtesy if she had been the foremost
lady of the land. He listened to her story of
the misfortunes of her nephew and her proffer
of all her savings-bank money if Mr. Lyle would
only get Frank out of his trouble.

"There, there, Mary, don't cry," he said.
"There has probably been some mistake, and I'll
try to straighten it out. Money does n't count
between old friends. I'll see what can be done
right away." But his words brought little comfort to Mary Green; Frank had been arrested,
and there were too many had seen him do it.
Her one hope was that Mr. Lyle, the great criminal lawyer, could somehow or other get him off
— she did n't expect him to prove Frank had n't
done it.

When Mary Green had left, Mr. Lyle sent for
Thomas Nash, a young man in his office.
Thomas was the third of the seven younger
brothers of Mrs. Hugh Ladd. To him Mr. Lyle
explained as much as he knew of Frank Merritt's
predicament and told him to get all the details.

"Hugh and Norman Dean were the two men who saw him run when the alarm was given," Tommy said.

"That sounds bad for Merritt," Mr. Lyle said, "but let's see what we can do for him."

Accordingly Thomas Nash investigated the case against Frank Merritt, which was this:

On the day of the theft Norman Dean and Hugh Ladd had talked for nearly an hour with Mr. Fiske in his office. Their talk finished, they said good-by and, with their minds still on their business, left Mr. Fiske's room and stepped into the private corridor. A man was approaching them. They let him pass and were following him toward the street door when they heard shouts which came from the rear of the banking rooms. Norman's mind, unusually quick to assimilate impressions, connected the man who had just passed them with the cries and dashed in pursuit of him.

The office itself was nearly empty, the corridor entirely so, and there was no one to stop the man. He would, however, to escape Norman, have to open a heavy door and close it behind him. He found the door difficult to manage, and Norman was upon him. The man turned, stepped quickly to one side, and put out his foot. Norman tripped and fell, striking ineffectively at the man's head. Before Norman could scramble to his feet the man had gone through the door and disappeared in the noonday crowds on Main Street. He had left his hat behind him as the result of Norman's wild swing at his head, but afterward no one could be found who remembered seeing him or any hatless man on the street.

The evidence against Merritt started in the stock room of Fiske & Co., of which Walter Jones had charge, he being the only employee in it at the time of the robbery. He stated that Merritt had left the room just before the cashier's shouts were heard. Merritt had gone through the swinging doors, and so far as Mr. Jones knew might have turned to the right into the public corridor of the office building or to the left into the private corridor of Fiske & Co. Mr. Jones stated that Merritt had been wearing a blue serge suit, a red tie, and a dark-green felt hat, such as the one the thief had left behind.

Arthur James, the cashier, admitted that he had carelessly left the grill of his cage open and the package of bonds on the flat desk within reach from the corridor. He had heard a step, looked around, and had seen a man just disappearing. He noted the open grill, went to close it, saw that the bonds were gone, and yelled. He could not identify the man he had seen, as he had caught only a glimpse of his back as he turned the corner.

When Merritt had been arrested he was wearing a blue suit, red tie, and dark-brown felt hat. Within another hour Hugh Ladd and Norman Dean had seen and identified him as the man who had passed them in the corridor and who had run when James had shouted. The hat left behind had been positively identified as Merritt's by one Ferdie Schwartz. It was quite new, and a clerk in the store in which it had probably been bought had looked at Frank Merritt, shaken his head, and said he thought he had sold him a hat like that, but he was n't sure.

That, in outline, was the evidence on which the State expected a verdict against Frank Merritt.

Tom Nash tried arguing with Merritt, with no success. He simply stuck to his guns, saying that he knew nothing whatever about the business. Nash tried to work out an alibi and failed, for no alibi was possible whether Frank was guilty or not, for the whole affair had not taken over a minute. Merritt said he had left the stock room and had gone into the public corridor and thence to the office where he worked. He had dropped into the stock room just at twelve o'clock, his lunch-time, and stayed there maybe ten minutes. Nobody could tell when he had come in or gone out of his own office; he was in and out all the time anyway, especially around lunch-time.

When Thomas failed, Samuel Lyle tried his hand on Frank with no better results. Mr. Lyle explained that he would be convicted sure as shooting; there were three witnesses against him whose character and testimony would undoubtedly withstand all assault, and there was a fourth, Ferdie Schwartz, whose identification of the hat was positive and probably could not be shaken, no matter how much his character could be damned.

Mr. Lyle said that if Frank would confess and return the bonds, his youth, previous good character, and the fact that Mr. Lyle had great influence with Mr. Fiske and the district attorney would, taken together, undoubtedly make possible at least a suspended sentence, and he might even go scot-free and be given another chance.

But Frank was obdurate; he said he had n't taken the bonds. Mr. Lyle therefore told Mrs. Green that he would defend her nephew at his trial, but that he could offer her mighty little hope of his acquittal.

Mr. Lyle was at a loss for an explanation of Frank's attitude and told Tommy Nash so:

"There's something wrong somewhere, Tom, and I admit I don't know what it is. The man seems to be a commonplace fellow with no great strength or weakness, no particular imagination. No exception can be taken to his previous conduct. I am convinced that if he took the bonds he did it on the spur of the moment. The theft was not planned; no thought of stealing had ever entered his head.

"What I can't understand is his apparent indifference to what happens to him; why in the face of the evidence he should shrug his shoulders and give up his only probable chance of keeping out of jail, I don't know. Men like Merritt, if they are guilty, almost always confess.

"And what can he have done with the bonds if he did steal them? A thorough search has not discovered them, and the immediate deduction is that he gave them to an accomplice. He certainly could not have given them to an innocent person, for an innocent person would come forward and give them up.

"An accomplice, too, would be likely to give them up, for one receiving stolen property, knowing it to be stolen, is guilty of a crime, and such a holder would be afraid that Frank Merritt might confess at any minute. His refusal to confess cannot be based on his inability to return the bonds, for he could, under threat of exposure, compel his accomplice to return the bonds to him. The existence of an accomplice is, I think, very unlikely. If Frank stole the bonds simply because they were there to steal and not as the result of a well-laid plan, how could he so quickly find some one to deliver the bonds to? Such a person must be a friend, and a friend would know that Frank could not have owned the bonds himself and would have asked questions unless he was himself a crook. In that case would he stand his chance of prison for the sake of protecting a crook when in all probability the crook would never return the bonds to Merritt, but would keep them for his own benefit?

" No, Tom, there's something wrong somewhere. If Frank Merritt was a criminal at heart, if he had the cunning of a clever, experienced thief, we might be able to analyze his mind and discover the nigger in the woodpile. But he is n't — he has no great mentality, no ability to grasp facts in their true light, no broad vision, and what the train of thought of such a man may be, what motives he may have, what ideas he may evolve, are extremely difficult for us to comprehend. You and I can't understand how any one can be fool enough to steal, but there are lots of people who do steal.

" Frank Merritt has n't had much show to succeed. He did n't get much of a start from his parents; his education did n't amount to much. He has always been poor, and he lives in a world where money is god and the only god; the ticker, the baseball scores, and the racing-sheets are his Bible. To be poor in his world is a sin; the

possession of money is the only success; there are
no refining influences whatever. What effect
that sort of life has produced in Merritt you and
I can't know, but I make the guess that there's
something you and I don't know about this business. However, there's nothing that we can do
but let the case go to trial. Perhaps something
will turn up."

But nothing did turn up.

The evening of the day before the trial Tommy
Nash dined with the Ladds, and, of course, he
entirely ignored the professional side of life,
though the fact that the next day his much
respected brother-in-law was to be a witness for
the other side did add a bit of spice to the occasion. Tommy, however, made several mental
notes of things which seemingly could have
nothing whatever to do with Frank Merritt.

Mr. Lyle dined with Norman Dean and threatened him with a grilling when he was on the
stand next day, such a grilling as would try his
soul, at which threat Norman laughed. Mr. Lyle
also made certain notes which, it seemed, could
hardly have concerned Frank Merritt.

At eight o'clock that same evening a boy rang
the doorbell of the house of Mr. Walter Jones,
Fiske & Co.'s stock-room man, asked to see Mrs.
Jones, and walked into the house for that pur-

pose. He delivered a box of flowers to Mrs. Jones, took her receipt, and departed, but not until he had made one mental note. Mrs. Jones did not know who had sent her the flowers, nor did she or Mr. Jones suspect the taking of that one note, but Mr. Lyle knew all about both.

The trial commenced. The prosecution outlined its case and called Arthur James, the cashier, who swore to and described the theft of the bonds. Mr. Lyle did not cross-examine him. Then came Mr. Jones, who swore to Merritt's presence in the stock room and departure from it just before the theft had been committed. Mr. Jones was sure that Merritt had worn a blue suit and a red tie, but would not swear as to his hat.

Mr. Jones was then turned over to the defense for cross-examination. Mr. Lyle elicited from him that he knew Merritt, his name, and his business, and that Merritt dropped into the stock room virtually every day, sometimes two or three times during one day, and that Mr. Jones had no objection to his so doing, as his deportment was always perfectly proper. On that particular day he had stood up in the back of the room, perhaps for ten minutes, and then gone out by the swinging doors. Mr. Lyle then annoyed Mr. Jones by making him admit that he really did n't know how long before the theft Merritt had left the stock room. Mr. Lyle finally made him say that it *might* have been as much as fifteen or twenty minutes, though he did n't think so.

Having gone this far, Mr. Lyle hesitated for a moment. Then he turned back to Mr. Jones.

" You dine at home usually, Mr. Jones? " he asked.

" Yes."

" And you did so last night? "

" Yes."

" And spent the evening at home with Mrs. Jones? "

" Yes."

" Then will you please tell the jury the color of the dress Mrs. Jones wore last evening and something of its design? "

Mr. Lyle waited. Mr. Jones laughed, tried to think clearly, and immediately looked foolish. Mr. Lyle went back to his task.

" Of course I must ask you not to speak hastily and to be absolutely sure of your statement before you make it; I can hardly contradict you."

Mr. Jones stammered and finally said: " I think —" but Mr. Lyle interrupted him.

" Not what you think, Mr. Jones — what you know, please."

" I don't know; I don't remember."

" And yet you have been willing to swear that your description of what Frank Merritt had on

that day is based on what you saw before the
crime was committed and not on your observa-
tions when you saw him after his arrest and
heard what others had to say. That's all." Mr.
Lyle dismissed the witness and sat down.

There was a titter in the court-room.

Hugh Ladd took the stand and identified Merritt as the man who had passed him in the corridor and then run, but the identification had one
small flaw in it: Mr. Ladd could not swear that
the two men were one and the same beyond any
possible shadow of a doubt. They were similar
in size; they had the same type of face; the man
in the corridor wore a blue suit and a dark-
colored felt hat. He believed Merritt to be the
man.

Mr. Lyle made short work of Hugh Ladd. He
would not swear absolutely to the fact, and so
long as he would n't do that his testimony did n't
amount to much. Mr. Lyle was about to sit
down when he turned back to Mr. Ladd.

" Do *you* know the color of the gown Mrs. Ladd
wore last night? "

Hugh did not hesitate. " I do not," he said
and laughed, and every one else laughed. Every
married man in the court-room was trying to remember what his wife had worn the previous
evening.

Ferdinand Schwartz took the witness stand.

Ferdie knew Frank Merritt well, had known him for several years, and had met him by chance the night before in the bar-room of the Palace Hotel, which was next to the Arena, where they had all been to the fights.   Ferdie and Merritt and every one else drank beer.   Somebody spoke of Frank's new hat and said it was a good hat for a dollar, which raised a laugh.   A little later Ferdie happened to be near Merritt, and when Merritt tipped his chair back Ferdie reached over, took off his hat, and looked at it.   Merritt made no objection, and answered Ferdie's banter about the green lid with good humor.   Ferdie remembered the hat perfectly — could easily have picked it out from among a thousand like it.

When he heard about the robbery and the hat, and that Frank Merritt was suspected, he had had a look at the hat.   It was exactly the same sort of hat that Frank had been wearing the night before, but he would n't have said it was the same hat just for that; what made him positive was that there was a spot on it.   The spot was still plainly to be seen on the hat.

Ferdie was turned over to the defense for cross-examination.

"You are a friend of Frank Merritt's?" Mr. Lyle asked.

"I know him."

"Do you like him or dislike him?'

"I like him all right," Ferdie said.

"Then why were you so anxious to testify against him?"

"I thought I oughter," the witness admitted reluctantly.

"Were you discharged by Amos Swift and Company a year ago?"

"Yes."

"Because you stole postage-stamps and padded your expense account?"

"Yes."

Mr. Lyle wanted to show that Ferdie was antagonistic to Merritt, and that his character was not beyond reproach, but his main object was to get Ferdie mad. He accomplished that.

"You were drinking the night you say you saw Merritt's hat in the Palace bar?" Mr. Lyle asked.

"Yes."

"What did you drink?"

"Beer."

"Now, recollect carefully. Had you been drinking before you met Merritt?"

"I had not!" Ferdie was on safe ground now and was emphatic.

"Are you absolutely sure?"

"Certainly I'm sure. I went straight there from the A—"

"Never mind that, please.   Simply answer my questions.   Did you have more than one drink?"

"Yes."

"How many?"

"Three."

"Are you sure you did n't have more than three? Tell the truth."

"Ain't I tellin' the truth?   I had three and no more."

"But you were drunk, were n't you?"

"Drunk on three beers!   I was not."

The court-room laughed at Mr. Lyle, and Ferdie beamed.

"Were you absolutely sober?"

"I was!"   Ferdie was enjoying Mr. Lyle's discomfiture.

"Sober enough to know it was a green hat?"

"It was a green hat."

"You 're jealous of Merritt, are n't you?"

"No, I 'm not."   Ferdie grinned; he knew what Lyle was driving at. The court-room laughed again. Ferdie was getting the best of the great Lyle, and Mr. Lyle hardly knew which way to turn. In desperation he went back to the hat.

"You examined Merritt's hat very carefully that night and remember it so well that you can swear this to be the same one?"   Mr. Lyle picked up the hat and held it out toward Ferdie.

" It is ! "

" It was green ? "

" It was."

" And new ? "

" It was."

Mr. Lyle examined the hat again.

" And you saw a spot exactly like this one on it ? "

" I did."

" And the same sort of ribbon and bow on the outside ? "

" I did."

" And the brown leather sweat-band ? "

" I did ! "

" And the —" Mr. Lyle adjusted his eye-glasses and turned a little so as to get a better light on the hat. " And the maker's trade-mark stamped on the sweat-band in gold ? "

" I did ! " Ferdie was more emphatic than ever.

" And all you 've sworn to here is absolutely true ? "

" It is ! "

" That 's all ! " Mr. Lyle snapped the words at the vicinity of the witness-box. Then he turned to the jury. " Gentlemen, if you will examine this hat, you will see that it bears no name or trade-mark whatever, on the sweat-band or other-wise."

Mr. Lyle sat down, thankful that the prosecution had n't been quick enough to foil him. He knew that the jury would look on Ferdinand Schwartz's testimony with grave suspicion.

And then came Norman Dean, president of the great Lee Bridge Company, a man of wonderful intellect and pretty nearly Alden's foremost citizen.

Mr. Lyle listened as he gave his testimony, clearly and positively, with no reservations whatever as to the main point, namely, that Frank Merritt was the man who had run away from Fiske & Co.'s office. He swore unqualifiedly to the man and his suit and tie, and Mr. Lyle was afraid that the facts were exactly as Norman Dean stated them. But what he thought about it had nothing to do with it; what the jury thought was what counted.

He took Norman Dean back over the ground already covered, simply to emphasize that when Dean left Mr. Fiske's office his mind was on the business he had been discussing, that he had been naturally much excited while pursuing the thief, and that the whole episode had taken not over fifteen seconds.

That accomplished, Mr. Lyle smiled at Mr. Dean.

"Will you tell the jury what was the color of the dress Mrs. Dean wore last night?"

" Black."

" Exactly — an evening gown, simple in design, but having a small amount of, say, metallic scales on it and a bit of red, a velvet rose perhaps, on the waist. You remember them, of course — in fact, you may have noticed them particularly? "

" Yes, I did, at the suggestion of a friend." Mr. Lyle himself had spoken of them the night before.

" Quite so. Mr. Dean, there is a fireplace in your library with a mantelpiece over it. There is a clock on it. Will you tell me the color of the clock? "

" Black."

" And the face? "

" Black, with bronze letters and a bronze rim."

" Exactly. And the hands? "

" Bronze."

" Very good. Now we come to the point. Will you describe the shape of the clock, roughly, and tell me whether it is plain black or whether there is any ornament on it, and what type of numerals denotes the hours? "

" It 's clock-shaped, and there is a little gold ornament, a little tracery, on it. The numerals are Roman, ones, fives, and tens."

" Clock-shaped is excellent." Mr. Lyle smiled broadly. " You can do no better than that? "

Norman shook his head. " That's the best I can do," he said.

" Will you take my word for it that the clock, except for its face, is as plain as your derby, or must I produce the clock? "

" No, I think perhaps you are right."

" If you wish, I will also prove that there are no numerals whatever on that clock face, but instead that there are simply straight lines, heavier than the minute marks. Shall I do so or will you admit that you know little or nothing of the appearance of the clock you have looked at every day for these many years? "

" I admit that you are probably quite right."

" Your powers of perception are not at all good, are they? Suppose we forget the clock and go to something else. You carry a watch and chain, I believe, watch in one pocket, knife in another, chain between, connecting them? "

" Yes."

" You know, of course, the manner in which the hours of four and six are shown on your watch face — every one knows that — but tell me about your chain. How long is it? "

" About twelve inches."

" With closely woven links. How many links would you say there are in it? "

" Fifty or sixty."

" Won't you count them? "

Norman counted them. "One hundred and four," he said, "and it's about seventeen inches long."

"How long have you worn that chain?"

"Twenty years."

"And you've seen it a dozen times a day for those twenty years and yet underestimate its length forty per cent. Good. Now let me ask you another question. You eat cereal for breakfast every morning, I think?"

"Yes."

"And you have a small pitcher for cream; you have had the same pitcher for some years?"

"Yes."

"What color is it?"

"Red and white."

"True. Will you describe the handle, the shape of the pitcher, and the nature of its decoration?"

Norman described the pitcher as being white with two red bands around it and with a red handle. The pitcher came straight down from the top for about an inch, bulged almost at right angles, and then tapered inward and downward; the handle was very small and square, running outward from the top at right angles and then straight down to the bulge; the spout was sharp and projected about a half inch.

"Anything else?" Mr. Lyle asked, and when

Norman said he could think of nothing more, Mr. Lyle reached into a bag, took from it a red-and-white pitcher and handed it to Mr. Dean. "Is that the pitcher you have just described?"

Norman examined it and handed it back. "Yes, that's the one I tried to describe," he said, with a rather sheepish expression.

The assistant district attorney made an objection; he had been making objections right along. But the judge overruled him, and Mr. Lyle asked the stenographer to read Norman's description of the pitcher. He held it before the jury as the stenographer read. The pitcher was shaped like a barrel, not like a jug; the handle was white, not red, and it curved from the top to the bottom of the pitcher instead of being small and square; the spout was so small it could hardly be called a spout at all, and there were six red bands about the pitcher itself, not two.

"And you have seen and handled that pitcher virtually every morning for several years?"

"Yes," Norman admitted.

"And you dare tell this court that you remember the color of the real thief's clothes and tie and that you remember his face, when you saw him only once and for only a few seconds when you were under great mental strain? Bah!"

Mr. Lyle did not wait for an answer. He turned as though to speak to Thomas Nash, be-

side him, and found him gone.   He turned back
to Norman Dean.

" I see that my associate, Mr. Nash, has left the
room. You know Mr. Nash intimately, I
think? "

" Yes."

" You have seen him here beside me for some
hours? "

" Yes."

" What was the color of his suit? "

" I don't know."

" You mean that you have been looking at him
for two or three hours and don't know the color
of his suit? "

Norman laughed with perfect good nature.
" No," he said, " I don't remember, except that it
was dark."

" Dark, you say! We all wear dark suits;
can't you do better than that?   What color necktie was he wearing? "

" I don't know."

" Was it a bow tie or a four-in-hand? Please
know something."

" Four-in-hand, I think."

Mr. Lyle waved his hand over his head and
waited. Thomas Nash came down the aisle.
wearing a light gray suit and a bow tie. The
judge, the jury, and spectators laughed. Norman enjoyed the joke immensely. Mr. Lyle did

not even smile.   He handed a book to Norman.

" You are in the steel business, I think? "

" Yes."

" You are an engineer? "

" After a fashion," Norman admitted.

" That is common knowledge — please read the first line on page forty-four."

" ' The prisoner, Simon Samuels, stated that at one o'clock —' " Norman read.

" There are two large S's in that line; choose one, examine it closely."   Norman did so.   " Now you have discovered that a printed S is composed of two loops, the upper and the lower.   Which is is the larger? "   Norman went back to the printed S.

" They are about the same — the upper is possibly very slightly smaller."

" Correct, but only microscopically smaller. In other words, it requires close examination to discover the difference in size? "

" The difference is extremely slight."

" Thank you.   Your estimate is most interesting."   Mr. Lyle took the book to the jury and showed them the S's upside down.   The jury laughed.   Mr. Lyle took the book back to Norman and let him try the experiment.   " I recommend a visit to the oculist, sir," he said.

He walked back to his place.   " Another question," he said.   " You read the Alden

' News ' every day — have done so for years, I 'm
sure? "

" Yes."

" Then make me a sketch, quickly, of the ' E '
in Alden, as it appears in the paper's name at the
top of the first page in black letters an inch or
more high."

Again Norman laughed. " I don't know
whether it is block, script, or fancy," he said.

" Then let me show you." Mr. Lyle turned his
back on Norman, reached for a copy of the morning paper, faced him again and held up the paper
where the letter " E " might be seen.

" Mr. Dean," he said in solemn tones, " the defendant's future depends to a very large extent
upon your identification of him as the man you
pursued in Fiske and Company's corridor and
your absolute certainty as to the clothes and tie
that man was wearing. The other witnesses are
uncertain; one is not trustworthy. Your character is beyond reproach; you have told the truth
to the best of your ability. The question is not
of your veracity, but whether or not you are mistaken. There are many reasons why you might
be mistaken; we may discuss them later; now I
will ask you one question, and when you have
answered it I want you to tell the jury whether
or not you are absolutely sure the defendant is
the man you saw in Fiske and Company's office."

Mr. Lyle leaned forward to the table before him and then quickly stood erect. The Alden " News " hid his necktie from view.

" Will you please tell me what color necktie I am wearing? " he said.

Norman Dean did n't know, and for the first time showed signs of embarrassment.

" At least say whether it is of a bright color," Mr. Lyle begged.

Norman Dean shook his head. " I think it is a dark tie," he said.

Mr. Lyle drew the newspaper down slowly — his tie was light gray.

" That 's all," Mr. Lyle drawled, and shrugged his shoulders.

The prosecution rested, the defense offered no evidence, the district attorney and Mr. Lyle addressed the jury, each belittling the other's efforts, the judge charged, and the jury retired.

Mr. Lyle went back to his office. For a few minutes he sat deep in thought, puffing the cigar that he had lighted when he left the court-room; then he rose and took two or three books from the cases along the walls and laid them on the desk before him. They were not law books, but scientific works on the eye, optical illusions, color blindness, and powers of perception.

It was an old, old story to Samuel Lyle. For thirty years a constant stream of criminals had flowed past him; days in court were to him as days in the country are to farmers; the only thrill left in his professional life was the thrill of a dramatic situation planned by him and clearing up the mystery surrounding an event or an accusation. For hours he would plod along, apparently dull and methodical, but the opposing lawyers never knew when the lightning would strike, when he would suddenly send his voice vibrating to the farthest corner of the court-room and put an entirely different complexion on the case being tried. No one could ever tell what Sam Lyle was going to do.

But for all his experience, for all the contempt that familiarity breeds, Mr. Lyle had never become hardened to the pathos of the young and first offender.

The approach to vice is gradual, almost always; step by step the man nears the border line, and until he has actually crossed it and taken up his abode on the other side there is always the chance of saving him.

Mr. Lyle had been reading for half an hour when Tommy Nash came in, smiling. " Not guilty," he said.

" H-m," muttered Mr. Lyle, " apparently the jury had a sense of humor."

Tommy laughed. " Merritt's outside," he said. " I told him you wanted to see him."

Mr. Lyle shrugged his shoulders. "Will he talk now?" he asked.

"I don't know. Maybe you can make him. He has n't said anything to me; he does n't seem particularly elated."

"Bring him in," Mr. Lyle said, and in a moment Frank was in the room.

"I'm very much obliged — for what — what you 've done for me," he stammered.

"Do you really mean that, son?" Mr. Lyle said.

"Why, yes, of course I mean it."

"Do you mean it enough to prove it to me?"

Frank did not answer; his eyes wandered nervously about the room, and finally rested on Mr. Lyle's as though held there against his will. Slowly a smile crept across the great lawyer's lips, and his face became very kindly.

"My boy," he said, "you have a long way to go before you finish this life. The way may be smooth and pleasant; it may be rough and cruel. It depends largely on yourself, and you may take an old man's word for it, a man who has seen more than his share of this world's troubles, that the truth will always make the way happier and easier, and concealing it will always, in the long run, make it very much harder.

"You have been declared not guilty of the charge against you. The jury ignored the evidence; the jury was tricked, but now you can never be punished for that crime. But that is not the end; if you stole the bonds, you will be unhappy until you have confessed and made such restitution as is in your power; you cannot forget it, you can never be at peace with yourself until you have cleansed yourself of that black stain.

"Perhaps you did not take the bonds. All the evidence goes to show that you did, but for some reason which I do not know myself I believe you did not take them. I have acquitted you in my own mind, just as the jury did, but for a different reason. But I do believe that you know something about those bonds; I do believe that you were the man who ran when the cashier shouted; I do believe that you know the thief, and I believe that you are shielding him for some reason known only to yourself, and which is a crime in itself."

Frank Merritt had sunk into a chair as Mr. Lyle was speaking; his eyes were fixed on the older man's, his hands trembled, his face was flushed. Mr. Lyle made his final appeal.

"And so, my boy, if you will take my advice, you will tell the truth, all of it, all you know, and some day you will thank me for advising you to do it."

"I did not take the bonds," the boy muttered.

"No, but you were the man who ran away and

left his hat behind." Mr. Lyle's voice was soft and low, but very positive.

"Yes, I was."

Mr. Lyle's expression did not change. "And why did you run if you had not stolen the bonds?"

"Because I knew who did it." The strain had become too great; Frank had to talk. "I saw him come in from the office corridor and go to the cashier's cage, and I saw him take something and go out again. I could see him through the door of the stock room. I did n't think much about it then, but when I started to go out I saw the wicket of the cage was open, and I knew he 'd stolen something and —"

"You kept on going," interrupted Mr. Lyle, "because you did n't want any one to know what you 'd seen, and when you heard the cashier shout you were afraid that you 'd be made to tell if they caught you. You were crazy mad, you did n't stop to think, you just bolted, to save your friend. Is that it?"

"Yes, that 's it, except that he is n't any friend of mine."

"Not a friend of yours! Then why on earth did you want to protect him?"

"Because —" Frank stopped.

"Tell me, my boy, tell me," Mr. Lyle cried.

"Because — because he was a friend of a

friend of mine, and I won't say any more than
that."

Mr. Lyle's finger had been playing with a button hidden under his desk, and as a result just at
that moment a young woman came in and gave
Mr. Lyle a slip of paper, on which was written
that Sarah Neely wished to see Mr. Lyle. No
names of callers were ever announced aloud in
Mr. Lyle's offices when other people were there.
Mr. Lyle knew a good deal about Sarah Neely,
for Tommy Nash had unearthed her when he was
digging out facts regarding Frank Merritt's life
and associates, and he knew that Frank had been
very attentive to her. The shop-girl had been the
only feminine element that Tommy Nash could
discover.

"Ask Miss Sarah Neely to come in," Mr. Lyle
said quietly, and watched Frank Merritt as he
spoke. He saw the boy start and flush, and his
suspicion was confirmed. He sank back in his
chair, his eyes half closed, his hands hanging
limp.

Miss Sarah Neely came into the room slowly
and stood by the door, nervous and embarrassed.
Mr. Lyle's half-closed, dreamy eyes were on
Frank Merritt, and they saw what he had expected to see. He waited for a full minute and
then turned slowly to Sarah Neely.

"Well," he said, almost harshly, "tell me what

you know." The poor girl was too frightened to speak, and again Mr. Lyle waited.

Finally Sarah, in a voice so low and husky that they could hardly hear her, said: " I would rather talk — with — with you by yourself."

" Very well, in a moment. You know something that would have helped Frank. You are too late, he has confessed, he has confessed that he shielded the thief to save you from disgrace. He was a fool to do it — you don't care a snap of your finger for him — but he took a chance on prison because he loved you. It is easy to see that a man you love stole the bonds and that Frank was fool enough to protect him for your sake. Bah, how ridiculous you both are! "

Mr. Lyle's voice vibrated through the room as he shot the words at the man and the girl, but he himself was thinking very little of what he said — he was simply calling them names, and any names would do. He was watching them, and saw what he wanted to see; he saw the girl shrink from him and move slowly to Frank Merritt and then suddenly, when he cried that Frank had confessed, he saw her bury her head on his shoulder and Frank take her in his arms as though to protect her from Mr. Lyle's abuse.

Mr. Lyle stopped and sank back in his chair, smiling, and again he waited. Finally he rose and went to them.

"It's all right," he said gently. "I'm not going to ask you to tell me anything more. It looks as though everything had turned out all right for both of you. Run along and don't ever do anything foolish again."

Sarah was n't frightened any longer and Frank Merritt was n't mad or obstinate; they were both experiencing quite other emotions. They went out, Frank looking straight ahead of him and with his face crimson, but Sarah Neely, before she closed the door, turned and smiled at Mr. Lyle.

Tommy Nash was alone with Mr. Lyle.

"What perfect damn nonsense!" Tommy exclaimed. "Imagine his standing trial when all he had to do was to stop when the cashier shouted, let himself be searched, and deny any knowledge of what had happened."

"It's easy to imagine what you would do," Mr. Lyle said, "but not easy to imagine what a man like Merritt would do, especially when he is dead sure that the girl he loves loves another man, and the world is accordingly all wrong from beginning to end. I confess that it did n't occur to me that Merritt had stuff enough in him to sacrifice himself in that foolish, melodramatic way, until I saw him looking at her in the courtroom to-day — it's a good scheme to watch for things like that during a trial; you get all sorts of hints. That was when I got mine. I told you that it is almost impossible for us to guess at the working of a mind like Merritt's: you have to get it out in the open where you can see it before you can get anywhere. That's why I had Sarah come here and kept her hidden till we needed her. My guess happened to be right."

What happened to Ben Scullin, Frank's rival, and how Frank and Sarah overcame the very evident obstacles in their path, are other stories.

THE ALIBI

ARTHUR FRENCH, District Attorney of the County of Oxford, sat in his office in the court-house, with his feet on the table, his coat off, and his hair rumpled, thinking harder than he had ever before thought in his life, and, turn and twist the problem as he would, he could not satisfy himself which of the roads that lay before him led to success, honor, and justice before the law. He was a young man, ambitious, energetic, intelligent, and he had an overwhelming horror of letting the innocent suffer. Hence the problem, which was this:

The highway from Alden to the west runs through Hopedale and Stockton and then into the open country. A few miles beyond Stockton there branches from it a hard, wide road that runs north, curving through the rolling farm-lands for forty miles, and no more fertile land can be found anywhere, nor more thrifty and wise farmers.

Thirteen miles from Hopedale on the right of the road going north is the farm of John Parrott, five hundred acres of it. The house in which Parrott lived is about fifty feet from the road and

is of red brick and square; the front door is in
the center, entering a hallway which divides the
house in two.   On the right is the living-room.
The first floor of the house is two steps above the
level of the ground; in the living-room there are
three windows, the sills of which are level with
a man's elbow as he stands outside.   In the living-room was a small round table, with a kerosene lamp on it.   John Parrott's chair, in which
he sat in the evening, was between the table and
the door to the hall, and he always sat facing the
front of the house.

In this position, fallen slightly to the right, he
was found by his wife, Mary, shot through the
heart, at quarter after nine, on the evening of
Tuesday, October 2d.

Henry Parrott, John's younger brother, had
been accused of the crime and was in jail awaiting the action of the grand jury.

John Parrott was fifty years old; Mary, his
wife, twenty-nine.   Her story was that at quarter
before seven that night she left her husband with
his brother, and went to spend the evening with
Walter and Jennie Wendel, who lived a little
more than half a mile southward, along the main
road.   She returned at quarter after nine, discovered her husband's body, and telephoned Walter Wendel.

Wendel telephoned the police at Oxford, the

county-seat, six miles away, and the chief and two of his men arrived at a little before ten, bringing with them the county physician, who, after an examination, stated that John had died at about half-past seven.

The news spread rapidly, and before the police arrived there was a crowd of people about the house. Jennie Wendel was among the first to arrive and found Mary Parrott in a state of collapse. She put her to bed and sat up with her all night. The next day Mary's mother arrived and stayed with her, Mary recovering quickly so far as her health was concerned, and acting as any normal, grief-stricken woman would act.

John Parrott had been shot with a 32-caliber revolver and had himself possessed such a revolver, which could not be found. He had always kept it on the shelf of the closet in his bedroom upstairs. A few days later this revolver was found in the mud on the bank of a small pond, hardly more than a widening in a brook, which touched the road and flowed under it about a quarter of a mile south of the Parrott house. It had evidently been thrown from the bridge with the purpose of having it fall in the pond. The thrower's aim had been poor, or he had judged the direction badly in the dark, for the revolver had struck in a bush which overhung the bank and dropped through it to the mud beneath, where it was hidden from casual observation.

Mary Parrott had arrived at the Wendels' before seven o'clock. Henry Parrott admitted that she left him alone with her husband. Henry admitted that he had had a more or less heated argument with his brother and had left him and gone to the Eagle Hotel, a small country tavern a few hundred yards beyond the Wendel house. He thought that he left the house at about half-past seven and reached the Eagle at about quarter to eight. Three or four men at the hotel confirmed the time of his arrival, but their confirmation was based on mere guesses and proved nothing of value. Henry's admission that he left the house at half-past seven was damning evidence against himself, for John had been killed at just about that time.

Certainly no one had any knowledge of the location of John's revolver except Mary, Henry, and the cook. It was admitted that Mary could not have fired the fatal shot, and the cook had been away all day and did not return till the following morning and her whereabouts during that time had been proved.

Of the three men who lived and worked on the farm two, Fred Smith and Andrew Gregg, were away with the automobile truck in Alden, and the other, Mike Foley, had gone to the Eagle Hotel about seven o'clock and in passing the house had heard the two brothers talking together with some signs of anger. He left the hotel before nine, and in passing the house on his way to the dairy noticed that there was a light in the living-room, but he heard nothing and did not look in. Two other men who worked on the farm by the day had gone to their homes in time for supper and had not left them.

There had been no robbery, no struggle. John had been shot by some one standing in front of him, either in the room or outside of the house. The latter was quite possible, as the night was unusually warm, and the window which John had faced was open and at a convenient height. The presumption was that John and Henry had quarreled and that Henry had gone upstairs, gotten the revolver, come down, shot John, gone down the road, thrown the revolver toward the pond, and gone on to the hotel.

John Parrott had been an honest, industrious man; he was well known and well liked. So far as could be discovered, he had n't an enemy. There was no imaginable motive for his murder, except Henry's. John was not a brilliant man; he was slow of speech and cared nothing for even such limited gayety as the farming country afforded. He stayed at home, except when at rare intervals he went to Alden for a day on business. It was generally believed in the com-

munity that he had made no will, a fact which
various people said he had mentioned to them.
He had made a will, however, which was dated
the September 20th previous; that is, only two
weeks before his murder.

There was evidence to show that Henry Parrott knew nothing of the existence of this will
and that he had good reason to suppose that no
will existed. Now, if no will did exist, Henry
would, at John's death, fall heir to about half
of John's property. Under the existing will
everything was left to Mary Parrott. But Henry
knew nothing of that will. Here was the foundation of a strong motive.

John Parrott had been a religious, sober, and
exceptionally moral man. Henry had no scrap
of religion in him, he worked only by fits and
starts, and he had a weakness for drink, which
was considered to be the cause of his other fail-
ings. He was a genial, happy-go-lucky man,
with no sense of responsibility, who turned up
periodically at times of financial stress. Henry
was seldom drunk, but he was often under the influence of liquor, which made him happy and
never morose. He was never vicious, always
meek; never combative, always peaceful. There
was plenty of evidence that he loved and admired
his substantial elder brother, and there was no
question whatever that, while John was greatly

disappointed in him, he loved Henry deeply. It was one of Henry's weaknesses that he made people like him and was satisfied with that and seemed to care nothing for their respect.

Thus Henry Parrott had had the opportunity of killing his brother, the weapon was at his hand, he had been arguing angrily with him shortly before his death, and had had the opportunity of throwing the revolver into the pond; there was ample motive, there was no known motive for any one else to kill him and no apparent opportunity. Who could, for instance, have obtained John's revolver?

As to the cause of the heated discussion between the brothers, Henry refused to discuss it. He said that there had been no ill feeling and that he would tell nothing of it. It had been suggested that John had just told him of the will, but that seemed improbable, for John's death would then be the last thing in the world Henry would desire. On the other hand, there was a remote possibility that that news and John's refusal to change the will caused Henry to lose his temper and murder John in a fit of anger. Henry was admittedly a little under the influence of alcohol at the time, and while this was known to have previously made Henry jovial rather than otherwise, a man in that condition follows no precedents.

Feeling against Henry was high in the community, his guilt was generally accepted, and the clearing up of the whole thing was demanded. Arthur French had little doubt that he could convict Henry of murder in the first degree and that the verdict would be universally approved, but he was not convinced that the thing would be proved beyond a reasonable doubt, a jury to the contrary notwithstanding.

He recognized the weakness of " If Henry Parrott did n't do it, who did? " and he was strongly of the belief that Henry was not the stuff of which fratricides are made.

So the district attorney of the quiet county where there had been no other murder for a generation had a real job on his hands as he sat in his office in the fall twilight, thinking hard. He had been there an hour when he suddenly made his resolution and acted upon it.

He called Samuel Lyle on the telephone, and Lyle asked him to come to Alden the next morning and tell him the whole story. The great criminal lawyer was a very old friend of Arthur French, whose father and Samuel Lyle had been chums for many years.

The next morning Arthur told the story just as it has been told here. Samuel Lyle listened without interrupting him; then he asked a few questions. In answering them Arthur said that

John Parrott had been married six years and was childless. Everything pointed to the fact that his domestic life was happy, that his wife loved him, although it was possible that originally she had had her eye as much on John's worldly goods as on the man himself.

Mary was tall and strong, with unusually fine development; she had some degree of rustic beauty, which was enhanced by the bloom of perfect health. She was keen of mind, smiled much, and laughed often.

The men on the place were of the usual type of farm-hand; four of them had unquestionable alibis, and the fifth a good one, and he was a man of excellent character and could have no imaginable reason for killing his employer.

Henry Parrott admitted the correctness of all the evidence against him, was willing to answer every question, except to explain the argument with his brother, and denied that he had committed the crime, or knew anything about it.

"You know, Arthur," Mr. Lyle said, "that some crimes, even when the evidence is not absolutely complete in the eyes of a trained lawyer, are so plain that a jury will cast aside quibbles and convict. That is one reason for juries of laymen. A mathematician recognizes the fact that if we match pennies I might win a hundred times in succession; you and I know that such a thing is utterly impossible." Mr. Lyle got up and walked to the window, leaving Arthur to turn that idea over in his mind. For some minutes Mr. Lyle blew cigar smoke against the window-pane. Then he turned back to the young district attorney.

"However, it is a beautiful day, and if you're not busy, I should like nothing better than a ride in the country. Suppose I get my car."

This was more than Arthur French had hoped for. Advice he had had from Samuel Lyle many a time, but the great lawyer had never before left Alden and gone professionally out to Oxford County. Arthur spoke of that to Mr. Lyle.

"But this is the first crime of moment in Oxford County within the memory of man; perhaps we may be able to turn up something interesting. Crimes in cities are seldom picturesque; they are dull matters of routine following well-established lines. I don't get a thrill in Alden once in a blue moon, but in the country, where emotions are elemental and minds simple, there must be some extraordinary circumstance to bring about a murder. In this case we undoubtedly have a man whose moral fiber has been weakened by drink, killing for money. But — who knows?

"Your proof is not complete; perhaps there is something more to be discovered, and it is a perfect day, and how precious warm, sunny days are just before winter comes! Suppose we go to the Parrott place."

They were there within an hour and walked slowly about the farm. Samuel Lyle saw the five men who worked on the farm and spoke to them. They were very evidently depressed, which was to be expected of men who had lost not only a good master but a good friend. From them Mr. Lyle learned nothing, except that at various times they had seen John and Henry Parrott talking together earnestly, but only once, just before the murder, had there been any unusual feeling exhibited.

They found Mary Parrott with her mother. Mr. Lyle offered her his sympathies and explained that he was well aware what a terrible shock she had suffered, and how bravely she had withstood it and that nothing was farther from his desire than to annoy her with more questions if they would in any way add to her unhappiness.

But Mary was not at all averse to talking; she told Mr. Lyle the story that she had told everyone else, a story that even the accused man admitted was true. She ended by saying that her one wish was that she might be able to do something for her brother-in-law, Henry, for notwithstanding his faults she was very fond of him and was sure that he was innocent.

At this Mr. Lyle nodded and said that he hoped

so too, but that it seemed impossible the crime could have been perpetrated by any one but him. Then he asked Mary a few questions which led nowhere, except one, which disclosed that so far as she knew her husband had loaned no one any money, which closed another door to freedom for Henry.

Arthur said that John Parrott had not only owed no one any money, but had a surprisingly large amount of money of his own.

They declined Mary's invitation to stay to dinner and drove south along the road till they came to the bridge across the brook that ran from the pond, at which, but not into which, John Parrott's revolver had been thrown. Mr. Lyle took from the tool box two wrenches, which Arthur thought approximated the revolver in size and weight, and sent the car on with orders to the chauffeur to return in half an hour. Then he climbed the fence and walked along the bank. Cattle came to drink there, and the soft earth along the banks was pitted with their hoofprints to where the bushes began. Arthur showed him where the revolver had been found and he sent Arthur back to the bridge with the wrenches and he himself stood beside the bank. At his direction Arthur threw a wrench toward him, with the intention of having it fall close to Mr. Lyle. It fell well short of him. Again Arthur threw the wrench, this time as far as he could, and still it did not reach Mr. Lyle.

Then Mr. Lyle walked along the banks of the pond, prodding the bottom with his walking-stick. In every case he found it very soft, there being no sign of stones or gravel. He went back to the bridge, and, taking the lighter of the two wrenches, threw it as far as he could into the water, and marked the distance with two twigs stuck on the banks. Then he climbed the rail of the bridge, sat on it, and lighted a cigar. "Arthur," he said, "I did not see any water along the road except this. Did I miss any?" Arthur said that he had not.

"Then I want you to send half a dozen men here with long-pronged rakes and have them go over the bottom of the pond. It is shallow; they can do it comfortably in rubber boots. Have them begin on the line we have marked and work away from the bridge. If they don't find anything, let them work this way, but be sure they do a thorough job. They had better do it at night, when they will not be seen; they can work as well then as in daylight, for the water will be muddied in any case, and they will have to depend on their sense of touch, anyway. You will send the men from Oxford, I suppose, in charge of an intelligent officer."

"All right," Arthur said; "I'll have them here

to-night," and then he waited, hoping that Lyle
would say something more, but he sat and
smoked, and said nothing.

"What do you expect to find, Mr. Lyle?"
Arthur asked, his curiosity being too strong for
him.

"I don't expect to find anything, but I don't
like to overlook any chance; if nothing is found,
that information may be valuable in itself. Of
course the whole thing must be absolutely
secret."

Arthur nodded.

The car came and they drove to Oxford.
Arthur arranged for the search; they had a late
lunch and went to see Henry Parrott. Henry
was playing solitaire in his cell and was a sorry
figure of a murderer. Mr. Lyle put the matter
to him squarely.

"Parrott," he said, "I have no intention of
bulldozing you. I have no right to: I have no
official connection with the case; I am simply a
friend of the district attorney. His duty is to
discover the truth, not to convict innocent men.
If you killed your brother, I advise you to say
nothing, apply to the court to have counsel as-
signed to you, if you have no funds of your own.
If you are innocent, you will, beyond all reasonable doubt, never be convicted even if you
are brought to trial, but it is your duty, if you

are innocent, to lend all the aid you can to the authorities who are trying to find the guilty person. You have told the truth, but not all of it. It is your bounden duty to do all you can in support of the State, to assist the law which protects you and your fellow men, which even now is doing its utmost to protect you, to discover the truth, to bring the guilty to justice and save the innocent. You, as an American citizen, cannot shield the guilty; you cannot obstruct the true course of justice, no matter where guilt may be, without yourself becoming not only a man guilty of a crime in the eyes of your fellows, but a man who must always be dishonored in his own heart.

"That is the broad, honorable view of your situation. If you are innocent of this crime, but have knowledge of it and do not reveal it, you become a partner in that crime and are only less guilty than the perpetrator himself. I have been long in this business, and never yet have I known of a case in which good was done, where suffering was lessened, where harm was not done by the withholding of knowledge which would throw light upon the truth and reveal it. Perhaps you do not know who killed your brother, but you have strong suspicions: that is perfectly evident from your manner and behavior. What are they?"

Henry Parrott smiled, an inconsequential, indifferent, good natured smile.

"I 've told Mr. French all I know. I s'pose he 's told you."

"Yes, he has told me all you have told him, but you have not told him why you were quarreling with your brother."

"That 's between him and me."

"Was it about the will?"

"I never heard of the will till he was dead."

"Money, then?"

"No, it was n't money."

"Something about the farm, or the men on the farm?"

"Nope," Henry spoke positively.

"Drink?"

"No, he spoke to me about that often enough, but not then." Henry Parrott was willing to give negative answers. It is hard not to answer questions at all, and he took the easy way out; he answered when the answers did not reveal the secret.

"Your plans for the future, then?"

Henry shook his head. "No," he said. "I did n't have any plans."

Samuel Lyle exclaimed: "Come, Parrott, tell us; it is bound to come out sooner or later." Mr. Lyle was very evidently without hope.

"No, I 'm not goin' to tell you. It 's between John and me. I promised I would n't ever tell a livin' soul."

"As you will; be it on your own head. It can-not help John now."

"That depends on how you look at it," Henry said, and would say nothing more.

Alone in his office with Samuel Lyle, Arthur looked at him expectantly.

"Well?" he exclaimed.

"Well, well, well," laughed Mr. Lyle. "Par-rott told us exactly what we wanted to know, did n't he?"

"Did he? Somehow I did n't get it."

"Arthur, if you know that one of, say, six things is the truth and the man who knows the truth says that five of 'em are n't it, what 's the answer?"

"Clear as crystal, except that nobody has limited this to six possibilities, and five from, say, a hundred does n't leave one. Do you get me?"

"Of course, but my statement was probably correct; note that I say probably. Think it over: what other reason for a quarrel could there have been? Come and see me, or telephone me to-morrow morning, when you have worked it out; the will, money, business, drink, Henry's plans for the future — that makes five — what's the sixth? And if you fish up anything in the pond to-night, let me see it, just as nearly in the condition you find it as possible."

Early the next morning Arthur French rushed into Samuel Lyle's office. Arthur had gone to bed at five o'clock and had risen at seven. His appearance suggested that he had not slept and that he had not taken off his clothes. He placed a bag on Mr. Lyle's desk and took from it a towel wrapped about a small object.

"There it is, just as we found it, mud and all," he exclaimed.

Mr. Lyle examined the object casually, screwed up his mouth, and gazed at Arthur.

"Well, well," he said, "what do you think of that?"

Arthur shook his head. "It's too much for me, Mr. Lyle."

"Then suppose we call in an expert or two," he murmured, "and see what they can tell us." He reached for his telephone, called Orchard 20, and asked for Inspector Gibb. The inspector answered promptly. Mr. Lyle asked if the inspector would do him a favor. Apparently the inspector would, for Mr. Lyle asked him to come at once and bring with him his best man on firearms.

Inspector Gibb arrived in five minutes, saw

Arthur, and said: "Parrott case?" Arthur nodded.

"What's up?" asked the inspector.

"There," said Mr. Lyle, "is a revolver found in the pond near the Parrott place. It looks like a thirty-two. The other was a thirty-two and had one chamber discharged and the others loaded. The same conditions seem to exist here. All I want you to do is to tell me whether this is a new gun, how long it has been in the water, who sold it, who bought it, and any other points in connection with it that occur to you."

"That's some contract," the inspector laughed. "How about it, Gene?" Mr. Eugene Schalk was the inspector's best man on firearms.

"Oh, I don't know," Gene said. "We can make a try at it. Suppose we take it over to the shop."

"Being very careful not to lose it," Mr. Lyle suggested.

"Never fear," the inspector said; "maybe you'd better take the number of it, so's you can identify it later."

The number was noted and the officers departed.

Three days later Eugene Schalk made his report.

A week later Arthur French was in his office, but this time he was not sitting wrapped in thought in his chair, with his feet on the table. He was walking about nervously, moving chairs, arranging papers on his desk for the tenth time, and giving other signs of extreme agitation. Murders in the quiet county of Oxford were rare, and Arthur was a very young man.

Presently Samuel Lyle came into the room with Inspector Gibb, and a moment later Ben Greatly, chief of police of Eastdale Township, followed. Ben had been shaking his head sadly since the night of the murder, which was the only part he had played in the tragedy.

The four sat about the table, Samuel Lyle at the end of it, facing the door to an adjoining room. The transom of that door was open. They spoke in whispers, when they spoke at all, and waited. Finally, the door to the corridor opened, a man appeared, nodded and withdrew. Arthur walked to the corridor door, threw the bolt, and returned to his seat. Samuel Lyle, who had slumped in his chair until his clothes were a mass of wrinkles and rolls, drew himself up, breathed inward deeply, and spoke, not to the men about the table, but to an invisible jury across the room, by the door whose transom was open.

" An English judge once said that the prisoners tried before him were just like other people, and that, but for different opportunities and other ac-

cidents, they and he might very well be in one
another's places. And a French judge wrote:
'Greed, love of pleasure, lust, idleness, anger,
hatred, revenge; these are the chief causes of
crime. These passions and desires are shared by
rich and poor alike, by the educated and uneducated. They are inherent in human nature, the
germ is in every man.'

"We have in this case a striking example of
the dual crime. The murder of King Duncan by
Macbeth and his wife is such a one in undying
literature. There are many dual crimes in real
life, in the highest and lowest strata of society,
in all lands, in all ages, crimes famous, crimes
sordid and forgotten. Remember Cassius and
Brutus, Antonius and Octavius, Ferdinand and
Isabella. Scipio Sighele, an Italian, has written
of dual crimes that he finds an *incubus* and a
succubus, the one who suggests the crime, the
other on whom the suggestion works, until he
or she becomes the accomplice or instrument of
the stronger will; 'the one playing the Mephisto-
phelian part of tempter, preaching evil, urging
to crime, the other allowing himself to be over-
come by his evil genius.' In some cases these
two rôles are clearly differentiated; in some
cases they are not. This, I think, is a case of
the latter class, but I am not sure.

"A great French judge, speaking of such a

dual crime as that with which we are dealing, said that it was necessary to seek an explanation of it in any abnormality which was negatived to all appearances by the antecedents of the guilty pair. It was necessary to ask it of anatomy or physiology. The crime was the result of moral degradation gradually asserting itself in two individuals, whose moral and intellectual faculties were the same as those of other men and women. It is by a succession of wrongful acts that a man first reaches the frontier of crime and then at length crosses it.

"In the case before us we have to deal with impulses which we can hardly criticise, impulses with which nature cursed us. At first the woman was as far from criminality as the most innocent among us. She was hardly more than a child, primitively reared, knowing nothing of the world, used to hard work and few pleasures. She married a man twice her age and thought little of the future, except that she was assured of comparative luxury and a release from everlasting housework. She soon found material comfort a sham, she found her husband cold, unresponsive, self-centered. She was a large, strong, well-formed woman; in her childhood she played with material dolls, in her youth she thought of dream babies, in the first years of her wedded life she dreamed of the reality. If she had had children, this crime would never have been committed.

"So she met the cold facts of the barren world face to face. She was as much alone as though she had been alone on an island in the sea. She had no healthful recreation, friends were few and difficult of access; the future was dark and drear. She had been enlightened and she was unhappy, but she was still innocent of a degrading thought.

"Then, when she was twenty-seven, she met by chance a man, casually and properly. He amused her; she fascinated him. They met again and again openly, in her husband's sight, with no objection from him. The result was inevitable. She was a wife with passion instilled in her, with the craving for love strong within her, crying for a strong man to hold her, comfort her, and protect her. Her husband treated her as a father might treat a child whose devotion he required, but did not openly return.

"In the eyes of the man she was a beauty, and, in fact, she has fine beauty of a sort; her body is lithe and graceful, her eyes alluring and crying aloud to those with sense to understand.

"The man and the woman became friends. They found little opportunity to talk confidentially and met clandestinely. She confessed that she was lonely and unhappy. The man was young, and the woman tempting. They walked together, he held her arm occasionally, and she made no objection. He soon did it constantly. They stood close together, his hand resting on her; she protested mildly at first, then consented. He kissed her, against her will, then against her ever-weakening resistance. Finally she considered it no crime to lie in his arms and receive his kisses. She reasoned that she was entitled to such innocent happiness. They met in the secluded woods, made safe by darkness.

" The man confessed love for her and asked for hers. She sprang from him and left him, but sent for him again and listened to him over and over again. The barrier between them was a mere convention, unholy in the eyes of God, a thing to be swept away. The man proposed the consummation of their love. Her brain reeled, her heart throbbed, her blood was on fire, she was consumed by a mad desire, of mind and body, for the young, strong man.

"Yet, gentlemen, she refused, but told him of her love, spoke openly of sacred things, of her passion, her longing for him.

" In the man there was but one all-controlling, overwhelming desire, and that the possession of the woman. He, an ordinary man, such as we — of spotless reputation, clean living — was as a feather in a gale. His sense of right and wrong was numbed, he was conquered as prehistoric man was conquered; he would stop at nothing to gain the body and soul of the woman.

" She held her virtue sacred, yet proposed or consented to the removal of the obstruction that kept them apart. It matters not which proposed, the man or the woman; their minds became cool and calculating; she did her part with all of her woman's artifice. John Parrott made his will leaving all his property to her; the scene was set, a man to suffer for them was ready at hand. With unearthly cunning the thing was planned so that there would be no suspicion thrown on them.

" But they planned too cleverly. They evolved schemes that were so complicated and so impossible of natural occurrence that the accidental discovery of one item of their schemes has led to the uncovering of all, and they forgot that while murder, contrary to the old saying, does not always out, yet it never fails to leave its trace, to set up such an unstable state of equilibrium that a simple touch is enough to bring the crime toppling down upon its perpetrators, and they forgot, too, that it is impossible to prove a murder against a man who has not committed it."

Samuel Lyle raised his right hand, and In-

spector Gibb stepped quickly and noiselessly to
the door, the transom of which was open, and
all the time Lyle was speaking.

"And so, gentlemen, I have tried to lay before
you the —"

Mr. Lyle nodded and Inspector Gibb snapped
open the door, of which the transom was open.

"Won't you come in, Mrs. Parrott?" Lyle
said, and then in a whisper to Arthur French:
"Watch her eyes, watch her eyes."

Her eyes were well worth watching.

The woman was in the doorway, her hand on
the casing of the frame, as she had been when
Inspector Gibb had opened it, as Samuel Lyle's
words were still pouring into her ears. She had
been surprised with her face ashen, her bosom
sunken deep, her eyes crying defiance and great
despair.

"Won't you come in, please, Mrs. Parrott?"
Arthur French's voice was husky.

Slowly, one foot dragged after the other, she
passed the inspector and approached the three
men standing beyond the table. Behind her
walked a matron, who took her arm and led her
to the chair that was waiting for her. She sank
into it, holding herself weakly by a hand on its
arm and another on the table. Then, seated, she
drew herself up, drew her breath sharply through
her teeth and her eyes met the eyes of Samuel

Lyle. For her there was no other person in the room.

"Madam, you are under arrest for the murder of your husband, John Parrott, on the night of the second of October of this year, and I warn you that anything you say may be used against you."

As Arthur French stopped speaking the woman turned slowly toward him; for a moment she stared at him as though she had no conception of what he had said. Then her lips curled derisively and she turned away from him, back to Samuel Lyle.

The silence in the room was profound. It had been arranged that after Arthur French's warning they should wait until Mary Parrott spoke, if it took an hour. Arthur was motionless in his chair, his eyes fixed on the woman's eyes.

They waited, and waited, and waited, every man of them in torture, except Samuel Lyle, whose eyes never left Mary Parrott's. She dropped hers to the table before him and, lifting them again after a long interval, found his waiting for her — deep, gray eyes, cold and remorseless.

"Well?" Mary's voice broke the silence.

"Remember that anything you say may be used against you," Samuel Lyle said in a voice so low that it was almost a whisper.

" You 're a fool — you 're all fools," and Mary
Parrott tried to laugh at them and achieved only
a hoarse cry.

" No, Mary, we are not fools. You were in
love with Frank Warner; you are not to blame
for that; it was beyond all your powers of resistance. If, instead of marrying John Parrott
six years ago, you had married Frank Warner,
you would have married a good man, and you
would undoubtedly be a good and happy woman
now. But you married John Parrott and gave
him your vow. Instead of keeping that vow, you
plotted against him and killed him."

" You lie!" Mary Parrott leaned forward,
her clenched fist on the table beyond her.
Samuel Lyle shook his head slowly.

" No," he said, " I do not lie. Your decision
to kill your husband came slowly, as slowly as
your acknowledgment of your love for Frank
Warner, but when that decision was made, you
never wavered, and plotted skilfully. You stulti-
fied your love by thinking of money; you per-
suaded your husband to make a will leaving all
his worldly possessions to you.

" Then you took from the closet five cartridges
and gave them to Frank Warner. Whether you
then proposed to manufacture evidence against
Henry Parrott, we do not know, and it is not important. You did manufacture it finally.

" Frank Warner took the cartridges to Alden and purchased a revolver which they would fit and a box of extra cartridges. Instead of going to a large store where many sales are made and customers come and go, leaving no trace, he made the mistake of trying to be seen by as few people as possible, and went to a small store, the proprietor of which remembers the sale, has a record of it, and remembers the man. Then Warner tried his new revolver so as to be sure of his aim.

" On the fatal Tuesday you telephoned him to come that night, that all the men would be away. In the meantime you had evolved the hideous plan of placing the guilt on your brother-in-law. Frank Warner fired one of the cartridges taken from your husband's supply and gave you the empty shell. This you put in your husband's revolver under the hammer, and you both forgot that the hammer marks of the two revolvers might not be alike.

" On Tuesday night you left home with the revolver hidden on your person. Either you met Frank Warner and gave it to him, or you left it in a prearranged hiding-place, or you placed it under the bushes on the bank of the pond; it does not matter which of these you did.

" Frank Warner went to your house, not along the road, but by the path along which he had gone to meet you so many times. He waited in

the darkness, undoubtedly hearing the heated
argument going on within, and when the farm-
hand passed and heard it too, Warner rejoiced.
Fate was good to you. Warner gave Henry Parrott time to get beyond hearing, but no more time
than was necessary. He crept to the window.
If he was discovered, he had an explanation ready
at hand: he had been there often before. But
he was not discovered. Through the window he
shot your husband. He went back as he had
come, along the path.

" Perhaps he had with him your husband's revolver, and perhaps it was his part to place it
where it was found. It does not matter; either
he put it there or knew that it was there. He
reached the brook, and the desire to dispose of
the weapon of the crime seized him as it does all
criminals. He had an inspiration, a fanciful
conceit. The pond was at hand, why not let it
hide his revolver forever as it had cunningly
failed to hide your husband's? The thing burned
in his hand. He might by ill chance be found
with it in his possession if he kept it a second
longer. He threw it into the pond.

" Then he went to the place in the woods where
he had left, not his automobile, but one he had
borrowed in Hopedale, saying that his was out of
order. He wanted no one to recognize his car
on the road. There are thousands of the kind

he borrowed, as alike as two peas, and to make safety doubly sure he put mud on the license plates, so that the numbers could not be read. He forgot to clean them before he returned the car. His brain was too active; he overdid himself.

"All this time you were at the Wendels', and they say that they noticed in you no nervousness nor anxiety; that you acted normally, that you laughed and chatted. Yet you knew that, if your plans did not miscarry, your husband would be, had been, murdered, with your knowledge, with your approval, and with your assistance."

Samuel Lyle spoke the last words slowly, and in a low voice that yet was sharp as a razor's blade. The words cut deep and damned the woman; they were the malediction of humanity upon an outcast.

Mary Parrott's eyes were held to his as if by an invisible force. She was weak of body, her mind was stunned, but always her eyes saw only the eyes of Lyle, and she could not have turned them away if she would.

So they sat, the great, strong man facing the wretched woman. The men about seemed not to breathe, but stared and waited, waited, waited.

Mary Parrott's hands were clenched, the trembling fingers forced their nails into her flesh, her breath came fast and with a catch in it, as

though she could not breathe deeply; her breast
trembled, tried to rise and could not; her
shoulders drooped forward, and her head, so
that her eyes looked upward to Samuel Lyle's.

Suddenly a spasmodic tremor passed through
her body, as though her breath had gotten into
it; she gasped once or twice, and then jerkily
she sat upright, her fingers tearing at the throat
of her waist. She threw her head back, the color
rushed to her face, and she was a glorious animal
to see. And then she laughed, a long, loud,
screeching laugh, her arms stretched out before
her.

Her arms crashed downward to the table, she
leaned forward, and with the passion only such
a woman as she can possess, she cried:

"You fool, you fool. Frank Warner has an
alibi. He was —"

She did not finish. Samuel Lyle sprang to his
feet. He shrugged his shoulders, spread his
hands apart, and turned from Mary Parrott.

"You see, gentlemen, it is as we expected. An
alibi prepared and ready is a confession of guilt.
The innocent do not scream the word 'alibi' at
the moment of accusation."

Then he turned back to Mary Parrott.

"Frank Warner's alibi was cleverly conceived.
He and his friends told stories that fitted as a
hand and a glove, but they told the story of Wed-

nesday night, not Tuesday. They had no lies to tell, except the one lie of the night. It is a ruse as old as the hills. The alibi was clever, by itself, the using of another's car was clever, by itself, but the alibi and the car did not interlock. He was too clever."

The wild cry of Mary Parrott had ceased when Samuel Lyle turned his eyes from her. She heard him speak and understood, and then she screamed as she had never screamed before, a long, shrill, inhuman cry that suddenly died to a rasp of anguish as she fell forward against the table, slipped from it, and crashed to the floor.

She was unconscious but an instant, and as they lifted her the door from the corridor opened and Henry Parrott walked into the room, bewildered.

Mary Parrott saw him, but she was beyond all power of speech. Henry Parrott saw her and the men about her, and understood. He rushed forward and leaned across the table toward her.

"Mary, Mary," he cried, "tell me that it's not so."

But he needed no word from her; he knew the truth only too well. And the tears rolled down his cheeks, for a good-natured drunkard cries easily.

That night Arthur French sat in Samuel Lyle's study. The youth was weary, for never had he spent such a day. Mr. Lyle was calm and comfortable, and smoked his cigar, at peace with himself and the world. For him it was an old, old story.

"Arthur," he said, "it's my dog-gone craving for melodrama that makes me do those things. I can't get along without fool exhibitions such as we had to-day. Other men have the drink mania, or drugs; I have the theatrical, tragedical craving. Of course those two unfortunate creatures could have been arrested, jailed, tried, and convicted according to Hoyle; instead they both have confessed, the man's confession denying the woman's participation. He has regained his manhood; he has been delirious; he has been through hell. I am inclined to believe the woman wholly at fault, morally. She hypnotized Warner; she led him to the gates of Paradise, enchanted him, held him bound by her spells, and then offered Paradise itself, offered him herself forever, if he did her bidding." Samuel Lyle threw his head back and blew clouds of smoke into the air. "Arthur, would you mind if I defended him? I believe that I could get him a second-degree verdict. But I forgot, you prosecute, don't you? It wouldn't do; but don't be too hard on him."

They sat in silence for a long time, till the young man said: "Mr. Lyle, I don't understand how you got your first idea of the thing. It's all clear to me except that, but it seems to me that you knew what was what as soon as you'd heard the story from me."

"The frigid husband of fifty and the childless wife of twenty-nine was suggestion enough, was n't it?"

"Yes, I got that far myself, but there was n't a word of gossip about her, and I could n't find a suggestion of anything wrong."

"Exactly. Do you remember that I told you to-day to watch her eyes? You did and you saw enough emotions in them for a picture-play thriller, but you saw her under great mental strain; the natural, everyday expression was not there. The day that I went to her house and saw her for the first time I watched her eyes. I cannot possibly describe what I saw, but it was unmistakable and convinced me of the probability of what has become a fact.

"I have seen female criminals of the worst type whose eyes were clear and steady and sweet and innocent as a pure and beautiful young girl's. I have seen fallen women whose eyes were as honest and lovely as a child's. I have seen all sorts and descriptions of eyes that lied and would give no inkling of what was going on behind them, but I have never seen eyes like Mary Parrott's that did not tell the truth; they

are absolute proof of character. The eye itself
speaks plainly, but the lids and the skin at the
outer corners of them speak more plainly still.
I am sure that I can stand on a crowded street
corner and pick one woman with such eyes from
among every hundred that pass, and that all of
them will have the same weaknesses that Mary
Parrott has, and the same capability of doing
wrong. Many of them never do wrong, but they
need only the proper suggestion, the right circumstances, and the deed of passion will follow
inevitably.

"Thus I knew that Mary Parrott was capable
of the crime; it might well be the climax of her
original weakness. It was necessary that there
should be a man. It might have been Henry
Parrott, if he had been more of a fellow. He
would n't answer the purpose, yet he played a
heroic part. Of course he loved Mary; he tried
to save her by enlightening her husband, but apparently John was too self-satisfied to recognize
the truth when he heard it. Henry denied to us
that he was talking about five things; the only
other thing I could think of was the eternal
feminine, and Mary was the only female available for discussion. It will be interesting to
see how much Henry Parrott will disclose, now
that he knows we have the main facts.

"As to the finding of the second revolver, that

was pure luck. As I stood on the bank it suddenly occurred to me what a fine place that pond was to hide a revolver, and, knowing that Parrott's revolver had never been thrown from the bridge, I had an inspiration. It was an inspiration because it turned out right; if nothing had been found, I'd have been thought a fool."

NUMBER 14 MOLE STREET

IF you walk along Main Street in Alden, past
its big buildings, to Elm Street, and then turn
northward, you will notice, as you go on, Oak,
Ash, and Willow Streets, but you will not,
beyond all reasonable doubt, even suspect that
you have crossed Mole Street.

Yet there it is, between Ash and Willow, and,
what is more, on the wall of the saloon on the
corner is the name in white letters on a blue
sign, "Mole St." But it is a very narrow and
inconspicuous street, and it does not cross Elm
Street and never reaches Cedar Street at all,
which is the street parallel to Elm Street on the
west.

And Mole Street is now almost as it was many,
many years ago, for the great buildings which
have sprung up about it for blocks in all direc-
tions have ignored Mole Street and left its
antiquity undisturbed. But time has placed a
heavy hand upon it, for whatever its modest af-
fluence may once have been, now it is in terror
of the devastating hand that hovers over it.
Landlords can see no object in repairing and
painting buildings that soon must pass from

Alden to the heaven of old houses. Thus, shutters once a snowy white are gray or brown and often hang askew, with a hinge gone; bits of woodwork have fallen and passed away; iron railings are rusted and here and there bent with old age. Each house has six or seven steep steps up to its first floor, and the once white marble is dirty with the grime of years, worked in by feet and washed in by rain, beyond removal.

Commerce, too, has of late years worked its trembling and temporary way into Mole Street. A carpenter and builder has hung out an ornate sign; two florists, advertising " Wholesale," do a lagging business; and a quick-lunch restaurant has come, died, and gone away, leaving a " To Rent " sign behind. But all these are close to Elm Street and do not disturb those who live in the houses that are numbered from 16 to 32 on the north side and 13 to 31 on the south. Thus old Maggie Clancy, who sits on the landing of her steps with just room to squeeze her old rocker between its railing and the doorstep, thinks nothing of the stores, but only of whether any one will come and gossip.

But Mole Street had, only a few days ago, a store almost as ancient as the street itself, and no man living can remember when it was not there. Over its door is the century-old sign, " Adolph Bachman, Bookseller," and Herman

Swann, his nephew, had let it stay and never even put his own beside it.

And this store alone on Mole Street was bright and clean and in as good repair as house had ever been. Its steps were white, its window-panes shone with polishing, its paint was all that good paint should be. Curtains starched and trim were at the windows, a row of red geraniums smiled down into the street, and the brass door-knob and knocker were yellow as burnished gold. This was Number 14 Mole Street.

So it was on the afternoon of October 29, 1918, a day as warm as midsummer. Children played in the street, boys at marbles, girls with dolls, and hopping from square to square marked out with chalk on the narrow sidewalk. Pigeons stepped along the asphalt, hoping for a crumb of food among the not quite cleanness. Mrs. Clancy dozed in her chair; a woman of savage mien, with head thrust through her window, rested, with her elbows on the sill; one colored woman on a door-step talked with another across the street. It was very quiet and very peaceful and very, very far from the turmoil of the city that was only a hundred feet away.

That was at four o'clock. At ten minutes after four Mole Street was in a turmoil and filled with people, many of whom, ten minutes before, had never heard of it. And the manner of it was this:

The door of Number 14 opened, and Hannah Swann, as clean and fresh as the house itself, came out. For an instant she stood on the topmost of the white marble steps, looking up and down Mole Street, and then she saw down at the corner of Elm the great figure of Andy Higgins, the cop. Then with a speed most remarkable for so old a woman, she descended the six steps and ran toward him. But her speed was not sufficient, for she had a wild fear that Andy might go on his way and be lost forever. Therefore Hannah screamed and Mole Street awoke, and, so quickly that it was almost beyond belief, the multitude poured into Mole Street.

Andy the cop went into Number 14, followed by Hannah Swann and many others, and from that moment there were only cold facts to deal with and the romance of old things went out of Mole Street completely.

In the room back of the book-store was a large iron safe, its two heavy doors wide open, and on the floor directly before it lay Herman Swann, a great welt across his forehead. Andy knelt beside him, felt swiftly over his heart, touched his eyelids, and rose.

"He's dead," he stated, and let it go at that. Then, realizing that death was but the beginning

of serious things and with a fine training to back
him up, he said: " Out wid yer, avery wan, and
touch nothin' as ye go."

The news that old Herman Swann had been
killed, and everything in his safe stolen, spread
through Mole Street in a flash, and the last edi-
tions of the evening papers had a note of it inserted on their front pages, which they qualified
by stating that it " appeared " to be murder and
robbery. Samuel Lyle read it and was sad, for
he had known Herman Swann and his books for
many a long year.

It was by the merest chance that Mr. Lyle,
walking along Orchard Street about nine o'clock
that evening, saw and recognized Henry Ward.
Mr. Ward was no more than a casual acquaint-
ance of Mr. Lyle's, chatted with a few times at
Herman Swann's, but that night there must certainly be a bond of sympathy between them, for
they had both been good friends of Swann.

Mr. Lyle stopped and spoke to Henry, and a
very few minutes later they were at a table in
Slavin's basement grill, Henry with a mug of ale
before him, Samuel with a pot of tea. Henry
was telling all he knew of Herman Swann's
death.

To tell the story as Henry told it would be impossible, for Henry was an Englishman and came
from the class which has a subtle way of add-

ing and dropping "h's" and using inflections
that defy cold print, just as Herman had always
come very near calling Henry "Heinrich" and
never had.

About two that afternoon, Henry said, Herman had left Hannah to tend shop and had gone
to the Alden Trust Company and perhaps to
other places, for he did not return until about
three. He brought back with him an afternoon
paper and a large envelope. These he took to the
back room and, opening the envelope, spread its
contents on his desk before Hannah's eyes and
smiled at her. There were ten one-thousand-dollar bonds of the Fourth Liberty Loan.

Hannah told him to put them in the safe before anything happened to them, and went upstairs. An hour later she came down and found
her husband lying before the safe. The newspaper was on the floor beside his chair, and
everything was just as it had been when she left
him, except that the Liberty Bonds were gone.
She had heard no one come in, but she probably
would not have heard it if any one had come in.
Herman's keys were in his pocket; the inner
compartment of the safe had not been opened;
nothing had been touched except the bonds.

So much Henry knew and told, and Henry's
mug was empty, a fact which Samuel Lyle
noticed and corrected.

"Who killed him?" Henry said, repeating the question Lyle had asked. "That I don't know and I can't think it would be any one but a stranger who came in and saw the bonds and —" Henry's gesture explained the rest.

"You have known him a long time?" Lyle asked.

"Forty years. We're the same age: 'e was seventy; I 'll be that in another month if I live."

Lyle was surprised: Ward looked not more than fifty.

"And we both came over about the same time, both of us to Mole Street, and we 've both been there ever since, 'e from Munich, I from Liverpool. I saw 'im sitting on 'is doorstep and spoke to 'im after we 'd been 'ere ten years, and we 've been the best of friends ever since. 'E came over to work with 'is uncle, Adolph Bachman, who was 'is mother's brother, and Adolph left 'im the bookstore. 'E was soon married, and every Saturday night I 'd 'ave supper with 'im and 'Annah. I 've always been a travelin' man, but I 've always took good care to lay out my route so I 'd be back 'ere by Saturday. And after supper we 'd play chess. Ah, but we 'ad some grand battles. Poor 'Erman!"

"And when the war came?" Lyle asked.

Ward shook his head slowly. "That was a bad time," he said, " a bad time indeed." Then his face brightened. "But it came out all right. I was away for two weeks when the war started; I could not get back that Saturday, and when I walked into 'is 'ouse I 'd made up my mind what was the thing to do. ''Erman,' I said, ' we 've been friends a long time; this thing shall make no difference with us.' 'That is right,' he said, ' it shall make no difference!' 'We will go on as though there were no war,' I said. 'You and I are Americans; we will forget what we were when we were boys. You and I will never speak of the war.' 'No,' 'e said, ' we will never speak of the war.'

"But it would not do. I would go to 'is 'ome, and 'e would sit and glare at me, and I could not speak to 'im. The thing was there, between us, and we could not 'ide it. I was afraid what would 'appen, for I loved 'Erman. Finally 'Annah saved the day. ''Enery,' she said, ' and 'Erman, this will not do. You two must talk. One night a month you must talk about the war. It is in you, and you must get it out. Talk one night a month, and then forget, and on other nights you will be 'appy.' And that is the way it was. One night a month we talked war and we were 'appy and liked each other as well as ever, but I was sorry for 'im when the 'orrible stories were told, and 'e shook 'is 'ead. ''Enery,' 'e 'd say, ' it cannot be; the German people would not act so.' I would n't argue that with 'im.

"I said that all was right between us after the war started, and we thought it was, but afterward we knew that we 'd been mistaken. That was when the United States went into it and a very remarkable thing 'appened. Two of 'Erman's grandsons, sons of 'is daughter Mary, who 'd gone West, volunteered, and a nephew of mine, my youngest brother's boy, did the same, and they came 'ere to Alden together, though they 'd never 'eard of each other before.

"'Erman and I saw them 'ere and saw them go on their way together, and afterward we went back to 'Erman's 'ouse, though it was not Saturday night, and all the while 'e was very quiet and said little, till after dinner 'e looked up at me and I saw tears in 'is eyes and 'e takes my 'ands in 'is and 'e says: ''Enery, 'Enery, you and I are not Bridisher and German, no part of us; we 're Americans and nothing else,' and in a minute we were both laughing and there were tears in my eyes too. After that everything *was* all right, and every Saturday night we 'd stick pins in a map and talk of winning the war."

Lyle was tearing bits of paper into minute particles, and kept on doing it after Ward stopped speaking. Ward filled his pipe and searched for matches, ignoring the match-safe on

At quarter after twelve, as Henry turned into Mole Street

no one else had gone in after three o'clock, till
Andy the cop and all the others went in and
found Herman dead.

If that story had been told by only one person,
perhaps it might have been questioned, but when
it was emphatically told by a lot of people and
details furnished, it could hardly be doubted.
So, of course, Henry was arrested and locked up
for the night, and the next morning he sent for
Samuel Lyle and told him the whole story.   Then
Mr. Lyle called a taxicab and kept it waiting
while he talked with Inspector Gibb and the
district attorney, who explained the evidence
against Henry.

Mr. Lyle drove to the plant of the Lee Bridge
Company and had a talk with Alex White, the
superintendent, and Donald Gregg, the purchas-
ing agent.   Then he telephoned Inspector Gibb,
and at eleven o'clock he wandered into Mole
Street.

Old Mrs. Clancy was again sitting wedged in
on the narrow landing of her steps.   A policeman
was at the door of Number 14, and strangers
were coming and going out of idle curiosity.
There was an ever-changing group of them opposite Herman's house, gazing up at it, just as
though it had not been there to see for nearly a
hundred years, just as it was then.

But none of them spoke to Maggie Clancy, and

the table. Lyle pushed it toward him, and
Henry was confused. " I was thinking of something else," he said apologetically.

" I 've known Herman a great many years,
too," Lyle said, " though not forty, as you have."

" Books brought you together? "

" Yes, and kept us together.   They are a hobby
of mine.   I have the finest library of worthless
law-books and criminal records in the world, I 'm
sure."

" And others besides that are n't worthless."

" A few," Lyle smiled, and they talked of Herman Swann and books till midnight.

At quarter after twelve, as Henry turned into
Mole Street, he was arrested for the murder of
Herman Swann and for the robbery.

There was undoubtedly sufficient evidence to
warrant Henry's arrest. Shortly after three
o'clock that afternoon half a dozen people had
seen him leave his house, which was Number 30,
and walk along Mole Street, carrying a heavy
walking-stick, such as might have struck the blow
that killed. He went up the steps of Number
14 and went inside; a few moments later he came
out and walked to Elm Street and disappeared.
He had not been seen again in Mole Street until
he was arrested. All the people who had seen
him go into Number 14 were absolutely sure that

knowing that it made no difference to her mother
what time it was, had done no such thing.

Mr. Lyle went to the kitchen door and looked
at the backs of Mole Street's houses, counted till
he identified Herman's and noted that there was
scant opportunity for entrance, either physical
or visual, to Herman's back room. Then he
talked commonplaces for a few minutes, for
courtesy's sake. Again in Mole Street he
managed to talk with Annie Macgregor — who
had seen Henry go into Number 14 and disre-
membered how she knew that it just after three,
but who knew it sure enough, for why would n't
one know the time of day? — and Hattie Rourke,
who had seen the whole thing and knew what
time it was because she had sent Tommy to the
store and he 'd took longer than he should, like
he always did, and she looked at the clock and
it was ten minutes of three, and ten minutes
after that, or maybe fifteen, she looked out the
window and seen Tommy coming, and Henry
Ward at the same time. When Mr. Lyle asked
her if she had waited long enough to see Henry
Ward go in and come out of Number 14, when
she was in such a hurry for the thread Tommy
was bringing, she said she 'd told the police what
she 'd seen, and she guessed that was enough.

It was quite enough for Mr. Lyle, and he set
about approaching the one inhabitant of Mole

Street in whom he had a deep-seated interest, and that was Tessie Murphy, who, when she heard, as she did promptly, that Herman Swann had been murdered and that it had been done after three o'clock, had rushed to the first blue-coated officer she saw and said that Henry Ward had did it, and the officer had passed her along, higher up.

Tessie was fourteen and smart as they make 'em, and if it had n't been for school's being closed, she would have been there then and not sitting on her steps, half playing and half watching the baby in the carriage, George on the curb, and Susie beside her.

Samuel Lyle had guessed what description of young woman she was and when he approached her it was with great admiration for what she had done. Tessie, being busy and at the very end of Mole Street, did not know that she had till then been slighted for less important people. Mr. Lyle did not waste words.

"You 're the girl that caught him?" he said, nodding down Mole Street.

"What 's that to you?" Tessie found further joy in suggesting that, great as the deed had been, it was nothing for her.

"I just want to get a photograph of the girl who caught him," he said. "Pictures of a girl like that get in the papers, you know."

" You don't say! " Tessie put every bit of
sarcastic disdain she could into that short statement, but it was far beyond Tessie's powers of
dissimulation not to show that she was deeply
interested.   " You a reporter? "

" Of course, I 'd pay something for the photograph," Lyle said.

" Would yer? "   Tessie spoke as though the
matter were quite uninteresting and beneath consideration, but she could n't play the game long.
Lyle waited.

" How much would yer pay? " she asked de-
fiantly.

" Five dollars, perhaps."

" I don't want no perhapses; I want to know."

" Well, it would be five dollars if the girl
should be nice and pleasant and tell me all about
it so that there 'd be something to write to go
with the picture."   It is quite possible that Mr.
Lyle was not acting honorably toward Tessie.

" Watch him," she cried, indicating the baby
carriage, and flew into the house.   In a moment
she returned, her picture, held close to her.

" Give us the five," she demanded.

" Tell me how you happened to catch him."
Mr. Lyle was not to be caught, himself.

" I was a-playin' here an' he comes out, an' I
sees him an' I says: ' His n't hit ha be-u-tifful
die? ' to him an'—" Tessie's rapid speech

showed anxiety to have the five dollars quickly.

" What were you playing? "

" Hop-scotch — where you see them white marks — an'—"

The marks were a house or two down Mole Street.

" He had his heavy walking-stick with him, did n't he, that he killed Mr. Swann with? "

" Yes, he did, an' he waved it at me like he was agoin' to hit me like he always does when I talks to him like he talks an'—"

" Did he laugh? "

" He made belief be mad like he always does, an' goes on down the street an' goes into the book-store, an' in a minute I seen he 's come out again an' walkin' toward Ellum."

" And did you see his walking-stick then? "

" Certainly I seen it, an' him a-swingin' of it, an' just then Mom calls me an' says have I give him his bottle." This " him " was indicated by another nod toward the baby carriage. " So I give it him, an' when I come back he 's gone."

Tessie finished with her eye on the five-dollar bill Samuel Lyle was holding in his fingers.

" Yer goin' ter give me it? " she demanded.

" I surely am, in just a minute, if you 'll tell me what happened when the people went into Mr. Swann's."

Tessie would tell anything to hasten the moment of possession.

"First off, I hears Mrs. Swann scream, an' I sees the cop a-runnin', an' I runs an' I gets there 'most as quick as them, an' then I remembers him "— again the baby carriage —" an' I starts back, but I see Mom's by him an' I goes back, but I can't get in on account of the crowd, an' I just stands round as close as I kin, like, an' I hears people talkin', an' after a while I hears a man say he must of been kilt just after three o'clock, an' then right off I remembers how I sees him goin' in the store right after three on account of me goin' fer his bottle what he gets at three o'clock an' was late."

"I see," said Mr. Lyle. "You knew it was after three because your mother called you and asked you if you 'd given the baby his bottle, and you had n't, and you knew that your mother would n't call you till it was time."

"That's right," Tessie exclaimed, "an' what's more, I knows 't was late because I 'd heard the clock in the parlor strike, an' I knew it was time, an' I'd orter of done it, only I wanted ter finish the game, an' when I went in I seen the clock, an' it was a quarter past."

"You did very well, Tessie, to remember all that so clearly. You have certainly earned your five dollars." And then, as though the Fates were playing a practical joke on Mole Street, Mr. Lyle heard the dull, wheezy notes of the clock in Tessie's parlor striking twelve. Mr. Lyle could just hear it, and he was on the door-step, and the door and a window were wide open. Mr. Lyle looked at his watch. It was quarter before twelve.

"There you are, Tessie," he said and, handing her the bill, he walked away, down Mole Street.

It was Saturday night, four days after the death of Herman Swann. Hannah, his widow, was upstairs with her sister, who had come to live with her at 14 Mole Street. Below, in the back room, where chess had been played and battles fought, surrrounded by shelves of fine old books that had been close to Herman's heart, sat Henry Ward and Samuel Lyle. They had been hard at work all day long, going over the affairs of the dead man, for they had been named his executors in the will. It was ten o'clock, and they were ready to call it a day.

Yes, Henry Ward was there, a free man and beyond suspicion, for he had told Samuel Lyle exactly what had happened on Tuesday afternoon, and Mr. Lyle had been able to produce proof that Henry's statements were true.

Henry had left his house on Tuesday afternoon at a quarter of three, carrying an umbrella which

he had borrowed from Alex White, superintendent of the Lee Bridge Company, and not a
walking-stick at all. It had been his intention
to put his head into Herman's door and say
" Good afternoon," but just as he was about to
climb the steps he saw Herman himself turn into
Mole Street. Therefore he spoke to Herman on
Mole Street and walked to the Union Station,
which must have taken not less than ten minutes
at the very least. At the station he took the
local train that leaves at three-two, and on the
train he sat with Dan Carrouthers, who was a
traveling man himself, and besides that he
chatted for a moment with the conductor, whom
he had known for years.

Henry had an appointment with Donald Gregg
at three-thirty, and he was there on the dot, and
mentioned the fact and noted the time to Alex
White, when, on the way, he returned his umbrella. Henry delivered to Donald Gregg a letter
which was a proposal for tool steel, and Gregg
stamped the letter with his recording stamp as
soon as he had read it. The stamp on the letter
was perfectly clear, and it bore the date " October
29–'18," and the time, " 3.40 p. m." Henry left
Donald Gregg and went out into the shops and
chatted a while with John Harvey, who had been
a wee lad in Liverpool when Henry sailed away,
and he went home to dinner with John and had

been on his way home when he met Samuel Lyle, having heard the story of the murder from John's son.

By the time Inspector Gibb and the district attorney had all those facts straight, they knew also that Herman Swann had died of heart-disease as he rose from his chair, and that he had fallen, and that his forehead had struck against the sharp iron sill of the safe.

So there had been no murder, and the only mystery was the theft of the Liberty Bonds, for they had not been found, and there was not the faintest evidence to show that any one had entered Herman Swann's store between three and four o'clock. No one but Henry Ward had been seen to enter the front door; and the back door, every window, and the scuttle to the roof were locked fast.

But the bonds were gone, and some one must have come in unnoticed and walked past Herman, lying dead on the floor, and taken them away with him. One could go in and out of Herman's store and the fact not be noticed or remembered, for a good many people did go in during a day. And, besides, Mole Street had been so sure that it had seen Henry go in, when he certainly had not, that it was n't taking any more chances.

"It is most remarkable, most remarkable,"

Henry said, and then after a moment's thought:
" And it was most remarkable how all the people
on Mole Street were sure that it was me."

Samuel Lyle shook his head. "No," he said,
" that was not surprising. It all started in the
brain of a child, Tessie the precocious. She reasoned cleverly, but she reasoned backward; she
jumped at the fact and then made the circumstances fit the fact which she had uncousciously
invented. She saw you; you usually carried a
stick, therefore the thing you had in your hand
was a stick. You walked toward Herman's;
often — usually — you went into Herman's;
therefore you went into Herman's that afternoon.
She saw you beyond Herman's; therefore you had
come out of Herman's. The clock had struck
three; therefore she had heard it strike, whereas,
as a matter of fact, she could not have heard it
so far away, and even if it had been audible she
would not have noticed it, for it was a familiar
sound and she was intent upon her game.

" And the clock itself gave false testimony, for
it was fifteen minutes fast Wednesday morning.
A witness that lies on one day is not to be trusted
on another. So Tessie, honest but ambitious and
romantic, wove a pretty tale and advertised it,
and women up and down Mole Street took it for
granted that it was a true tale, and their imagina-
tions ran riot. Maggie Clancy remembered that

she called to her daughter Sadie for the time, just as you passed by, and Sadie said that she had called back the time by the clock she couldn't see. Sadie guessed, as she did a dozen times a day for her old mother, a guess being close enough.

"And Hattie Rourke looked at the clock to see if it was n't time for Tommy to return, and ten or fifteen minutes after that she looked out at the window and saw both you and Tommy. The ten or fifteen minutes was a myth, the child of an effort to have her recollection fit Tessie's exciting tale."

Mr. Lyle rose and took a book from a shelf. "Listen, Henry," he said, and read the "Essay on Child's Play," by Robert Louis Stevenson, and after another trip to the shelves he read Hall's "Children's Lies."

"So you see, my friend, I came back here, just for my own amusement, for the stories people tell, the processes of their minds, their attempts to recall exactly circumstances that they cannot possibly remember with any degree of accuracy. All those and the proper interpretation of them are my stock in trade. I let you languish an hour in jail while I came here and found the flaws in Tessie's statement, and the women's. There are volumes on the subject, Henry. I recommend them to you if you would really understand your fellow man."

Samuel Lyle lighted a cigar, and Henry re-lighted his pipe. "And now, Henry, I am going to tell you something that must be between you and me. People call me a successful criminal lawyer; they say that I have an uncanny way of discovering the truth, of making men tell the truth. I do not think that I have anything more than a charity for human weaknesses, that I understand the minds of all sorts and conditions of men, their loves and their hatred, their hopes and their regrets, their strength and their weakness.

"I knew Herman Swann, but no better than you. We both loved him, you, I think, because of closer association, more deeply than I. You knew, as I knew, the workings of his mind, the greatness of his heart. Yet you do not tie up those things with the disappearance of ten one-thousand-dollar Liberty Bonds; I, with my idiosyncrasies, try to do that.

"Herman died between three and four o'clock; the surgeon, who arrived here very quickly, said that it was nearer four than three. Now, what are the chances, do you think, of a friend or customer, coming in here between three and four, being a thief? About one in ten thousand. Granted that a customer came in and was, at heart, a thief, what are the chances that he came to rob? Very small, I think you will agree; and, presuming that, what do you think are the prob-

abilities that he would notice the bonds lying on
the desk, when before him was a man dead?
Would he dare rob, even if he saw the bonds, and
take his chance of being accused of murder?

" Beyond all human reason, there was no robbery, and the bonds are here. I have sat and
reasoned; I have tried to determine logically,
knowing Herman, where he would put those
bonds. Herman was German-born, his blood and
the fiber of him were German, yet this country
had adopted him with his consent. He was for
Germany against the world when the war first
came, but when he had to choose between the land
of his adoption and the land of his birth, he made
his choice with no quibble. His head was high
and his heart proud. Hannah, his wife, who
knew of Germany only from her parents, rejoiced
in his quiet but very sincere declaration. He
brought the bonds here, and spread them out before her, and she kissed him and went upstairs to
her sewing, but she did not sew; she sat in her
chair with her hands in her lap, smiling and
dreaming; the memories of her long life were
sweet.

" Down below, Herman closed his eyes and saw
his two grandsons going away to give their lives
for his adopted country. He sat and dreamed,
smiling, as Hannah did above. Then he opened
his safe and, as he moved the heavy doors, his

eyes fell on a great book on a shelf just level with them. He stopped, and then he had a most fantastic thought. He went to the shelf and took the book down and opened it on the table and read for a moment. Then he took his bonds and, spreading them out flat, placed them in the book, which was very old, with the bindings soft. He put the book back in its place and stepped away and looked at it and smiled again, and there was a lump in his throat, and the stifling sensation we all have when there is great emotion. And then the darkness came and Herman fell, forward and down; there they found him."

Samuel Lyle stopped speaking. Henry Ward reached for a match and struck it and held it in his hand till it was almost burned out, and then tried to light his pipe. It was no use, and he gave up and wiped the tears from his cheeks with the back of his hand. His lips were twisting, and he was gulping. Slowly, like a man dazed, he turned in his chair to the great book on the shelf by the safe. Steadying himself by a hand on the chair, he rose and reached for the book. It was too heavy, and he took both hands and laid it on the table. It opened, as at a place marked, and there were the Liberty Bonds, face to face with the names of the ancestors of Herman Swann, written in the German Bible that had come down to him through generations.

For a moment Henry stared, and then sank to his chair; his head fell forward on his arms across the book, and he cried like a woman. Samuel Lyle, behind him, turned away, took a handkerchief from his pocket and blew his nose violently.

THE RACONTEUR

A. STUART TAIT was sixty years old and a
widower. He was short and somewhat
fat; his hair was gray; his mustache, to call it a
hard name, was a dirty, drooping yellow, his eyes
were greenish, rather small and peered more in-
tently than eyes usually do. Mr. Tait had poor
taste in clothes; his lacked that intangible something which makes a man's clothes disappear
completely from notice when one comes to know
him. They were good clothes, undoubtedly, but
Mr. Tait selected patterns usually seen in cheap
cloth, and he wore them with no grace whatever.

Mr. Tait's face followed the characteristics of
his clothes. Sometimes late in the day it needed
shaving, and it *always* looked as though it did.
It wasn't a prepossessing face; neither was it an
unpleasant face; it was simply a negative face
which suggested no special attractiveness in its
owner. It has been said, mostly by ladies, that
his face indicated no praiseworthy past, which
may have been a libel and is certainly of little
importance.

Mr. Tait had, a few years before his sixtieth
birthday, retired from active business. The

amount of his fortune was problematical, but he
certainly had had an income sufficient for his
comfort, and there was little if any blemish on his
business reputation.   He lived in the north part
of Alden, where it is neither city nor country; his
house had been ample in size for his large family
and was now much larger than he needed, for
there remained with him only his youngest
daughter, Clara, his other children having married and gone their various ways.

His establishment consisted of a maid, a cook,
and a man, who under Mr. Tait's tutelage had become the sort of genius that can be a butler and
clean spark-plugs and windows equally well, and
does so willingly.   Mr. Tait owned one large and
one small automobile and belonged to the Alden
Club and the Hopedale Golf Club, which he never
used for golf.

In the winter of Mr. Tait's sixty-first year, his
daughter Clara became engaged.   The man was
satisfactory to him, but the idea of being left
alone in his large house was not pleasing at all.

The wedding-day was set indefinitely for the
spring, and Mr. Tait had suggested to Clara that
it would be a good time to have certain old family
jewels reset, they then to be a present to her from
him, and accordingly he brought them home with
him one night.   Clara happened to be out, and
they did not find time to discuss the matter in de-

tail until one evening two weeks later, when they went to his study and Mr. Tait proceeded to open the iron safe, turning the knob with great deliberation. The combination failed to respond at the first attempt, but the second time the bolts turned back and the massive door swung outward.

Mr. Tait reached toward a compartment, hesitated, and drew back. A puzzled expression came across his face as he scanned the interior of the safe; he ran his hand into a dark cubbyhole or two and again stood upright, scowling. Then he turned the desk light so that it shone directly into the safe, and searched it carefully. It was useless, and Mr. Tait knew it before he started; the box was too large to be hidden in so small a space as the interior of the old safe. Again Mr. Tait straightened himself up and, turning to his daughter, said: " I have been robbed."

Would that some subtlety of print could convey even a small part of the intensity of Mr. Tait's voice. His four small words were spoken calmly, but with such conviction as a man might have were he pronouncing a solemn and important truth from the pulpit. Whether Mr. Tait's ability so to speak was a natural gift or whether it was a thing of his own cultivation matters not.

Subsequent investigation indicated that Mr. Tait had spoken nothing more nor less than the truth. The investigation was thoroughly and skilfully made. Inspector Gibb of the Detective Bureau and Mr. Thomas Higgins did the investigating. Mr. Higgins represented the insurance company which had insured Mr. Tait's property against " burglary, theft, and larceny " to the extent of one hundred thousand dollars, for Mr. Tait's house contained many pictures, rugs, porcelains, and books; much silver, and gold, and precious stones and valuable antiques.

Mr. Tait stated that he had, on Wednesday, December 6, 1916, gone to the People's Trust Company, opened his box in the safe-deposit vaults, and taken therefrom the box which contained the jewels. The fact of his opening the box on that date was proved by the trust company's records. Mr. Tait had then gone to the Alden Club and there, always keeping the box in his possession, he had spent an hour or two smoking, reading, and chatting. At five his car had come for him; arriving at his house, he had asked for his daughter and discovered that she had gone out for the evening unexpectedly. Mr. Tait had then opened his safe, placed the box in the lower compartment on the right-hand side, shut the door, locked it, and gone about his ordinary business. He had not opened the safe again until the evening of December 20th, when his daughter was with him and the loss was discovered.

There had been nothing else of value in the safe; it contained largely old account-books, canceled checks, expired insurance policies, and such accumulated rubbish. Mr. Tait's securities and other property of great value but small bulk were safely in the vaults of the People's Trust Company.

The great question was, of course, how the box had been abstracted. That the house could have been entered feloniously and no trace left was of course admitted, but the safe was another matter. Mr. Tait alone of those in the house knew the combination. He thought his son, A. Stuart, Jr., knew it, but he had not been within hundreds of miles of Alden for a year.

There was not the slightest indication that the safe had been tampered with, not another thing in the house had been touched, and not a soul but Mr. Tait and his daughter knew that the jewels were there. All these facts were indisputable, and in due course Mr. Tait pressed his claim against the insurance company, and the company asked for time. It wanted time in which to do a little quiet investigating, of which Mr. Tait would know nothing, unless evidence against him were unearthed.

There was no proof that Mr. Tait actually had had any old jewelry; it was simply known in the family that it had once been in their possession and that from time to time Mr. Tait had stated that it was in his safe-deposit box. Granting that the jewelry had been in Mr. Tait's box, there was no proof that he had brought it home, or, bringing it home, had put it in the safe. Perhaps the whole thing was a blind; perhaps Mr. Tait had disposed of the jewelry for cash to meet unexpected obligations; perhaps he had been in the market and met reverses; possibly his income was not sufficient to meet the greatly increased cost of living.

Mr. Thomas Higgins and the insurance company thought that, to be on the safe side, all that should be looked into. It would n't be the first time such a game had been played, and in, apparently, the most respectable circles. Furthermore, the proof of loss was a bit hazy. It was a nice question whether Mr. Tait's affidavit that he had put jewelry to the value of ten thousand dollars into that safe was sufficient evidence to require the payment of his claim.

That the safe could be opened without knowledge of the combination was admitted, but only a man who had studied the mechanism of combination locks for years and years could do it, and it might take the cleverest of such men hours or even days to accomplish it. On the other hand, it might be done in ten minutes.

But men who could open that safe with its

four-number combination by listening to the clicking of the tumblers and by the feel of the knob were few and far between, and Inspector Gibb was pretty sure he knew every one of them and that none of them had been in a position to do the job. And why should a thief spend time over that forty-year-old safe when treasure was lying at his hand with not even a key to turn?

So the insurance company staved off Mr. Tait and set about investigating him, which was a delicate job. They discovered that he was sound financially; he had no debts, paid his current bills with reasonable promptness, and did not lack cash in bank. It was true that he had found his income not quite sufficient for his own needs and for the contributions which he wished to continue to his children, and that as a result he did odd jobs for various men of means in the way of appraising objects of art, looking up the history thereof, or supervising the decorating or building of a house. This was in no way open to criticism, but rather to be commended.

On the other hand, certain men who had known A. Stuart Tait for years said that they had never been able to make up their minds whether he was the cleverest old crook alive or whether he was just a queer old duck with a mind that had a peculiar kink in it. But not one definite black spot could Higgins find on Mr. Tait's record.

That was how things stood when Paul Waters, insurance broker and general agent for the company issuing Mr. Tait's policy, went to Samuel Lyle. He told Mr. Lyle the story from beginning to end, and Mr. Lyle said nary a word till he had finished. Then he said: "Go to see Johnny Bowers, tell him your story boiled down to the limit, show him your policy, and ask him whether, as things stand now, Tait could collect at law. Tell him I sent you and that you want a curbstone opinion. He's in his office."

Paul went and came back within a half-hour.

"What did he say?" asked Mr. Lyle.

"'Yes.'"

"Anything else?"

"No, just 'yes' and 'good-by.'"

"He's the boy!" Mr. Lyle exclaimed. "No ifs, ands, or buts about him. Why don't you pay Tait his money — think it's another Farson case?"

"No," Paul said, "I suppose it is n't, but how do we know the old boy's telling the truth? It looks fishy — the company thinks so — that's why I'm here."

"All right, son, I'll see what I can do for you, but how to go about it I don't know. I'll think it over and let you hear from me."

Paul was going through the door when Mr. Lyle spoke. "There is something you can do,

Paul. Dig up two or three intelligent men whom I know, who know Tait well, and who would be willing to do us a good turn on the quiet if it came to a pinch."

Two days later, in the middle of the afternoon, Samuel Lyle pushed a chair a foot or two closer to the window of the Alden Club smoking-room, sat down, lighted a cigar, and began to read the afternoon paper. Mr. Lyle had been a member of the huge Alden Club for years, but never before had he sat at that window; nor did he go to the Alden Club except on rare occasions and for particular purposes. Such time as he had for clubs he spent at the Orchard, which was n't like the Alden Club at all and was lots harder to get into.

Mr. A. Stuart Tait was n't a member of the Orchard Club, but he did belong to the Alden Club, and that afternoon he was sitting on the other side of Mr. Lyle's window. Mr. Tait, too, was reading, but before very long his paper dropped to his knees, and he contemplated alternately the street and Mr. Lyle. Presently Mr. Lyle tossed his paper away, relighted his cigar, and watched the passers-by. Mr. Tait never suspected for an instant that Mr. Lyle was awaiting with great interest the result of his little experiment. Mr. Lyle had not long to wait.

"Samuel Lyle?" Mr. Tait asked Mr. Lyle.

Mr. Lyle turned, smiled his captivating smile, and nodded.

"Tait." A. Stuart said the word as though there were only one Tait in the world's telephone directory.

Again Mr. Lyle smiled and nodded, to explain that he understood. Mr. Tait relapsed into silence, and his face took on an expression of deep thought. Mr. Lyle waited again — waited for the flower to unfold — and again he had not long to wait. Mr. Tait spoke.

"There comes to my recollection an incident which occurred in 1894, when I was associated in business with Thomas Campbell in the firm of W. S. and T. Campbell. The morning was bitterly cold — oh, bitterly cold! — such a morning as Thursday of last week. I was engaged at the time upon the adjustment of claims which had been made upon us by a man who had undertaken certain work for us in the capacity of subcontractor. There was little foundation for his demands, but in accordance with my invariable practice I was giving them the utmost consideration. On the morning of which I speak I was in the office, when Thomas Campbell entered, having been driving since early in the morning. As I said, it was bitterly cold and he came in completely swathed in furs, which he removed one by one — gloves, hat, and coat — saying as he did

so that it was too cold for the comfortable transaction of business out of doors. He looked at
the thermometer and went to the stove, which
then furnished the only heat in our office. I re-
monstrated, but it was of no use, and presently
the iron of the stove was white-hot. Campbell
stood watching it, holding first his hands toward
it and then giving the seat of his trousers its
turn. Finally he said: 'I'll make the man's
stove burn just as the man who made it is burning this minute.'"

Mr. Tait stopped and became very solemn; his
eyes were fixed on Mr. Lyle. Mr. Lyle waited.

"The name on that stove was —" Mr. Tait
stopped for another moment —"'Lyle's Stove
Works.'"

Mr. Lyle laughed, not loudly, but with a sin-
cerity that did Mr. Tait's soul good.

"That certainly is remarkable," Mr. Lyle said.
"That Lyle was a distant cousin of my father's.
You did n't know him, I suppose?"

Unfortunately Mr. Tait had not known him,
but before Mr. Lyle left Mr. Tait had told him
of a great many men he had known. Mr. Tait
enumerated the virtues of one of them slowly and
in an impressive voice.

"A most remarkable man," he said, "a man of
wonderful ability, of keen insight, far-seeing, upright, an organizer, a most delightful gentleman,

and one —" (here Mr. Tait became sad, slower, and more impressive than ever) "one of — the — very — dearest — friends I have ever had." The memory of that friendship brought tears to Mr. Tait's voice if not to his eyes.

Mr. Lyle found Mr. Tait himself so delightful that he dropped in at the Alden Club for lunch every day and spent two hours over it with Mr. Tait; he played rubbers of auction with him, and even dined with him at his house. Mr. Lyle paid for most of the lunches. A. Stuart accepted his invitations at first. When they went into the dining-room together as a matter of course, Mr. Tait, about every fourth time, insisted that he must sign the check. Mr. Lyle always protested, and then the real Mr. Tait showed himself.

"I insist, sir!" he thundered. Yes, it was thunder though it was not as loud as atmospheric thunder, and he backed it up with an expression of such determination and his voice was so much like a man's calling on the mob to stop rioting or he'll order the soldiers to fire, that Mr. Lyle let him pay, about every fourth time.

Invariably after lunch Mr. Tait offered Mr. Lyle a cigar from his cigar-case, and invariably Mr. Lyle took cigars from his own pocket. The first time he smoked one of Mr. Tait's and confessed frankly that, though excellent, they were not his sort, they were too thin and a little bitter or bity, whereas Mr. Lyle preferred a large, free-burning, mild cigar. Yet Mr. Tait tried to force one of his cigars on Mr. Lyle at least once a day, insisted and was imperative if Mr. Lyle hesitated to accept, and paid little if any attention to Mr. Lyle's repeated statements that he preferred his own.

It was at lunch, too, that Mr. Tait first told Mr. Lyle the story of the late Mrs. Tait's roses. That story would, if written, fill a good-sized magazine. It began when Mrs. Tait was a girl and it wandered hither and thither over the face of the earth, each bloom worthy of a paragraph, each word carefully and slowly chosen, until long years afterward Mrs. Tait died and Mr. Tait laid one rose from her favorite bush on her coffin. That might well have ended the story; but no, a friend of Mr. Tait's, whose wife had been a dear friend, a very dear friend of Mrs. Tait's, came to Mr. Tait and made a very long speech, which Mr. Tait repeated word for word, inflection for inflection, tear for tear, comma for comma, even unto the time when the friend, too, took a rose from the favorite bush and laid it on the breast of his dead wife.

In a similar manner Mr. Tait explained that he had recently employed a famous artist to paint a portrait of Lucy, his late wife, from oral descriptions, good photographs, and snap-shots. In

great detail he described the perfection of the
artist's work, his skill in reproducing each line
and feature, and then stopped. The suspense
was great until Mr. Tait said, funereally: "But
it was not — Lucy."

So it was with many stories, such as that of the
Southern woman who reformed; of the man who
said that he had said good night to a ravishingly
beautiful woman in London and left her, and to
whom Mr. Tait said that "he was either a fool
or a liar"; the story of how his daughter designed
a booth at the fair; of Mr. Tait's great illness;
of how he voted the prohibition ticket and drank
a quart of champagne immediately thereafter to
square himself with the world; of how he had
taken four cottages in payment of a debt and how
they were paying him forty per cent. per annum;
and so on and on, stories whose point could have
been proved in a dozen words, but must needs be
approached through a dozen pages.

Yet, long as these stories were, and however
much they were encumbered with extraneous detail, Mr. Tait added to them the words "to digress," and then digressed for further orders,
usually on an anecdote of some truly great man
who was always a dear friend, a very dear friend
indeed, of Mr. Tait's. So far did the digression
carry him that ofttimes he was quite unable to
recollect from what he had digressed and many

times there were digressions within digressions.

Mr. Tait admitted modestly that he was the best teller of stories he knew and to prove it told how the great Junius Bacon, who held America in the palm of his hand, often sent for him in his last days and asked Mr. Tait to tell him this story and then that and then the other, just as he had told them to him before.

Mr. Lyle played auction with Mr. Tait, who by retrospection, introspection, analysis, logic, and common sense had convinced himself that the laws of probabilities did n't apply to auction, that conventions were snares and delusions, that it was better to fool one's partner than to give the opponents information, and that if he did n't win it was because he did n't hold the cards. He admitted also that he seldom, if ever, did hold the cards.

Mr. Lyle hesitated about going to Mr. Tait's house, for there is something holy about a man's home, where he has, if he be a decent man, spent the best part of his life, where he had raised his children and from which he has sent them out into the world and where he has sheltered the woman who loved him. That, of course, is sickly sentiment, but even an old rascally criminal lawyer like Samuel Lyle had some feeling of the sort. He went, finally, and eased his conscience by leaving his professional self on the door-step.

Having done that, he wondered why he had gone at all. Perhaps it was plain luck, for that night Mr. Tait made possible the thing which Mr. Lyle had considered, and had believed unwise to attempt.

Mr. Tait mentioned the robbery for the first time and, having opened the subject, dilated upon it. In the end he granted Mr. Lyle permission to have Angus Queen attempt to open the safe. Mr. Queen was the most skilled safe-artisan of whom Mr. Lyle knew. The whole thing was, of course, to be just an interesting experiment between friends; there were only three or four persons who knew that Mr. Lyle had any official interest in that safe, and Mr. Tait was n't one of them.

Notwithstanding Mr. Lyle's professional self being without on the door-step, the rest of Mr. Lyle's self could n't help noticing one little incident, try not to as he would. There were ducks for dinner, very special ducks, and Mr. Tait made ready for dismembering them by first selecting the carving-knife with great care and then preparing its edge with a great deal more care. Yet — horror of horrors — the ducks failed to respond even to such blandishments and Mr. Tait was in despair, covered with confusion, and very red in the face, until the situation was saved by the man-servant who whispered over his shoulder: "The other edge of the knife, sir."

Several days after that dinner, Angus Queen told Mr. Lyle that he had spent thirty hours on the combination of Mr. Tait's safe and had not been able to open it, and that he believed it very unlikely that any man could open it in that time. But Mr. Queen admitted that a man *might* hit it the first time he tried it, the chances being roughly one in six thousand million.

Two months after Mr. Lyle met Mr. Tait, Mr. Lyle stopped going to the Alden Club and went back to his cronies at the Orchard. There he gave a little luncheon for Paul Waters, David White, who was a builder; Norman Dean, Thomas Higgins, Inspector Gibb, and Mr. Bowers, all of whom knew Mr. Tait and were greatly interested in the matter of his old jewelry. The luncheon was on a Saturday when it was snowing and there was an afternoon to waste, and it was in a small room, safe from interruption. Mr. Lyle had previously talked with David White and Norman Dean, whom Paul Waters had selected as intelligent men who knew A. Stuart Tait and were friends of Mr. Lyle.

It was a very pleasant party, and the talk drifted hither and thither till the cigar time came. Then Mr. Lyle gave them fair warning.

"I have n't made a speech out of court in years," he said, "but I 'm going to make one now. I 'm going to get square with the world by

boring you to death for an hour or two, just as
I have been bored to death for an hour or two five
days a week for two months.

"To begin with, two months ago Paul Waters
gave me a job of work; the work is n't finished,
but I am.   The facts which Mr. Waters — curses
on him! — gave me are these."   Mr. Lyle outlined the facts.   "So far as I can see, things are
just where they were then: not a single, solitary
new fact has been unearthed.

"I have been working on the case steadily,
and I have nothing to report but an opinion and
that opinion is n't worth one per cent. of what
I 'm going to charge for it.   For two months I
have chummed with A. Stuart Tait, the man who
demands   compensation   for   certain   jewelry
claimed by him to have been feloniously extracted
from his locked and undamaged safe, and for two
months I have been bored beyond my powers of
description; only the thought of the good cause
in which I was engaged sustained me in my task.
I have listened to stories innumerable, long-
drawn-out, windy, wandering, stilted, lugubri-
ous; stories told so slowly and with so many digressions and with so much of the egotistical
story-teller's affectation that they were painful
beyond expression.   And that is not all.   Permit
me to refer to my notes, which I assure you are

accurate. I have heard various stories, as follows:

"The story of the roses, six times; the story
of the portrait, eleven times, three times in one
day; the story of the Southern woman who reformed, eight times; the story of the prohibition
vote, four times; the story of the man who said
he left the woman in London and was either a
fool or a liar, eight times; the story of the arrangement of the booths at the fair, twelve times;
and David White states that he has heard it four
times in the same day; the story of a certain illness four times; and the story of four cottages
taken for a bad debt, six times. And that is not
all; there are many, many others.

"During those two months, too, I have — I
again refer to my records — heard anecdotes of
thirty-seven very remarkable and notable men,
leaders in their respective spheres and all of them
dear friends, very dear friends indeed of the defendant — or perhaps I should say offendant. I
have had opportunity of checking up twelve of
these thirty-seven great men and have discovered
that six of them never heard of the raconteur, five
knew him very slightly, and one said: 'Are you
up against it, too?'

"I have lunched almost daily with the subject
of this investigation, and he was able to convince

himself that he had made me believe that he believed — yes, I mean just that — that he had
paid for every other lunch, whereas I paid for
seventy-five per cent. of them. He offered me
cigars, day after day, which I explained to him
over and over again I did not like; yet he came
to the attack each time with a mind free from our
previous conversations on the subject.

"I played bridge with him and discovered that
he had manufactured a set of fallacies and made
them so much a part of his inner being that he is
absolutely unable to discard them. In fact he
knows not that they exist, hidden under his epi-
dermis of infallibility, and he denies the laws of
mathematics by blaming his luck because he loses
nine times out of ten.

"I saw him take a quarter of an hour to prepare a knife for carving ducks and then apply
the back of the knife to said ducks and struggle
on and on, unconscious of the absurdity of the
whole thing till his servant straightened him out.
I have seen him dilate on the beauty and merits
of his walking-stick, held up for inspection, only
to have him discover later that he had some one
else's. Four times I have seen him go off and
leave his store teeth behind him. I have seen
him write his name with as much care and as
slowly as an engraver would hew it out of metal.
I have seen him, yes, seen him choose his words

in ordinary conversation as though he were manufacturing an epitaph for a dear friend.

"Norman Dean tells me that he will discuss a matter of business for hours and then take the whole thing ' under consideration.' A day or two later he will have had no time to give it sufficient thought, and another couple of days later he will have forgotten it completely. One day he will argue over a client's dollar for hours and the next spend ten thousand for him without a thought.

"David White tells me that one day Mr. Tait is the soul of honor and considers his employer's interests to be a sacred trust; the next day he says the old man client has all kinds of money — what difference does it make how he spends it? One day it has been his lifelong practice to adhere strictly to the terms of the contract as the only safe and proper procedure, the next day it is manifestly unfair to make *him* live up to the same contract; one day he is the soul of honor, the next 'What is the Constitution between friends?'; one day he considers his word sufficient, for never has he gone back on it, the next day he does not recall having given his word. He will come to a definite agreement, state that in his opinion it is fair and satisfactory, and before the formal papers are drawn up he will have changed his mind on the theory that if the other side is satisfied they must have got the better of him, and the whole thing has to be done over. He professes to be most methodical in all matters and has method in none whatever.

"Such, gentlemen, is my view of the ponderous, dreamy, chaotic, wandering, topsyturvy mind of A. Stuart Tait. And now — oh, lovely word! — let us digress.

"A. Stuart Tait deposed that upon the sixth day of December last he did enter the vaults of the People's Trust Company and remove from his box one package containing old jewelry and that he did nothing else whatsoever with the contents of that safe-deposit box, that he spoke to no one and tarried not. Yet the record of his entry and departure reads ' In at two-twenty-three and out at two-thirty-eight,' an elapsed time of fifteen minutes. How in Heaven's name did he use up the time?

"He then signs a proof of loss and swears to it, wherein he states that he placed that box in his safe at home and that two weeks later it was gone.

"It disappeared as the morning mist, as water falling upon sand, as a man's soul, leaving no trace but memory. He asks us to believe that a thief of great skill, of skill so great that there are no more than a dozen of them in the whole land, entered his house through an unlocked window, in the dead of night, and with an hour or two before him set about opening that safe, a task which a thief skilful enough to accomplish it at all must know would take, in all probability, days of patient effort. And staring the thief, and us, in the face, were all the silver and gold that he could carry, or that ten men could carry, while for all said thief knew there might not be ten cents' worth of plunder in the safe. Gentlemen, again we digress.

" Memory is a highly complicated and variously organized function which it is difficult to understand, even in everyday life. One Herbart had the idea that memory consists in the possibility of recognizing the molecular arrangements which have been left by past impressions in the ganglion cells and in reading them in identical fashion. A Mr. Wundt says the problem is one of the central organs. You may draw your own conclusions — personally, I think it is halfway between the two; and now that you know exactly what memory is we can discuss the subject intelligently. There are all sorts of memories, good, bad, and indifferent. Some people have such memories for all kinds of detail as to stagger us, but as a rule people have good memories for items in a narrow field. As a rule, specialists, such as stamp-collectors, zoölogists, and botanists have stupendous memory for their particular matters, but no memory at all for anything else; there are people who can remember only faces, rimes, titles, figures, relationships or — stories.

" It is a well-known fact that aged persons have a good memory for what is long past and a mighty poor one for recent occurrences. To digress, gentlemen, a man of sixty may be very old. To return to the subject, old age is accompanied by a decrease of energy in the brain; it no longer accumulates facts, but it retains those assimilated in younger days.

" A man's retentiveness of mind is unchangeable; it seems that no amount of culture is capable of modifying it. An ignorant man or a semi-idiot often has a far more trustworthy memory and makes a better witness than the most learned professor.

" Our memories trick us all; it is often impossible for us to say how much of our recollection is memory and how much inference. Memory is an impression; if we go farther than that, we add inferences, which may well be wrong. A month or a year from now it will be possible for me to recall in ten seconds the whole event of this luncheon, which has already occupied two hours and will use up another before it is through.

" When men recall events distinctly, they are certain of three things: something happened, it happened the way they think it did, and it hap-

pened when they think it happened. If they
want to get at the truth of the matter, they must
look elsewhere than in their own minds.

"The most frequent source of false memory lies
in the dressing up of our own experiences; we
talk to entertain, therefore we amplify the facts,
wander from the narrow path of truth, elaborate
our tales to make them more interesting, and no
harm and perhaps some good is done at the time,
but before long we come to believe that we are
telling the plain truth without embellishment.
That is what A. Stuart Tait does; he has little, if
any, idea that he is the most profuse liar extant.

"I have done my best to explain to you my
opinion of Mr. Tait and his memory. I have
done it much as I think he himself would have
done it — at great length. Between you and
me, the whole thing may be stated concisely. A.
Stuart has the poorest memory in the world —
for everything but stories. He has concentrated
his memory on stories; he tells them hour after
hour, over and over again, and he never changes
a word, a comma, an inflection or a digression in
one of them; he tells them with all the studied
effort of an actor repeating his lines, and he believes them to be miracles of the art.

"He says he got the jewels from the safe-deposit box, took them to the Alden Club, keeping
them in his possession while there, took them

home and put them in his safe, from which he
insists that they were feloniously extracted.
They were not feloniously extracted from his
safe; he did not put them in his safe. I say that
positively because I am quite willing to take one
chance in ten million of being proved wrong.

" What happened or what became of the jewels,
I don't know. That he did open his safe-deposit
box is sure; after that nothing is sure. I can
cook up a fanciful tale of what happened. For
instance, he bought a box of cigars, put it in the
capacious pocket of his remarkable overcoat, went
to the trust company, read his will or looked over
his securities, closed the box, remembered what
he had come for, felt the box of cigars in his
pocket, and presumed that it was the jewel-box
put there when he had first opened the safe-deposit box. He returned the safe-deposit box to
its place, carried his cigars to the Alden Club,
and then went home, opened his safe, saw something that recalled old times, took it out and
perused it, hunted for a cigar in his pocket, found
none and opened the box on his desk, finished his
perusal of his old account-book, or what not, put
it back in his safe, locked it and went upstairs.

" That, or something equally ridiculous, is
what happened. Perhaps the jewels *are* gone;
perhaps he left them about and a servant took
them; perhaps they are in the house in a little-

used drawer or an out-of-the-way corner, but I will bank my hopes of salvation on the fact that they were never stolen from his locked safe. He is honest, fundamentally; he did n't steal his own property for the insurance. Integrity consists of a mind ordered on honorable lines. There A. Stuart fails: he has no desire to be dishonest, he undoubtedly intends to be honorable, but the trouble is that his mind has no order in it.

"Paul, my advice to you and yours is to fight the case, provided I do the fighting in court. I can imagine no greater joy than to have A. Stuart Tait on the witness stand, where I can tell him and the world exactly what I think of him and his stories — the damned old bore!"

And so it was that the insurance company decided to let Mr. Tait collect his claim in the courts, if he could. But the case never came to trial. One day Paul Waters walked into Mr. Lyle's office, sat down and grinned and grinned, and then laughed out loud.

"Well, well!" exclaimed Mr. Lyle. "What 's all this monkey business?"

"Old Stew Tait has his jules —"

"Has he?" said Mr. Lyle.

"He has; and where do you think they were?"

Mr. Lyle's eyes began to glow and then he began to grin.

"Really?" he said.

" M-h-m."

" Well, well, well! "

" And he 's the sickest-looking old rooster you've ever seen. He dropped into my office about two hours ago and began a tale of how his mind was losing some of its youthful vigor; he was not able to think clearly; his mental processes were getting all gummed up. He talked that for an hour, and laid it mostly to the loss of his Lucy, but partly to the anticipated loss of his daughter, and then as an incidental example of his pathetic state, for which he wanted huge gobs of sympathy, he told me of his discovery, and admitted that he had been to his box in the trust company's vaults several times since Christmas, and had failed to note that the dear old box was there in its cozy corner. Then he started to digress, and I threw him out. He has added another two-hour story to his collection."

Mr. Lyle worked his lips round and round till he got them into a very solemn position.

" What time do you think I may expect him to digress through my door with the sole purpose of honoring me with his mental processes? "

" 'Most any minute. I think I passed him on the way. He 's a slow walker."

Mr. Lyle's door opened. " Mr. Tait," said the young woman.

"Out!" said Mr. Lyle, "and — I never expect to be in." The young woman smiled sadly; she suspected that she had a man's-size job on her hands.

JUROR NO. 5

JUROR No. 5 was a very able man of thirty-
five. He was the head of an excellent business; he was a sportsman of fine reputation; he
read intelligently; he loved dogs and children
and his charming wife, each in the proper degree
and in the proper manner, and had a delightful
personality. You might travel many a long mile
before you would find a pleasanter, more honest,
and more capable man than Juror No. 5.

Juror No. 7 also was a gentleman of intelligence and refinement. The other ten were a sad
lot, a very, very sad lot indeed, and Juror No. 5
was entirely aware of it. Juror No. 5 was conscientious; the fact that he had made no effort
to be excused from jury duty was conclusive
proof of that.

The jury filed into their room, made a few remarks, and took a ballot, the result of which
showed that ten of them were for conviction.
Juror No. 5 met the glance of Juror No. 7 and
both of them understood: they were the two
against the ten. It was four o'clock, and Juror
No. 5 wanted to go home at five, but he was conscientious, very conscientious. He and Juror

No. 7 must change the vote from ten-to-two for
conviction to twelve to nothing for acquittal. It
was some job, but Juror No. 5 set about it. It
was a job that must be done even if it took all
night.

Back in the court-room the story had unfolded
itself slowly. It began with the confession of a
young man named Albert Warren who had been
married and out of a job, and very nearly broke.
He 'd had a war job and while he was working at
it his wife had gone to live with her family. In
the meantime they had stored their furniture, and
Warren's one thought was to get enough money
to get his furniture out of storage, put it in a
home of his own and get his wife back again.

But the best he could get was odd jobs that
did n't pay very well and the future did n't look
very bright. He met Frank McCabe, a young
man he 'd known a long time, and Frank was up
against it, too, so they decided to save money by
doubling up in the matter of rooms, and accordingly they took one small bedroom in a cheap
rooming-house. The room had two beds in it,
one small bureau, a table, and two or three chairs.

They had been there together about two months
when Warren got what looked like a steady job
with a future to it, but McCabe had no luck at all.
Warren got twenty dollars a week, and one Saturday, with his pay, a twenty-dollar bill, in his

pocket, he stopped and bought two pair of socks from a peddler. He counted the change, put it in his pocket, and went to his room. McCabe was n't there and Warren went out for his dinner.

In the restaurant he found that instead of having one ten-dollar bill, one five, and four ones, he had the five and the ones and a bill that had been raised from a one to a ten. He did n't wait for his dinner; he hurried back to where the peddler with the push-cart had been, but the peddler was gone and Warren could n't find him or find out anything about him.

He got something to eat and went back to his room and took out the raised bill and examined it. Of course he 'd been a fool to take it, but the probabilities were that the peddler had n't known it was phony and that his very innocence had disarmed Warren. He remembered that, when he had counted the change, he had just looked at the numerals in the corner. He must have done that because " ONE DOLLAR " was in black letters across the face of the bill and there were smaller " ONES " scattered all over it. What he or any one else looks at are the big numerals in the corner.

It was a clumsy job, that raised bill. The big 1's had been cut out and 10's had been stuck in their places: the bills of that issue were so designed that it could be done without changing

the general design appreciably. Warren doped
it all out. It was a fascinating thing to do and
looked easy. He folded the raised bill over on
itself in the middle so that the ONE DOLLAR was
hidden and wondered whether other people would
take it just as he had, if it were handed to them
in that fashion.

He went out to a cigar store where he was n't
known and tried it. It worked, and he was
square with the world. His conscience was
perfectly easy; the argument now was between
the peddler and the cigar-store man. Warren
had stepped from under.

But he was n't satisfied with that; the idea
stuck in his mind. Twenty dollars a week did n't
go far, it was hard to save anything, and he
wanted to get his furniture out of storage and his
wife back from the up-state town. His process
of reasoning and the various stages through
which he passed between the time temptation laid
hold of him and the time when he succumbed are
not important. But succumb he did.

He tore the corners from ten-dollar bills one at
a time and passed the mutilated bills, taking his
change, until he had a stock of 10's in sets of four,
one for each corner, and with infinite care he cut
the 1's from the corners of one-dollar bills and
inserted the 10's in their places, and passed some
of them, making nine dollars on each transaction.

So much Warren confessed to the federal agents, and they could not find any flaw in his story, though they questioned him for hours. The rest of the story, as it came to Juror No. 5, was in the form of testimony from witnesses on the stand.

Frank McCabe, Warren's room-mate, was on trial for the same crime to which Warren had pleaded guilty.

August Dietz testified that on a certain evening at about six o'clock Warren had come into his store and made a small purchase, offering, as Dietz thought, a ten-dollar bill in payment. He took the bill, put it in the cash drawer, and gave Warren his change, and Warren went out. Just as Dietz was giving Warren the money Mrs. Dietz came in. Dietz, on the stand, was shown a raised bill and identified it as the one Warren had given him.

Hannah Dietz testified that she lived over the store which she and her husband ran, and that at the time in question she came down the stairs to the street and entered the store, there being no other way from their apartment to the store. While she was on the sidewalk she saw a man looking into the store through the show-window. She saw him distinctly.

She went into the store, meeting Warren com-

cash-drawer open, and was about to close it when by the merest chance she saw the spurious ten-dollar bill and knew at once that something was wrong. An instant's examination of the bill was sufficient to show exactly what was wrong and she spoke to her husband and they rushed out of the store in pursuit of Warren. They saw him and ran after him, and, as luck would have it, a plain-clothes man was close by and he arrested Warren.

Mrs. Dietz, later on, was taken into a room in which were about a dozen men and as she stepped into the room she picked out McCabe instantly as the man she had seen looking into the store. She admitted on cross-examination that she had not seen McCabe after she had entered the store and that of course he was not with Warren when Warren was arrested.

A detective testified that on searching Warren he found two more of the raised notes and that on searching his room he found in a bureau drawer a bottle of mucilage, some gum, some safety-razor blades, and three pairs of scissors, two them being curved manicure scissors. On the floor he found minute slivers of paper which under the microscope proved to have been cut from bank-notes. The presumption was that most of the waste cuttings had been collected and carefully disposed of, but that these slivers had

been brushed or blown to the floor and been over-
looked, and had stuck to the carpet when the
room had been swept.

The woman who ran the rooming-house testified that Warren and McCabe had lived there together for five months previous to their arrest
and that in the last two months they had spent a
great deal of time together in their room, much
more than they had at first. She could not, naturally, make any statement as to the exact
amount of time they had stayed in their room,
but generally they had, at first, gone out in the
evening and then had generally stayed in. Her
statement was perfectly frank, and made without any suggestion of malice.

That was the Government's case, its contention
being that as Warren was guilty McCabe must
also be guilty, that he had worked hand in glove
with Warren. It was impossible that, living in
the same small room with Warren, he should be
ignorant of what Warren was doing.

Frank McCabe was represented by Samuel
Lyle's law firm, his active counsel being Mr.
Thomas Nash, one of Mr. Lyle's junior partners.
McCabe's case was of no great importance; perhaps it presented no unusual features, and yet
the great Lyle had wandered into the court-room
and taken a seat beside Tom Nash. He had a
way of keeping an eye on the young men under

him, guiding and helping them whenever he could. He sat there quietly. Nash paid no attention to him. The elderly man seemed almost to be asleep. But the prosecutor developing the Government's case kept his eye on him. No case was easy to win when Sam Lyle was on the other side, and the more Lyle dozed the less the Government's attorney liked it. If Lyle kept wide awake, cross-examined witnesses, badgered the opposition, harangued the judge, and made the jury laugh, then Lyle might have a bad case, but when he kept quiet and appeared to be paying no attention to what was going on, then — look out; the lightning was likely to strike.

Thomas Nash did not cross-examine August Dietz at all, and he asked Mrs. Dietz only a few questions, that in no way touched on her desire to tell the truth.

" You remember distinctly the man you saw looking into your shop through the window when Warren was inside? " he asked Mrs. Dietz.

" Yes."

" Was he clean-shaven? "

" Yes, sir."

" What color was his hair, light or dark? "

" Light."

" Very light? "

" Yes, sir."

" Was he young or old? "

" Young, sir."

" Somewhere about thirty? "

" I could n't say exactly, sir."

" Of course not, but he was about thirty, rather than forty or fifty? "

" Yes, sir."

" That 's all."   He asked her nothing about her having picked out McCabe from a lot of other men in a room at headquarters.

Thomas Nash did not cross-examine the detective who had arrested Warren, nor the men who had searched him and his room, but when it was testified that Mrs. Dietz had been taken into a room where there were a dozen men and that she had instantly picked out McCabe as the man she had seen at her window, then Nash made the witness give him the names of the other men who had been there, and then quickly made the witness admit that they were all detectives, that there was n't a light-haired man in the lot, that they were all over forty, and that nearly all of them had mustaches.

" The prisoner must have stood out prominently, a white lamb among a lot of black sheep," Nash said, laughing.   " That 's all."

Nash said nothing to the woman who kept the rooming-house, but he recalled Warren to the stand and asked him at what time he had left his room when he went to Dietz's store.

" About half-past five."

" Was McCabe with you? "

" Yes."

" Did he go to the store with you? "

" No."

" Where did he leave you? "

" At the corner of Elm and Scott streets; he went down Elm Street."

" And you went up toward Main? "

" Yes."

" You did n't see McCabe again that day? "

" No."

" Did he know where you were going? "

" He knew I was going to the movies."

" But he did n't know you were going to Dietz's store first? "

" No, I did n't know it myself, then. I just happened to see the store when I was going by and thought it looked like a good place to pass a bill. I 'd never noticed the store before."

" That 's all."

The prosecuting attorney could n't shake Warren's statements.

Nash spoke to McCabe, telling him to take the stand. McCabe went into the witness-stand and was sworn, and then Juror No. 5 saw Samuel Lyle say a word to Nash.

Then Nash withdrew the witness and McCabe left the stand. The district attorney jumped to

his feet, exclaimed, " Your Honor," and stopped.
He looked at Lyle for an instant and sat down.
Juror No. 5 saw the faintest suspicion of a smile
on Mr. Lyle's face. He could not see the prosecutor's face.

The defense rested and the attorneys addressed
the jury.   Juror No. 5 knew Samuel Lyle by reputation; he had heard much of his wonderful ex-
ploits at the bar and he had been hoping that the
great lawyer would take a hand in the trial, that
at least he would make the address to the jury.
But Nash made the address.   Just before he began Juror No. 5 saw Mr. Lyle speak to him and
saw Nash look into the jury-box. It seemed to
Juror No. 5 that Nash searched about for an instant with his eyes until he saw him, and then
as though satisfied he turned back to Mr. Lyle
and they spoke together for a moment.

Nash spoke to the jury for only a few minutes
and Juror No. 5 felt as though Nash were speaking directly to him and to him alone, in an ordinary conversational tone. Certainly there was no
attempt at oratory, no appeal to heart, simply a
quick analysis of the testimony and a straightforward statement that Nash himself believed,
and was sure that the jury would believe, that the
Government had not proved beyond a reasonable doubt that McCabe had had any part in the
raising of the bills or in issuing them, or even

that he had had any knowledge of what Warren was doing; in fact, the Government had proved nothing except that Warren and McCabe had known each other intimately, and that was far from sufficient evidence on which to convict a young man of so serious a crime.

Juror No. 5 would have bet at odds of ten to one that McCabe was guilty, but ten to one was not in his mind equivalent to " beyond reasonable doubt." A thousand to one was closer to Juror No. 5's idea of " beyond reasonable doubt." Juror No. 5 had a keen mind and he reduced " reasonable " to bold figures.

Juror No. 5 had sized up Warren as being inefficient and rather weak; if he had had a strong and honest hand to guide him he might have done well enough, have been a rather pleasant, commonplace man. But he had been turned loose in a big city and had succumbed to the first temptation he had met. Juror No. 5 was very sure that Warren, when he confessed, had told the whole truth — his manner indicated that — and, besides, Juror No. 5 did not believe that Warren was clever enough to make up all or part of his story without contradicting himself and getting caught, and he certainly had not been caught in any contradiction.

On the other hand, Juror No. 5 thought that McCabe was a pretty good-looking man; he had not been able to find anything in his face that suggested a criminal tendency.

Thus it was that Juror No. 5 set about convincing his ten fellow jurors that they must not declare McCabe guilty. His plea was that the Government had not proved its case against him. He said nothing about his personal feeling that McCabe did not look like a crook because he thought that would weaken his argument.

The foreman of the jury said he did n't see how two men could live together for five months, in one small room, without one of them knowing what the other was doing, especially when the thing was done at night, and must have been done nearly every night for two months. Why had n't the defense proved that McCabe was out a lot of nights, so as to show Warren had had the chance to work alone? Five other jurors approved that view of it, and emphasized their belief that the two men had worked together.

Juror No. 5 said that it was n't up to the defense to prove McCabe had n't done it, but that it was up to the Government to prove that he had, and the Government had shown only that McCabe might have known what was going on.

Juror No. 11 said that Warren, having been caught with the goods on him, had to confess and that naturally he 'd try to protect his chum. To that Juror No. 5 said that Warren knew if he turned state's evidence he would get a lighter sentence. He had n't turned state's evidence and it was therefore apparent that he was telling the truth. All the other indications were that Warren was telling the whole truth. Four of the jurors said they thought that was so and Juror No. 5 considered those four won over to his side.

Juror No. 12 spoke of Mrs. Dietz's identification of McCabe, and that raised Juror No. 5's wrath. He did n't question Mrs. Dietz's honesty, but it was a cinch that all any woman would notice, who saw a man as she had seen the one by the window, would be his more prominent characteristics, such as the color of his hair and whether he had a mustache. She had n't looked at him carefully; she 'd just seen him for an instant as she went around the post that was between the entrance to the stairs and the entrance to the store. As for identifying him later, that was nothing. In the first place, the cops were out for a conviction and had forced McCabe on her just as a man who knows how can force a card on another in sleight-of-hand tricks. Besides, the cards were stacked on Mc-Cabe, anyway, when they put him — a young, thin, light-haired, clean-shaven man — in a room with a dozen heavy, dark, older men. Further, if McCabe had been before the store window he must have been waiting for Warren, and yet they had n't seen him with Warren or anywhere else when they rushed out of the store. There was nothing to that identification. The jury agreed that there was n't much to it.

Juror No. 5 raised another point. Warren had been caught with two raised bills in his pocket. If he had had any sense he would n't have let that happen, because otherwise he could have pleaded, if he were caught passing the raised bill, that he had n't known it was raised, that he had come by it in the ordinary way. It was remarkable that one man should be such a fool; it was more than unlikely that McCabe, if he were working with Warren, would overlook such an obvious thing, too. It would have been simple for McCabe to keep the two bills while Warren was passing the third. That made it look as though McCabe had known nothing of it.

It all came down finally to the fact that Warren and McCabe had been chums and had lived in one small room for five months: that was the point most of the jury could n't swallow. The scissors and gum and the rest of the stuff was in the drawer of a bureau that they both used. McCabe *must* have asked Warren what those things were for, if he had n't known without being told. Then the question came up whether or not McCabe might not have known what Warren was doing and perhaps told Warren to stop it

"It looks to me as though the case wasn't proved"

and himself refused to have anything to do with
the game. If that were so, was McCabe guilty
of anything? The jurors thought that perhaps
he was, but that he could n't be blamed for not
squealing on a pal. They were willing to ignore
the guilty-knowledge issue.

By that time Juror No. 5 thought that eight
or nine of the jurors were for acquittal and he
made his speech.

"I don't want to stand out against the rest
of you," he said, "and keep us all here till all
hours of the night. I 'm willing to go along with
the crowd, but it looks to me as though the case
was n't proved. McCabe *may* have had a part in
it — I know that 's a possibility — but, on the
other hand, it is possible that he did n't. He 's
young, younger than any of us, and if we say he 's
guilty he 's done so far as this world is concerned. He 'll go to prison and that will end
him for ever and ever. He 'll be on the records,
he 'll be watched, wherever he goes he 'll have
the mark on him. The mark will be on him because we put it there, and if we put it there we
may do wrong. I know there can't be any sentiment in this business — we are on our oath —
but I believe it 's our duty to give a young man
like McCabe the benefit of every doubt and to
be as merciful as we can without going against
our oath. Even if he 's guilty, he has had his

lesson and he won't forget it in a hurry. If he's a crook they'll get him sooner or later, and they'll get him right so that there won't be any question like this one for a jury to decide. I'm for giving him a chance to make good. And, besides all that, I don't want him on my conscience. I don't want to think all my life that I sent a young man to prison for ten or twenty years because I *thought* he had done wrong, not because I *knew* he had."

It was n't much of a speech, perhaps, that appeal of Juror No. 5, but it was good enough for the purpose. He made the appeal because his conscience ordered him to do it and because he believed that it was his duty to make the verdict his verdict, not the verdict of those ten men who had voted guilty on the first ballot. They were dull men, those ten — stupid, careless, thoughtless, uneducated men, with none of the finer susceptibilities, with no power of analysis, with no sentiment, with no great sense of responsibility. Each one of them was anxious to arrive at the easiest verdict and get away.

Juror No. 7 was not one of them; he was the same sort of man as No. 5, and No. 5 knew that No. 7 had sat back and let him do the talking, not because he, No. 7, could n't talk, but because he was keeping his arguments in reserve, to come to No. 5's aid if it turned out that No. 5 could n't quite put it over alone.

They took another ballot and it resulted in an eleven-to-one vote for acquittal. No sooner was the vote announced than Juror No. 2 spoke up.

"I'll change my vote," he said. "He did it all right — there ain't any question about that in my mind — but I guess maybe they did n't prove it. Besides," he added with a grin, " I ain't for stayin' here any longer than necessary; I got a date."

As the jury walked back to the court-room Juror No. 7 patted Juror No. 5 on the back.

"You did a fine job, I congratulate you," he said. "A pretty tough crowd, that bunch. I was afraid they might get obstinate and keep us here all night. I think the Government made a mistake in trying the case with only such flimsy evidence, but at that, if you had n't been on the jury, McCabe would have been convicted sure, and it would have been a grave miscarriage of justice."

Juror No. 5 as he took his seat felt that he had done a good job. The Government had tried to put one over on him, and failed. He had not dodged his duty; he had made no attempt to evade serving on the jury; and he was glad he had n't, for he had had a large part in giving

a young man a chance, a young man who did n't
look like a crook and who, Juror No. 5 was sure,
was n't a crook at heart. He might have done
wrong this one time, but Juror No. 5 was very
sure that if he had he 'd never do it again.

Juror No. 5 had a vision of a man coming to
him, perhaps five or ten years hence, and saying:
" You gave me my chance to make good. I 've
come to tell you that I have made good. I have
a wife and children and I have a good job and
my share of friends. My prospects are good, I 'm
happy, I 'm proud that I 'm straight and doing
well. I thought you might like to know it."

Juror No. 5 would be glad to know it. He was
very sure that McCabe would make good, even
if he did not know of it specifically, and the
thought pleased him. He, Juror No. 5, would
go home to his wife and children with a light
heart, pleased with his day's work.

The foreman pronounced the verdict: " Not
guilty."

McCabe smiled, a very little; he seemed to be
almost indifferent to the words that gave him his
freedom. Juror No. 5 understood that. The
young man had courage, and he had confidence in
himself, in the law, in the jury, in Juror No. 5.

Samuel Lyle was gone, but Tom Nash glanced
at the district attorney and Juror No. 5 saw the
Government prosecutor shrug his shoulders.

And he saw an expression on his face that said that such things were all in the day's work; he'd taken a chance and had n't gotten away with it, that was all.

Juror No. 5 did n't quite like the district attorney. He thought he'd gone too far with McCabe, had tried to get a verdict that he knew was not warranted by the evidence; he thought the district attorney might well look upon his fellow man with a little more mercy, with a little more kindness and generosity and not simply as a means of promoting his own professional record and reputation. Juror No. 5 was glad that the district attorney had failed.

Then the elderly, soft-spoken Judge called McCabe before him.

" You have heard the verdict," he said, " and I have no choice but to discharge you from custody. The jury, on the evidence presented to them, have acquitted you, and I cannot take exception to their decision. But let this be a lesson to you. Do not forget this day as long as you live. You have escaped the law, not because you are innocent but because the law surrounds every one brought before it with every safeguard. It has laid down rules of evidence to protect, to the utmost limit, the rights of the accused, and I am sure that in your case you have been declared not guilty because the law has protected

you, the very law which beyond a scintilla of
doubt you have yourself broken, in this instance,
as you have broken it before.

" If all the facts could have been given to the
jury you could not have escaped, and you would
have received a long sentence in prison — a
sentence which would, at its expiration, have left
you an old man, broken in spirit and useless to
yourself and your fellows; an outcast, disgraced,
forlorn and alone in the world. You have been
convicted of forgery and served a term in prison
for it. You have been convicted of counterfeit-
ing and because of your youth and the then apparently extenuating circumstances you received
a very light sentence. On another occasion you
have been before the court, on trial for check-
raising, and were acquitted because the jury considered the evidence insufficient. On still another occasion you were accused of passing worthless checks and again you escaped on a techni-
cality.

" And therefore, I say, let this be a lesson to
you to mend your ways. If honesty does not appeal to you for its own sake, let the fear of the
fate that awaits you cause you to lead an honest
life. I warn you that the way of the transgressor
is hard. You cannot always be as fortunate as
you have been to-day. Your record is known
and if you are ever convicted of a crime the

severest penalty the law allows will be inflicted upon you."

Juror No. 5 walked slowly from the court-room. Just ahead of him were the district at-torney and Tom Nash. Juror No. 5 heard them talking together.

"Why did n't you put the crook on the stand?" the prosecutor asked. "If you had I could have gotten his record to the jury and they would n't have been out ten minutes before they soaked him. As it was it took them over an hour to swallow the pill."

Tom Nash smiled. "Yes, I know it. I 'd have put him on, but Lyle would n't let me take the chance. He said the jury probably would n't convict on your evidence and he thought we ought not to take a chance on spoiling things. Our best chance was to let the case stand as it was. The jury did n't look very intelligent. Never mind, you 'll get him soon enough."

"The sooner the better. He 's bad, through and through. Warren would never have raised those bills; it took an old hand to do it. Damn Lyle, anyway!"

"He saved me from making a fool of myself," Nash said, laughing.

"It 's a rotten business, defending a man you know is guilty, is n't it?" the district attorney said. "So long, Tommy, see you to-morrow."

Juror No. 5 went out into the darkness, sadly.
On his way home he remembered that Samuel
Lyle had spoken to Tom Nash and that Nash had
looked over the jury until he had found him,
Juror No. 5, and that when Nash had addressed
the jury he had in reality spoken to Juror No. 5.

"He made a damn fool of me, right enough,"
mused Juror No. 5, humbly.

"COMPROMISE, HENRY?"

LYFORD is a town of a few thousand souls, some two hundred miles west of Alden, with little to commend it. Industrially, farming comes first, a paper-mill second, a flour-mill third, and after that, nothing, or next to it. It is the county-seat, and on court days the hotel does a good business and Main Street perks up a bit. The country about Lyford affords sport in season, trout, wild turkeys, and deer existing in sufficient numbers to give sportsmen a gambler's chance.

Aaron Miller was the villain of Lyford, the sort of villain who always has a grouch and grinds his neighbors under the iron heel of mortgages and loans. A book could be written about Aaron and his grouch and his hard heart, and if it were properly written Aaron would be very roughly treated in the last chapter. In that chapter, too, Sophy, his second cousin, would come to her own. Left penniless and alone at the tender age of forty-odd, Aaron had taken pity on her and offered her simple fare and a hard bed if she would pay for them by becoming his one domestic servant without other compensation.

One day, after twenty years of hard labor, Sophy packed a paper suit case and left for Alden, to spend two weeks with an old friend. Let it be known that she departed on a Saturday morning in the late autumn and that no one in Lyford knew the name or address of her Alden hostess, and Sophy is done with.

On the following Tuesday Aaron concealed in his house certain valuable documents and something over one thousand dollars in cash, and looked carefully to see that every door and window was securely locked. He left by the back door, went to his barn, hitched his horse, and drove to a neighboring town, where he transacted certain business, supped at the local hotel, and started home. As he neared Lyford in the dark he saw an automobile with glaring headlights coming toward him. Aaron disapproved of automobiles and took delight in crowding them to the side of the road.

In this instance he followed his usual practice and reaped the whirlwind. Coming from behind was another automobile, and there being courtesy ofttimes between automobilists, both of them extinguished their bright headlights. Aaron's buggy, carrying no tail-light, melted serenely into the darkness and was never seen at all by the driver coming up behind until a collision was unavoidable. The front wheel of the automobile struck the rear wheel of Aaron's buggy. The automobilist was very decent about it; he picked up Aaron's unconscious form and rushed it to the hospital in Lyford and saw that the horse was properly taken care of at the livery-stable. Aaron was pronounced not to be seriously injured, but he persisted in remaining unconscious.

Even if he had recovered consciousness promptly Dr. Watts would certainly not have permitted any word of the fire to reach his patient's ears, the fire having occurred that very afternoon. Mary Preston, who lived near by, saw it first and did the screaming; others took up the cry and the telephone, and when it was all over Aaron's house was in rather bad shape. Experts diagnosed the origin of the fire as having been in wood-boxes containing ashes with live coals in them and let it go at that. There was nothing for it but to patch up the house and wait till Aaron recovered or Sophy returned.

On the following Friday night at ten-twenty Samuel Lyle, coming from Alden, left the train at Lyford and, toting his own grip, walked the two blocks to the Mansion House, where a bed and his trunk awaited him. Saturday morning Walter Mellor, a young man of thirty, called for

Mr. Lyle in an automobile in which Mr. Lyle placed certain necessary luggage and two guns.

They drove to the office of Henry Smiley, District Attorney of the County of Lyford, and Sam and Henry greeted each other warmly, for their friendship ran all the way back to school-days. They chatted for a while, and then the little car chugged Mr. Lyle and Walter far into the mountains. There they hunted turkey and deer, and it made very little difference to them that the game was very scarce indeed, for the sport was the thing — not the prize.

On that same Saturday, too, Aaron Miller sat up in bed and tried to straighten things out in his head, but it was not until Monday that his condition permitted him to be intrusted with the news of the fire. The shock, instead of causing a relapse, seemed to bring about a complete recovery, and Aaron begged to be allowed to depart at once to the scene of the conflagration. Denied permission to do this, he demanded that certain trustworthy persons be despatched at once to discover and put into a safe place two boxes, one containing cash and the other papers, which they would find concealed in the bottom drawer of Aaron's desk, the key thereto being in the pocket of Aaron's coat.

The two trusted persons departed and shortly returned, saying that the bottom drawer of

Aaron's desk was substantially empty, and that certainly no boxes were in it.

Within the hour every man, woman, and child in Lyford knew that Aaron Miller had been robbed and that the thief had attempted to burn down the house to conceal the crime. The live-coals-in-a-wooden-box theory was exploded and District Attorney Henry Smiley took matters in charge.

Although the fire had surely originated in the cellar, Aaron insisted that all the ashes from the house were carried outdoors and never went into the cellar at all, which made people wonder how the live-coal idea had ever started. From Aaron's description of the cellar it seemed more than likely that the contents of a kerosene can had been thrown on the pile of kindling and ignited.

Then a clue was discovered. A large jack-knife was found on Aaron's desk, and Aaron said that he had never seen it before. Marks on the desk drawer indicated that it had been forced open with the large blade of the knife. Then the key to the back door could not be found. Aaron said that he had locked the door and put the key in his pocket, but it was not on his person when he was brought to the hospital, and it could not be found elsewhere. Members of the Lyford Fire Company said that when they got

there the door was unlocked and that there was
no key in the door. The key matter was mys-
terious and beyond explanation, but the knife was
something concrete to go on, and Mr. Smiley was
trying to discover its owner when Stephen Coale
walked into Mr. Smiley's office and sat down.
Mr. Coale was manager of the paper-mill, president of Lyford's only bank, a town supervisor,
and other important things. Yet on this morning Mr. Coale was troubled. " Morning,
Stephen," Mr. Smiley said, and when Mr. Coale
failed to respond in his usual genial manner,
Mr. Smiley asked him what was wrong.

"Something on my mind, Henry," Stephen answered, "and I guess I've got to get it off. I
can't ask you to consider it confidential, of
course, so suppose we just agree that it won't go
any farther unless it is necessary. It's about
that Aaron Miller matter."

Mr. Smiley promised secrecy so far as his official duty would permit.

" Well, then," said Mr. Coale with evident re-
luctance, " I saw Walter Mellor walking away
from Aaron's just before the fire was discovered.
I didn't think anything about it at the time,
naturally, and it wasn't till after I heard about
the robbery that I remembered I'd been by that
way late Tuesday afternoon. Walter was quite a
way off, but I'm sure it was he. Even then I

did n't think much about it till yesterday, and then one of the boys mentioned offhand that Walter had put over a thousand dollars in his savings account last Thursday. That set me thinking where he would obtain so much money, all in bills. I 've always considered Walter to be an honest man, and I 'm not suspecting him now, but I thought it was my duty to tell you about this."

As soon as Mr. Coale was gone Mr. Smiley sent for Arthur Sims, who was a close friend of Walter Mellor's, and showed him the knife. Arthur examined it carefully and said that he supposed that there were lots of knives like it.

"But do you know anybody around here who has one like it?" Mr. Smiley asked. Arthur was not enthusiastic.

"Come, son," Mr. Smiley urged, "this is just between you and me, for the time being, anyway. Whose knife do you think that is?"

Arthur stuck to his position that there were lots of knives like it.

"Yes, probably there are, but this knife has had the point broken off the smaller blade, and it 's been ground down; also, one of the three rivets holding on the wood handle is gone. Suppose you had found this knife somewhere, would you think of anybody special it might belong to — Walter Mellor, for instance?"

Mr. Smiley did not need Arthur's reluctant admission that Walter had a knife something like it to convince him that Arthur was pretty sure it was Walter Mellor's knife. He went to the bank and discovered that the bills Walter Mellor had deposited corresponded, at least pretty closely, with the denominations of the bills that had been stolen from Aaron Miller.

It is well-nigh impossible to keep such a matter secret in a small town. Nobody talks, but rumors start and take on speed and body and become gospel truth, and every one knows what's what and what is going to happen.

So it was in Lyford. Comments were made at noontime at the Mansion House, and by three o'clock Walter Mellor's name was on everybody's tongue. Hank Gross flashed into prominence because he knew that Walter had bought a gun for two hundred dollars from Skinner over in Hibbsville on the Friday after the fire, he having seen Walter with the gun Friday afternoon coming back on the train, and he'd thought it queer Walter could pay that much for a gun, unless he was lying. Skinner promptly stated that Walter had not lied.

Walter Mellor was a carpenter by trade, but did n't work steadily at carpentering, making most of his money taking city folks hunting and doing a little trading in dogs and getting a commission for selling a horse or cow or an automobile once in a while.

No sooner was the story of money rampant than Fred Shontz remembered that Walter had come into the Mansion House and bought cigars Thursday after supper. Fred had caught sight of a roll of bills big enough to choke a hoss.

All of this was pretty good proof that immediately after the robbery Walter had had a lot of money. Possibly Walter could explain satisfactorily where he got it, but certain individuals who may have been a little jealous of Walter and who may have taken a certain joy in the troubles of others doubted it.

Then came John Sharp and Mary Preston bearing tales, Mary being the woman who had first discovered the fire. John Sharp, who lived in the rear of Aaron's house, said that on the Tuesday afternoon of the fire he had seen Walter Mellor come around Aaron's house. He had knocked at the back door, waited for a minute or two, and then gone to the stable. From the stable he had gone back to the door and stood there a while and then gone in. In maybe fifteen minutes he came out and disappeared around the corner of the house.

John Sharp himself went away a few minutes later and did not get home till everybody was in bed, and he never thought anything whatever of

Walter Mellor's visit to Aaron's house until he heard people talking about Walter, and then it all came back in a flash.

When Mr. Smiley asked him whether he was absolutely sure that it was Walter, John said he was certain; he 'd know Walter anywhere as far as he could see him, " just as any one would, on account of his shape and way of walking, that was different from other people's," and furthermore Walter had been dressed, as he almost always was, in mackinaw, corduroys, and felt hat, up on one side and down on the other.   As to the time of day, it was five o'clock or a little after, just at twilight.   Mary Preston saw the queer light in Aaron's kitchen when she was just getting supper, which would be at about quarter of six, and the fire company knew as a matter of official record that word had reached the firehouse by telephone at seven minutes of six. So everything checked closely enough.

Mary Preston now added to her original statement that just before she went to the kitchen she saw Walter Mellor pass by. She admitted that it was pretty dark, but she knew him well and could not be mistaken; she could n't tell just why she knew it was Walter, but she was sure it was, just as she 'd recognize any one she knew without knowing just how she did it. That seemed reasonable enough. She would n't say for sure that Walter had come out of Aaron's place, but he was coming from that direction.

Mr. Smiley discovered that Walter had left the flour-mill on one side of town at half-past four that afternoon. It looked as though he had gone by the river path, because no one remembered seeing him go through the town. Walter boarded with Mrs. Pringle, and she could not remember at all what time he reached home that evening, except that he was there when the fire-bell rang.

Such was the case against Walter Mellor when he and Mr. Lyle arrived at the Mansion House with one deer and three fat turkeys.

The news of his arrival flashed up and down the street, and the hotel loafers jumped to their feet and made for the front steps.

Benny Riggs, Lyford's one policeman, was there, and it had been many a long day since Benny had had such a delicate and weighty job to perform. If Benny and his friends knew that Samuel Lyle was one of the country's greatest criminal lawyers, they forgot the fact in the excitement of the moment. On the other hand, they did not forget that Mr. Lyle was a stranger from a large city, and that it would be indelicate to embarrass one of their own number by accusing him before that stranger. Therefore Benny waited for a moment till he had a chance to speak to Walter quietly. Then he said: "Wait, Mr. Smiley wants to see you."

Walter knew at once from Benny's voice that something was wrong. A glance at the faces all about him made him doubly sure, and the atmosphere had suppressed excitement in it.

"What's up, Benny?" he asked.

"Have to let Mr. Smiley explain that, Walt," Benny said.

Samuel Lyle heard that statement and suddenly he too became aware of the tenseness all about. His expression of geniality vanished, and his face clouded for an instant; then it became as though Mr. Lyle was very tired and very much bored. The corners of his mouth dropped, his eyes took on a look of sleepiness, his huge frame lost all its strength, and his shoulders sagged. Mr. Lyle's mind and body were relaxed completely. It was a condition that years of effort made it possible for him to assume, and when he was in that condition nothing on earth, so far as ever had been discovered, could make him so much as bat an eyelash. He was absolutely emotionless; no lawyer fighting against him, no witness, no criminal, no judge, could ever tell whether Samuel Lyle was worried, jubilant, perplexed, disappointed, happy, sad, or anything else. His face was inscrutable.

Mr. Lyle waited for something to happen. "Right now or after supper?" Walter asked.

"Better be right now," Benny said.

"Nothing doing, Benny; I've got to eat. You tell Mr. Smiley I'll see him after supper." Benny shook his head positively, and Mr. Lyle walked over to him. "Walter killed anybody with premeditation?" he asked.

Again the chief of police shook his head. Mr. Lyle took out his glasses and, fitting them carefully to his eyes by holding them between his thumb and finger, examined Benny's badge.

"Umph," hummed Mr. Lyle. "Do you know the penalty for arresting a man in a hotel after dark for anything less than a capital crime? You don't, do you? Suppose you go ask Mr. Smiley and tell him I sent you, and you tell him that Walter Mellor has just retained me as counsel and that if he bothers us till after dinner, I'll — I'll — you ask him if he remembers what happened in the Wikkers case. I'll see that Walter does n't run away."

Benny hesitated; he had his duty to perform, but there was something about Mr. Lyle that worried him. He'd never heard about not arresting a man in a hotel after dark. Benny started for the telephone booth.

"Wait a minute," Mr. Lyle said and, taking Walter aside, they talked together for a moment.

Then he said to Benny: " Ask Mr. Smiley to come over and have dinner with us."

Mr. Smiley asked to speak to Mr. Lyle, and when Mr. Lyle left the booth he motioned Benny to enter it and Walter to come to dinner.

After dinner Benny was waiting, and every one marched to the court-house, but the entire procession stopped in the corridor except Benny, Walter, and Mr. Lyle, who went into the district attorney's private office.

Mr. Smiley greeted them with some small indication of nervousness. He knew Samuel Lyle only too well, and never in his experience had such a lawyer come to the aid of a malefactor in Lyford County.

After certain introductory remarks Mr. Smiley asked Walter two questions: was that his knife, and where had he gotten more than a thousand dollars in bills the week before? At both of these questions Mr. Lyle shook his head, and Walter refused to answer. Mr. Smiley then said that there was nothing for it but to arrest Walter and bring him to trial. A conference ensued between Walter and Mr. Lyle, and it was then agreed between Mr. Lyle and Mr. Smiley that Walter should remain in Mr. Lyle's custody until the morrow, when bail could be furnished and everything fixed up shipshape.

Bail was furnished, and the trial of Walter

Mellor was set for the next term of court, which would open on the first Monday of January. Samuel Lyle visited Lyford half a dozen times before Christmas. Walter Mellor went on his way, finding men who believed in his innocence in the face of the overwhelming evidence against him, and finding men who chuckled at his predicament and got an unholy joy out of it.

Henry Smiley looked forward to the trial with no calm spirit. In the first place, he liked Walter Mellor; he did n't entirely approve of Walter's happy-go-lucky life — working one day, loafing the next, and hunting the third — but Walter was a pleasant man and had a kind heart.

Such were Mr. Smiley's reflections as he stood at his window in the court-house, after lunch one day just before Christmas, staring his disagreeable duty in the face, which explained why a very small funeral cortège passed before him without his giving it a thought. Mr. Smiley was very sure that if Walter Mellor could have explained that he had come into the possession of all that money honestly he would have done so, and that if he could have honestly denied that the knife which had forced the drawer of Aaron Miller's desk was his he would have done that too. He was also sure that if Samuel Lyle could have gotten Walter out of his trouble without a trial Mr. Lyle would have done that. But if Mr.

Smiley had admitted what was troubling him most, he would have said that it was appearing in court as a prosecutor when Samuel Lyle was counsel for the defense.   Mr. Smiley had a strong suspicion that his dear old friend would forget their friendship and make a monkey of him.

Therefore Mr. Smiley returned to his desk sadly and did very little work that afternoon. He had just lighted his desk lamp when his clerk came into the room saying that Mr. Samuel Lyle craved an audience.   Mr. Smiley prayed fervently that Mr. Lyle's business would be personal and pleasant and not professional.   Again let it be said that William Smiley's love for Mr. Lyle the man was equaled only by his fear of Mr. Lyle the counsel for the other side.

Mr. Lyle did not describe at once the purpose of his call.   He put down his bag beside Mr. Smiley's desk, took off his heavy overcoat, laid it on a chair, and sat down.

" Well, Henry, how are you to-day? "

" Pretty fair, Sam.   You 're looking fit."

" Yes, I' m in good shape for an old fellow, but I 'm a wee bit sad.   I 've just come from Leander Webb's funeral."   Mr. Lyle opened his bag and took from it a box of cigars.   " Smoke, Henry? " he asked.   They both took cigars, and Mr. Lyle laid the open box on the desk.   As he did so something in it caught his eye.   He leaned forward

and took a key from among the cigars and, taking
his glasses from his waistcoat pocket, examined
it closely.

" Where do you suppose that came from? " he
exclaimed, looking at Mr. Smiley inquiringly as
though Mr. Smiley could solve the problem.
" Must have picked it up in the hotel absent-mind-
edly," he finally decided, and, laying the key on
the desk, he sank back in his chair, twisting his
lips as though he were trying to work his face
into some queer shape. Before he spoke his eyes
became sleepy and a little sad; his mouth drooped
at the corners.

" Henry," he said, " how 'd you like to settle
this Mellor case out of court? "

Mr. Smiley jumped as though a bomb had gone
off under his chair.

" Don't be worried, Henry," Mr. Lyle went on,
" I 'm not going to try to bribe you; I 've no
doubt I could, but I 'm not going to. You and I
know that when one side 's got a bad case it
usually wants to settle on the best terms obtain-
able. I thought maybe you 'd like to settle."

It was just as Mr. Smiley had feared all along:
Sam Lyle was going to make a monkey of him.

" Now, look here, Sam," he exclaimed,
" there 's no settlement possible in a case like
this, and you know it. Walter Mellor 's guilty
or he is n't, and a jury 's got to decide that."

"That's nonsense, and you know it," replied
Mr. Lyle. "If Walter's guilty, he's guilty right
now, and what a jury says about it won't affect
the fact one way or the other."

"You know perfectly well what I mean."

"You mean you're willing a jury should make
its guess and relieve you of the responsibility.
All you've got to do is to do your sworn duty and
wash your hands of the result. Now, I happen
to know that the fair name of the law is likely to
be smirched something scandalous if you try to
get out of it that way. I'll have to prove that
the state has a lot of perjurers working for it, and
I'll have to cast suspicion on the district attorney. Then what happens? The defendant is acquitted, and who robbed Aaron Miller and burned
down his house? What will justice do then?
Where will the law find a victim? Henry, my
old friend, you'd better compromise."

Poor Henry! Only too well he knew that Sam
Lyle was throwing no cheap bluff. He knew as
sure as shootin' that Sam would make a monkey
of him if it came to the test. But Henry Smiley,
for all his simple life in Lyford County, was no
fool.

"Sam Lyle," he said, "you've no business
coming up here and meddling in my affairs, and
you know it. But you're here, and I can't send
you away. You're entitled to appear before any

court in this state and maybe some others, but I'm not going to have any nonsense. Tell me what you know and be quick about it."

Mr. Lyle smiled broadly, and his eyes lighted up. "That's the talk, Mr. District Attorney, that's the talk! But you can't bamboozle me. If you're ready to compromise, say so; I'm not giving away something for nothing, not even to you."

"Compromise! How can any one compromise?"

"Have another cigar, Henry, and think it over."

"I haven't half finished this one," he exclaimed.

"So you haven't," said Mr. Lyle. "Suppose, then, instead of a cigar, you take that key. The state ought to have that key. It's the one that opens the back door of Aaron Miller's house."

Again Mr. Smiley jumped as though a bomb had exploded in the room.

"What's that? What's that? Where did you get it?"

"Slow, Henry! slow! If I were to give you my word of honor that Walter Mellor didn't have it, and never had it, what would you think of compromising then?"

"Who did have it?" Mr. Smiley went straight to the point emphatically.

"Not so fast, Henry. Answer my question first, while I hunt for something in this bag of mine. Somehow, everything always seems to get mixed up in my bag." Mr. Lyle laid on the desk the exact duplicate of the knife that had been found on Aaron's desk, except that the rivet was not gone from the handle and the small blade had not been repointed. "Compromise, Henry?"

Mr. Smiley sank back in his chair, a dejected figure.

"Sam," he moaned, "I knew all along that you'd make a — Sam Lyle, are you going to tell me what you know or ain't you?" Mr. Smiley allowed himself the "ain't" under great provoca-tion. "Where'd you get those things?"

"I got the knife from Walter; I got the key from the same man from whom I got this." Mr. Lyle was searching in the bag again. "From the same man — from whom —" He took a tin box from the bag and put it on the desk and opened it. "All Aaron's papers are there," he said, "and not one inch farther do I go till you promise me, so far as it is within your power and within the proper discretion of your office, that you will do as I want you to."

Of course Mr. Smiley understood the proposal that Samuel Lyle was making to him. It was that he should go before the court and ask for the discharge of Walter Mellor, that he should make restitution to Aaron Miller and make no explanation of his action nor divulge the name of the guilty man to the people of Lyford. Who that man was, or why Samuel Lyle should want to protect him, he had not the faintest idea.

" Man to man, Sam, do you know Walter Mellor is innocent? " Mr. Smiley asked.

" I do, Henry."

" But the evidence? " Mr. Smiley was ill at ease.

" You 're wondering what you 're going to do with that array of witnesses who were going to prove your case against Walter, are n't you? There are all sorts and descriptions of liars in this world, old friend; suppose we get one of them in here right now and convince him of the error of his ways. It ought to be just about time for Stephen Coale to leave his office: call him up and see if he won't stop here."

Mr. Smiley called Mr. Coale on the telephone, and Mr. Coale said that he would be in the district attorney's office in a very few minutes.

Samuel Lyle sank back in his chair. " Yes, Henry, there are many kinds of liars in the world. The knife you found in Aaron's house was a liar, an innocent one, just as was the money that Walter put in the savings fund of the bank. To be sure, this money was the root of evil, though, out of fairness to drink and women, it is n't square to charge money with being the root of all evil: it does n't deserve so much credit.

"Then, Henry, continuing the subject of lying, there are lies of invention or suppression, lies of addition or omission, lies of exaggeration or attenuation, just plain lies, and lots of other kinds. There are fallacies of memory which, unrecognized, force a liar to fill the gaps his poor memory has made, and he fills them for his own satisfaction as he believes they should be filled; he furnishes, from his own imagination, facts to fill his mental voids, and, once filled, he refuses to remember that those voids ever existed. The narrative he has pieced together becomes the truth and nothing but the truth; he cannot tell, himself, how much of his tale is fact and how much fancy; he forgets entirely his inventions and becomes a liar of purest ray serene. That sort of liar is dangerous because he is egotistically ignorant that he is lying, his character is beyond suspicion, and often he is testifying simply because of a magnified idea of his public duty.

"Now, in this case, Henry, you were up against various phases of this lying business. Mary Preston lied, under stress of emotion or bias. Walter Mellor was not within half a mile of Aaron's house on that Tuesday until after the fire was discovered; he went from the flour-mill to his house, *carrying his tool-box,* by way of the river path. Yet Mary Preston says she saw him at about five o'clock near Aaron's house. To begin with, she took it for granted that the proof against him was conclusive and that he was guilty. Once upon a time she had hopes of marrying Walter; recently he had transferred his attentions to another girl. Result — venting of her spite by shouting, "I too saw him," though she had in reality seen several men pass in the dusk, and satisfied her conscience by taking it for granted that Walter was one of them.

" Fred Shontz said he saw Walter with an enormous roll of bills in the Mansion House shortly after the robbery. That was a lie of exaggeration. Walter did not offer him a cigar, perhaps, and Shontz brooded over his own lack of ready cash and magnified Walter's wad accordingly. Walter had less than twenty-five dollars that night.

" Hank Gross said that Walter had bought a gun for two hundred dollars, an expenditure far beyond his normal means. That was a lie of omission, for he forgot to say that Walter had told him that he had purchased the gun for some one else. He was willing to lie for the sake of being in accord with, and more or less applauded by, others for his astuteness, and to that end methodically forgot the second fact, taking refuge in the possibility that Walter himself had lied. Walter bought that gun for me, with my money.

"John Sharp indulged in the pleasant recreation of lying for its own sake, the secondary motive being malice superinduced by jealousy. Walter was paying attention to his girl and was a competitor of his business in a small way. Sharp was just plain liar.

"Aaron Miller lied, for he said that he locked the back door and put the key in his pocket; that was a lie of supposition. Aaron intended to lock his house when he left it, therefore he said that he had done it, whereas if he were honest he would have said that he supposed he had completed the undertaking. His positive statement that he had locked the back door and put the key in his pocket was nothing more than a figment of his imagination, based on his ideas of his own infallibility.

"So you see, Henry, evidence doesn't always turn out the way the prosecuting attorney expects —"

At that moment Stephen Coale, leading citizen of Lyford, a gentleman of parts and of unblemished character, was announced by Mr. Smiley's clerk. In the moment before his entry Mr. Lyle said: "Now we come to the conscientious witness who is not satisfied with telling facts, but, much as he hates to do it, must take upon himself the burden of saving the state."

They greeted Mr. Coale, and Mr. Smiley explained that they were talking over the Mellor case.

"Very sad indeed, very sad, isn't it?" Mr. Coale said. "I cannot understand how Walter Mellor could have done such a thing."

"Yes," Mr. Lyle said, "it is too bad. I'm trying to find some way of saving Walter's good name, and Mr. Smiley has very kindly permitted me to ask you a few questions, provided, of course, that you don't object."

"Oh, no indeed, certainly not!" exclaimed Mr. Coale.

"Then, as I understand it, you left your office on that Tuesday at about four o'clock, walked down Main Street, turned and walked past the Miller house to the Warnocks'. You spent half or three quarters of an hour with Mr. Warnock, who was ill, and then walked to the Mansion House. On the way you saw Walter Mellor leave the Miller place by the drive. Is that right?"

"Yes, that is correct."

"You don't go to the Mansion House often, do you, Mr. Coale?"

"No; very seldom. I went that day to see a Mr. Clement, who was stopping there overnight, a business friend whom I had not had an opportunity to see during the day and whom I was especially desirous of seeing."

"Exactly. That is as I understand it. A week or ten days later you learned by chance that Walter Mellor had made a rather large deposit in your savings fund. It was then that you recalled seeing him leave the Miller place?"

"Yes."

"You had recognized him by his clothes, perhaps, as well as by his features and figure?"

"Undoubtedly."

"Did you speak with him?"

"No; to have done so I must have crossed the road or shouted."

"Quite so. You recall his gray mackinaw coat and his felt hat?"

"Yes, distinctly."

"And you would swear that it was he and no other?"

"Absolutely."

"But, Mr. Coale, Walter Mellor was on the Miller place that day only after the discovery of the fire. Furthermore, Mr. Clement did not register at the Mansion House till the morning after the fire — that is, on Wednesday — and on Wednesday afternoon at about five o'clock Jerry Waldron, wearing a *brown* mackinaw and a *cap*, left the Miller place and saw you on the opposite side of the street. Would those facts alter your testimony, do you think?"

Mr. Coale glanced from Mr. Lyle to Mr. Smiley; his expression was exactly as though some one had slapped his face. "There — er — er — must be some mistake."

"Yes," said Mr. Lyle, "there must be some mistake. Will you tell me this — think carefully before you answer — did you really mistake the man you saw coming from the Miller place on Wednesday or did you actually not recognize him then at all, but afterward, when you learned of Walter Mellor's possession of the money, did you say to yourself: 'The man I saw must have been Walter Mellor'?"

"I — I —" Mr. Coale began to stutter something.

"Just a minute. Did you actually see and make a mental note of the man's costume when you saw him, or did you, a week later, reason: 'The man was Mellor; therefore he had on the gray mackinaw and the felt hat Mellor always wears'? Was that the way you arrived at the facts you would have testified to?"

Mr. Coale was indignant. "Do you mean to insinuate, sir, that I invented —"

"No, no, no! Disabuse your mind of any such thought. Mr. Smiley and I simply were discussing, now, the value of the prosecutor's evidence,

rather than waiting and doing it in court.
Your character and reputation are so far beyond
reproach as to answer your own question."

Mr. Coale smiled blandly.

" Is there anything in what Mr. Lyle suggests,
do you think, Stephen? " Mr. Smiley asked.

Mr. Coale made some show of thinking deeply,
and finally delivered himself of this confession:

" I understand the fallibility of mortal man,
and I presume I am as susceptible to error as my
fellows."

A few minutes later Mr. Coale departed.

" A very pretty liar," Mr. Lyle muttered.
" Compromise, Henry? "

Henry Smiley nodded.   " Yes, Sam, anything
you say — provided only that I don't go to jail
for it."

" Might make you more merciful afterward if
you did. But you won't. I 'll begin at the beginning. About twenty-five years ago Walter
Mellor's father died and five-year-old Walter was
facing the orphan-asylum when Leander Webb
offered to provide for him. Of course Leander
could n't take the boy himself, but he paid his
keep and something more — in George Pratt's
family, was n't it? He saw that he got a good
start in life and taught him woodcraft too; used
to take him out in the woods when he was a
mere shaver. Leander never talked much, and I

don't know that he had any reason except plain
charity for what he did for Walter, but I always
suspected that Walter's father had done some big
thing for Leander. Anyway, Leander was very
fond of him.

"I was very fond of Leander, too; he had his
limitations, of course, but the world would be a
better place than it is if there were no worse men
than he. Many and many a day I've spent with
him in the woods, and no more honorable man
ever lived. The night I got back here with Walter Mellor and heard you wanted him, I did n't
know a thing about the robbery. I'm naturally
wary, Henry; it usually pays, and it paid this
time, for as soon as you'd asked about the knife
and the money and I'd talked to Walter, everything was pretty clear. He told me the knife was
Leander's and that Leander had given him the
money, saying that he owed it to him, which had
some truth in it, and that it had been paid to him
by a man he had lent it to long ago. Walter took
it and put it where the old man could have it if
he ever needed it. Leander had to be humored.

"It is undoubtedly a good thing, Henry, for all
of us to go into the woods occasionally, to get
away from the stress of life in crowds, but I think
that perhaps too much solitude, such as Leander
had, day after day, year after year, is too great
a strain on the mind; there is too much self-con-

templation, too little stimulus from other minds.
Leander's mind wore out before his body; you and
I probably shall go the other way.

"After we left you that night we found him in
bad shape — possibly as a subconscious result of
the deed he had done. He admitted it readily
enough, laughed at it, and said that Aaron had
skinned Walter's father out of the money years
before. After all these years he had gone to tax
Aaron with the fact and demand restitution, but
Aaron was not at home, and he found the key in
the back door. He went in and took the two
boxes, chuckling at the joke on the old skinflint;
he would hide the papers and tease Aaron about
them and give the money to Walter to pay the
debt and defy Aaron to get it back.

"I knew the night we left here and went to
Leander's that the courts could never harm him
and that he would either forget all about this
world or would be with his Maker before many
days were past. It would have been easy to explain that to the court, but it would not have
been easy to make all of Lyford understand it;
there are always some who will believe ill of a
man despite everything. Walter was not willing
that Leander's name should have even so white
a blot on it, and so we did not explain. Walter
carried the burden for the sake of the man who
had befriended him. And now, Henry, it's up

to you to straighten things out. I don't envy you the job.

"Incidentally, there is no power on earth that can make Walter Mellor return that money to Aaron if he does n't want to. He 'll do it if you say so, but knowing Aaron, if it were my business I think that I should arrange for the old miser to make an involuntary contribution to — say the fire company."

"You don't mean that, Sam."

"Don't I? How do you know what I mean? " Samuel Lyle grinned. "I 've got to go, Henry; my train 's about due, and there 's not another for an age."

"Speaking of the fire company," Mr. Smiley asked, "why did Leander set fire to Aaron's house? "

"He did n't; anyway, he says he did n't, and he told the truth about everything else. He went to Aaron's about two o'clock, and the fire was n't discovered till nearly six. I guess it was just plain fire. The fire company did good work; that's why it occurred to me that Aaron might like to express his appreciation materially. Come and see me in Alden, Henry, just as soon as you can."

"I will. Don't forget your cigars! "

"Keep 'em, as the consideration for compromising. A Merry Christmas to you, Mr. Dis-

trict Attorney," and the door closed behind Mr.
Lyle — and opened again. "Caution your police
force about making arrests in hotels after dark,
Henry." Then the door closed for good.

BEYOND A REASONABLE DOUBT

WE hold no brief for Mary West. We are not at all sure that she needs any defense at our hands or at anybody else's. Her early life had been none too easy and she had undoubtedly seen many a romance die a slow and painful death at the hands of hard work, many children, and a small income. She had been, once upon a time, Mary Booth, and she was the prettiest and smartest girl in Soleby and the neighborhood; though, to be sure, that isn't necessarily saying much for her, as Soleby has very few permanent residents and its neighborhood is sparsely settled. It is a small New England village, which in the summer is the resort of city people; except in the summer it is very quiet and very modest and it lives almost entirely upon the money the summer visitors leave behind them.

So far as romance was concerned Mary had had two suitors, Amos Rose and Harry Packer, who had grown up with her and who were, themselves, good friends. There had been some question in and about Soleby as to whether, sooner or later, the friendship of years' standing between the two would be broken by their rivalry for Mary's hand; but suddenly Mary had settled the question — temporarily, as it happened — by giving up all thought of romance and marrying William West, who was a widower and, as things go in this world, an old man. Whether Mary thought herself lucky or unlucky matters not; the fact is that William West died within a year after his marriage to Mary and left her with all her charm and brightness and, in addition, with a nice bit of property which, presumably, in no way lessened her attractiveness.

Within a year after William West's death Amos Rose and Harry Packer were again Mary's suitors, and again it was a question whether their friendship would stand up under the strain of their rivalry. There was a further question, of course, which was whether or not Mary would marry again. She insisted to her bosom friends that she would not, but that did not mean anything, and her bosom friends were very sure that not only would she marry again but that she would, in all probability, marry either Amos or Harry. It would be, in a way, a case of eating her cake and having it too: she had given up romance for the sake of ease and comfort and now she could, if she wished, have her comfort and her romance too.

Nobody really had any strong opinion as to

which of her two suitors she would take if she took either of them. From an unprejudiced point of view each had certain good points and certain bad points. Harry Packer was a little more attractive personally than Amos, but Amos was a little steadier. Harry Packer was a very pleasant man, a good-natured, easy-going fellow, kind-hearted, generous, and a little lazy; years before he had drunk more than was good for him, but he had stopped that, apparently for good and all, and people had said that he had done it because of Mary. And even when Mary married William West, Harry had not gone back to his old habits.

Amos Rose was a quiet, undemonstrative man who worked hard and was thought to be a little close. He built small boats and rented them; he had an interest in Soleby's summer fish-market and did odd jobs of carpentry and repair work in the cottages. He was a plain, matter-of-fact man, rather dull and with no superficial charms to attract a woman, but he was steady and he made more money than Harry Packer. All in all, it was a toss-up which one Mary West would prefer as a husband.

That was the condition of affairs when, one Sunday morning in the spring, Amos Rose and Harry Packer, clinging to their old friendship despite everything, went fishing together, at

the bridge where the Shore Road goes over Salt
River. At twelve o'clock that day Harry Packer
was seen, alone, going through Soleby. Amos
Rose did not return.

Mrs. Rose, Amos's mother, thought very little
about Amos's not returning for dinner; she was
surprised but not alarmed when he did not return
for supper and it was not until late Sunday night
that she began to wonder whether anything had
happened. He had, of course, stayed out late
many times before and she had always worried a
little about it every time, as mothers will, but
this time, as on other occasions, she went to bed
and slept soundly. When she awoke the next
morning and found that Amos had not returned
she made inquiries which led to the discovery
that no one had seen him return from fishing.
The first idea was to ask Harry Packer where
Amos was, and this idea disclosed at once the
fact that Harry, too, was missing. People said
that they had seen him come back alone at twelve
o'clock the day before, and suspicion was naturally immediately aroused.

Men went down to the bridge over Salt River
and found Amos's knife, his pipe, bait, the fish
he had caught, and an empty ginger ale bottle
on the bridge pier where the men had fished.
Later in the day a bamboo fishing-pole was found
floating in the river. There was nothing to

identify it positively as Amos's, but the presumption was strong that it was his. Then Soleby put two and two together and arrived at the conclusion that there had been foul play and that Amos had been the victim and Harry Packer the perpetrator.

The police were notified and the search was started, first for Amos or Amos's body and second for Harry Packer. Salt River in the vicinity of the Shore Road bridge was dragged and nothing found and no trace of Harry Packer was discovered. Nobody could be found who had seen him after twelve o'clock on Sunday.

Three or four days later Amos Rose's body was found about a quarter of a mile up Salt River where the tide, going out, had left it, partially hidden by the marsh grass on the river bank. An autopsy was immediately performed which proved that Amos had not been drowned but had been killed by a blow on the back of the head, a blow of such magnitude that the skull was crushed and deeply indented.

It was a mystery what manner of instrument could have been used in dealing such a blow. It must have been very heavy and blunt; it might have been done, for instance, with a heavy iron maul between two and a half and three inches across the end, such a maul as iron-workers use. The blow had been fairly struck, for the autopsy

showed that the wound on the head was round
and that the direction of the blow had been
straight against the head and not at an angle. A
thorough search was made all about the bridge
and along the Shore Road back to Soleby and
by a diver at the bottom of the river, but no instrument capable of inflicting such a wound could
be found. No one could think of any such instrument except an eight- or ten-pound iron
maul, and no such thing had been seen around
Soleby within the memory of man. That Harry
Packer should have had such a tool or, having it,
that he should have had it with him at the pier
seemed impossible. It was suggested that a cu-
riously shaped rock might have been used for the
purpose, but the country all about was marshy
or sandy and there was not a trace of a rock anywhere and it seemed inconceivable that if Harry
Packer had murdered Amos Rose he had employed so crude a method as throwing a rock at
his head. It was improbable, if not entirely impossible, that the blow could have been struck
with a rock held in a man's hand.

It was known that to all appearances a strong
and abiding friendship had existed between Amos
and Harry up to that Sunday morning. Fred
Clinch said that he had gone down the river in
his skiff about ten o'clock and had seen them sit-

ting side by side, fishing, and that while they were speaking to him they spoke to each other and that they were both in good humor and very evidently friendly. Other people had passed the two going to the bridge and said that they seemed happy and friendly.

There could be but one possible motive for the crime, which led, of course, directly to Mary West. Harry Packer might have been insanely jealous of Amos and been able to hide it, while he had actually been planning to do away with his rival.

Excitement ran riot in Soleby. Never before had such a crime been committed in the peaceful village; never before had its inhabitants been so thrilled, so aroused, so horrified. Soleby became important: city newspapers told the story and made Soleby famous, for a few days. Soleby talked it all over, and over and over and over, went back years and years to scrape up evidence, recalled little incidents that proved this, that, and the other thing. A Soleby man or woman who evolved a new theory of how the blow might have been struck, found ready listeners until the theory was torn to shreds and, perforce, abandoned. Where Harry Packer might have gone or not gone, when he would be caught, and why the police did not find him furnished topics of

conversation whenever two people met on the
street, at gatherings at the village store, at the
post-office, everywhere.

Summer came and with it the city people, and
the story and theories were told all over again,
dozens of times. Samuel Lyle came to Soleby
for a month's visit and heard all about it, facts,
theories and all. The case interested him. He
listened to the story and the theories, he heard
about Mary West, he went down to the bridge
over the Salt River and sat there for a long time;
but he said very little, until one day he spoke to
Mrs. Fox, who was Harry Packer's sister and
kept a store in the village.

"If your brother is ever found and brought to
trial, I will defend him, if he wishes me to."

"He did n't do it, I know he did n't," Mrs. Fox
cried. Mr. Lyle would not argue that point, but
simply said that, as things stood, her brother
would have need of a lawyer experienced in cases
of that sort, and that he would be glad to help
him.

The search for Harry Packer went on in every
part of the country, but not a trace of him was
found until late in the autumn, and then he was
arrested in Boston as he was leaving a vessel in
the harbor. He said he knew nothing whatever
of Amos Rose's death. He said that some time
after Fred Clinch had spoken to him and Amos

that morning Amos had said that Mary West had promised to marry him. He, Harry, loved Mary; he always had and he always would, and he could n't stay around Soleby and again see Mary married to another man, even if that man was his friend. He decided then and there to go away and stay away. He had left Amos fishing on the bridge pier and had gone home, put a few clothes together, taken what money he had, gone to Boston, and gotten drunk. Then he had signed up for a voyage on a freighter. During the months that followed he had changed his mind about staying away from Soleby and if he had not been arrested would have gone back of his own free will.

Such was the case against Harry Packer when he came to trial in a little court-house in the county-seat, and on this evidence the district attorney, sworn to perform his duty as prosecutor, expected to convict him of first-degree murder. The state's case was based on circumstantial evidence: no one had seen the crime committed and it was only by a process of reasoning and elimination that it could be brought home to Harry Packer. The strength of the state's case lay in great part in the weakness of the defense.

To all intents and purposes Harry Packer had no defense. It had required no keen mind to invent the story which he told of his actions on that

Sunday morning and thereafter: it was a simple denial, in the face of all the evidence, that he had committed the crime. His sole hope lay in the fact that the prosecution must prove the case against him beyond a reasonable doubt, and to do this the prosecution must prove the opportunity to do the killing, must show a motive and must produce a plausible theory of how the blow was struck, and then, perhaps, show that only Harry Packer could have killed Amos.

The court-room was crowded. All Soleby was there, tense with excitement, glorying in the horror of it, thrilled, nervous, ashamed, expectant. It was almost as though Soleby expected to see a hanging then and there, and yet as though Soleby were at a play, staged specially for its benefit.

Few had seen Harry Packer since his arrest and he was an object of curiosity — and an object of loathing. When he pleaded not guilty to the charge against him there was a hush in the room as though the lie were in itself a terrible thing.

As, one by one, laboriously, the jury was selected, a change came over the people in the court-room: slowly there came to them the sensation that they were in a place almost holy; before they had heard one word of evidence there came to them the knowledge that they should not judge lest they themselves be judged. It was not a hanging nor a play, but a house of justice, of honest men, freed of all prejudice, of rancor, of hate, of vindictiveness, holding in their hands the life of their fellow man.

Such were the personality and the voice of Samuel Lyle, the prisoner's counsel.

Finally the jury were chosen and the district attorney outlined his case to them; this done, he placed on the stand the man who had found the body of Amos Rose, who told when and where he had found it. Mr. Lyle asked the witness no questions.

Then came the physician who had made the autopsy, and he explained that death had been caused by the blow on the head and not by drowning and that death had been instantaneous. On cross-examination Mr. Lyle handed the witness a skull and asked him to show the jury the location, shape, and size of the wound which had caused death. The witness did this, in great detail, showing where the blow had been struck, and the exact dimensions of the indentation it had made.

The next witness was Fred Clinch, the last man with the exception of Harry Packer who was known to have seen Amos alive. By him the district attorney proved that the two men were on the bridge pier together at about ten o'clock on the Sunday morning. On cross-examination by

Mr. Lyle, Clinch said that from his position in his skiff he could not see the floor of the pier and therefore could not see any comparatively small article which might have been on it.

Mr. Lyle asked Clinch whether or not he had ever gone fishing with Amos Rose and Harry Packer, either singly or together, and Clinch said that he had, many times.

"I presume that you always took substantially the same things with you when you went fishing?" Mr. Lyle asked.

"Yes, sir."

"What did you usually take?"

Clinch said that they took poles, tackle, bait, basket, pipe, tobacco, knives, and that was about all. Mr. Lyle asked him to think carefully whether or not he could remember their ever having taken anything else with them. Clinch could remember nothing.

Mr. Lyle asked Clinch to tell on what part of the bridge pier Packer and Rose had been sitting, and Clinch said that they were very close to the bridge framework itself, not over ten or fifteen feet from it.

Mary West testified that Amos Rose and Harry Packer had proposed marriage to her, both before she married William West and after he died. Amos Rose had asked her only once or twice to marry him during the two or three months preceding his death, but he had called on her often and had indicated a great affection for her. On the other hand, Harry Packer had asked her over and over again to marry him: he had broached the subject at every opportunity.

Mrs. West admitted, under pressure by the district attorney, that she had teased Harry by telling him that if she ever married again she would marry Amos Rose, but she said that she had told him that she was not going to marry any one, and she denied emphatically that she had ever told Amos that she would marry him, or that she had ever said anything to him which might encourage him to believe that she would do so. She said that Amos was a man of good reputation, that he was a very serious man, that she believed he always told the truth, and that he was not the sort of man who would lie to his friend Packer about her or about what she had said.

Mr. Lyle did not cross-examine Mrs. West.

Mrs. Green, in whose house Harry Packer had lived, said that on the Sunday morning in question she had gone to church and had returned about a quarter before one, and had not seen Harry then. She had been the first to go to his room after his disappearance and had found that he had taken his clothes with him. He had left no word about going away; usually if he was to be away over night he told her.

On cross-examination Mr. Lyle asked her if she had seen Harry Packer leave to go fishing.   Mrs. Green said she had, and Mr. Lyle asked her to tell as nearly as she could remember what Harry Packer had had with him. She said that she could n't remember exactly, but that she knew he had a fishing-pole and tackle and he had said that Amos Rose was going to bring the bait.

" Packer went fishing rather often, did n't he? " asked Mr. Lyle.

" Yes, sir."

" You saw him leave your house many times to go fishing? "

" Yes, sir."

" Can you remember ever having seen him take anything with him besides his fishing-tackle, basket, bait, and such small articles as he may have had in his pockets? "

" No, sir."

" Think carefully, please, Mrs. Green. I know of course that you would tell nothing but what you believe to be true, but it is sometimes difficult to think clearly when one is not used to testifying on the stand, and I want you to take as much time as you wish to refresh your memory on this point. Please try to remember whether in all the times you have seen Harry Packer leave your house to go fishing he had with him any article except those which you have described and those which he may have had in his pockets where you could not see them."

Mrs. Green did her best to refresh her memory but could not remember Harry Packer's ever taking with him any articles except those already mentioned.

Then the district attorney proved by the police that a long search had been made for Harry Packer without success until he had been arrested on a freighter in Boston, six months after Amos Rose's death. He proved further that he had been on the same vessel all of that time, and that he had given another name than his own. He then proved that no letter had been received from him during that time by his sister, his only near relative.

Then the prosecution rested.

Mr. Lyle put Harry Packer on the stand and Harry Packer told his story as he told it when he was arrested.

"What did you and Rose take with you that morning when you went fishing?" asked Mr. Lyle.

"I took a pole and tackle and such things as I had in my pockets. Amos took a basket and the bait."

"Nothing else?"

"No, I can't think of anything else."

"You are absolutely sure that you had nothing

with you except the articles which you have described and such small things as you may have had in your pockets?"

"Yes, sir."

"Why did you give another name than your own to the steamship company?" Mr. Lyle asked.

"I was drunk when I did it, and I can't be sure, but I guess it was because I didn't want people to know I was doing that kind of work, or where I was. I'd made up my mind never to come back home then. When once I'd given that name I stuck to it."

"Why didn't you write to your sister?"

"I didn't want her to know what I was doing, not till I'd changed my mind and decided to come back, and then I put off writing till I'd 'a' got here as soon as a letter."

"Cross-examine," said Mr. Lyle.

The district attorney could not shake Packer's story. It was so simple and so easy to manufacture that the district attorney had no hope of catching Packer in any contradictions, and in the end Packer's story stood before the jury exactly as he had told it.

Mrs. Rose, Amos's mother, was the next witness and to her Mr. Lyle put the same question that he had put to Mrs. Green, and received the same answer. She had seen Amos leave to go fishing that morning as she had seen him leave many times before and she could not recall seeing him take any articles with him except those which had already been mentioned by preceding witnesses.

Mr. Lyle's next witness was Arthur Jones, a civil engineer, who said that he had made a plan showing the bridge, the river, the roadway, piers, etc., and he produced this plan. He stated that the floor of the bridge pier was twenty-eight feet below the driveway and that the pier itself was not visible to pedestrians on the roadway or to persons in automobiles driving along the road.

"Then," said Mr. Lyle, "if Rose and Packer were fishing at a point fifteen feet away from the bridge proper, or for that matter on any point of the pier itself, they could not be seen by any one passing along the Shore Road unless that person made a point of stopping, leaning over the concrete rail of the bridge, and looking down?"

The witness said that that was correct.

"You have examined the roadway where it crosses the bridge and for a distance of half a mile on each side?"

"I have."

"And you found it in good condition?"

"Yes, sir, in excellent condition."

"And straight and level so that it may be seen for a considerable distance ahead from any point within half a mile of the bridge?"

"Yes, sir."

"The roadway is such that automobiles might, with safety, drive over it at a considerable rate of speed, say thirty or forty miles an hour?"

"Yes, sir."

The district attorney saw no reason for questioning these facts and did not cross-examine Jones.

Mr. Lyle then placed the road supervisor on the stand and from him obtained the information that no repairs of any sort had been made to the road in the vicinity of the Salt River bridge since the previous year and that therefore the road had been in at least as good condition on the Sunday in question as it had been when the examination was made by Jones, the engineer.

Then followed two witnesses who had met Rose and Packer on their way to the bridge and Mr. Lyle asked both of them to tell as nearly as they could what those two men had had with them. Again he elicited the same information — rods, tackle, an open basket containing bait, and such articles as they might have had in their pockets and which therefore could not be seen.

Then one after the other, to the number of ten, Mr. Lyle placed men on the stand who had gone fishing with Rose and Packer many times, and he put to them the same question, namely, what were they in the habit of taking with them when they went fishing and had they ever taken anything except the articles enumerated by preceding witnesses? All of these ten witnesses testified that they could remember no article which they or Packer or Rose had ever taken with them other than those described.

Then Mr. Lyle asked the district attorney to produce such articles as had been discovered on the bridge pier on the Monday morning on which the search for Amos Rose had begun. One by one Mr. Lyle picked them up and showed them to the jury — the basket, the knife, the bottle, Amos's pipe, and then the fishing-rod and line which had been found floating in the water; and then he said, most unexpectedly:

" The defense rests, if your Honor please."

The district attorney addressed the jury, demanding a verdict of murder in the first degree, insisting that Harry Packer killed Amos Rose. The motive was plain and it was the strongest of all motives, a man's love for a woman and jealousy of a rival. Packer had the opportunity to do the deed. He was alone with Rose all Sunday morning, as far as any one knew. No one had seen either man from ten o'clock, when Clinch saw them, until twelve o'clock, when several

people saw Packer return to the village alone.
Packer evaded every one he met, he spoke to no
one, he told no one that he was going away. He
went away, giving a false name so that he might
not be traced, and while he was away he had with
him always the knowledge that he might some
day be caught and accused of the crime, and he
had accordingly concocted the story he had told
on the stand. He had said it to himself over and
over again, turned it and twisted it, memorized
it. He was cunning enough to so frame it that
it could not be disproved directly. But it had
been disproved by his own flight. It was beyond
human credence that an innocent man should do
what Packer had done.

The state had not produced the weapon with
which Rose had been killed, nor could it sur-
mise what weapon had been used. If Packer had
carefully laid his plans to kill Rose he might well
have previously concealed his weapon somewhere
about the bridge and, the crime committed, disposed of it in any one of a thousand ways. If
the determination to kill Rose had been formed
after they reached the pier, then Packer might
have found a weapon on or near the bridge and,
coming up behind his unsuspecting victim, struck
the blow which killed him. He knew well that
the instrument of death must be disposed of and
there were unlimited ways of disposing of it.

The weapon, what it was, and what had become of it, were unimportant. That which stood out from all the evidence was the motive, the opportunity to kill, and the flight from justice of a guilty man — a guilty man who, tormented, driven wild and overwhelmed by the horror of his act, had been drawn back by irresistible force to the scene of his crime.

The distict attorney addressed the jury for an hour and a half and during all that time Mr. Lyle sat slumped down in his chair with his hands hanging loosely over its arms and his eyes closed almost as though he were asleep. So far as any one could tell Mr. Lyle did not hear a word that the district attorney said.

Then Mr. Lyle rose and stood before the jury and spoke to them as he might have spoken to men sitting with him around a small table, and yet every one in the big court-room heard every word distinctly. He explained to the jury that it was the duty of the state to prove that the prisoner was guilty and that it was not the duty of the defense to prove that the prisoner was innocent, and furthermore that the state must prove the prisoner's guilt so clearly and so positively that a reasonable, unprejudiced, intelligent man, experienced in the everyday affairs of the world and with his share of common sense, could have no doubt of the accused's guilt.

"Not one contradictory statement has been made here on the stand," Mr. Lyle went on. "Every witness has told what he or she believes to be the truth, without fear and without malice. No statement made by one witness denies or even qualifies any statement made by any other witness. You are very fortunate in not being forced to decide whether a witness has been misled by his perception or whether he is lying. The facts, so far as it is humanly possible to know them, are clearly before you.

"You may take exception to my statement that no contradictory evidence has been given to you. Mary West has said that she did not promise Amos Rose to marry him. I believe that Mrs. West has told the truth; I think that you must believe so, for it is perfectly evident that Mrs. West is an honest and intelligent woman. Yet Harry Packer says that Amos Rose said that Mary West had promised to marry him. You will see at once that there is no contradiction here, for Amos Rose may have lied, he may have attempted to joke or to tease his friend. I do not know that he lied or joked or teased, but unless he did Harry Packer's story is not true, and if it is not true he is guilty of murder beyond all reasonable doubt. That is the issue which is being tried. I cannot analyze any man's mind, much less the mind of a man who is dead and whom I never saw. You must decide, from all the evidence, whether Rose lied or joked or teased that Sunday morning.

"Packer has told you his story. He alone knows whether or not it is true. There is no possible way to prove that it is not true, except by bringing forth circumstantial evidence to disprove it, and this the prosecution has attempted to do.

"First the state has told you that Packer had a motive to kill Rose. It cannot be denied that the state has shown a foundation for a motive, but can you rear a firm and strong structure upon that foundation? Once before Harry Packer saw the woman he loved become engaged to and marry another man, and in that case, although the man was not his friend, he accepted the condition calmly and with good sense, as any sane man would do. Was any one surprised that Harry Packer did not murder William West? I think not. And yet the state tells you that Harry Packer killed his friend, perhaps his best friend, because he was afraid that Mary West might marry him.

"How many of you have not loved and lost, been the victim of a woman's love for another man? And can you imagine killing the man, would the thought ever occur to you to kill your successful rival? I think not, and Harry Packer has always been known as the same sort of man that all of you are — a sane, reasonable, honest man.

" The state has laid before you a motive, but it is not a strong motive, except in stories of bandits, of pirates, of the bad men of the moving pictures, of lurid literature. It is not a motive at all among everyday, civilized, good men. And consider for a moment what purpose the crime could possibly have served Harry Packer. If he had desired his friend's death, if he had determined to bring it about, would he have killed him by striking him on the head with some instrument the nature of which even the district attorney and all the sleuths of the state cannot even guess at? Would he not have killed him in the dark of the night, with a knife, or a revolver, with some sure and quick instrument, instead, as the state claims, of attempting to kill him in broad daylight, beside a well-traveled road, with automobiles passing constantly, when many people knew they were together? Can you imagine a sane man committing murder in that fashion?

" Suppose that Harry Packer did not plan the murder of his friend and rival, but committed the deed in a moment of anger, of passion, where did he obtain the instrument, and what instrument did he obtain? Every witness without ex-

ception has told you that to the best of their
knowledge and belief Rose and Packer had with
them only the things with which they fished and
such things as pocket-knives and pipes and
tobacco. The bridge and the piers beneath it
were as clean as a penny whistle. Not a word
has been said of a bolt or a bar or a blessed thing
being on it, and the district attorney would have
suggested something of the sort to you if his conscience had permitted, but he is an honorable
man and would not — he could not, by inference
or otherwise — lead you to believe that such a
thing was there. Where, then, did Harry Packer
find it, whatever it was? I cannot imagine and
I doubt if you can.

"Harry Packer fled. The state says he fled
as the guilty fly. I say that Harry Packer, if he
had killed Amos Rose, would have stayed here
and denied it. Harry Packer did not kill Rose
— of that I am sure — but if he had, would he
have fled? If he had killed Rose would he not
have known that flight would be a confession?
Would he not have known that his only hope
would be to stay in Soleby and deny the act?
He did what any man might have done: his sor-
row, his fancied humiliation, got the better of
him and he went away to Boston. And there he
got drunk and, drunk, or suffering from the after
effects of drunkenness, he went on board a ship

about to sail and sailed with her. You must,
before you render your verdict, make up your
minds whether or not Harry Packer told the
truth on the witness-stand. I believe he did. I
ask you to consider only whether his acts were
the acts of a murderer or the acts of a disappointed lover.

"What good could Harry Packer do himself by
killing Amos Rose? A motive has been suggested
by the state. Compare the motive for the crime
with the object of the crime. Bear these two
words clearly in mind during your deliberations:
' motive '—' object '— or perhaps you may prefer
the word ' purpose ' to ' object.' What purpose
would Amos Rose's death serve Harry Packer?
Revenge? No, you may put that aside. Murder
and flight? What purpose would they serve?
Would they win for him the hand of Mary West,
would they bring him peace and comfort, would
they give him wealth or fame? You know that
they would not, you know that they would bring
him only hell on earth — and eventually, if the
law were successful, death. That is so evident
that I need say not one word more about it.

"And so I say to you that the whole theory of
the prosecution falls to pieces of its own weight.
It is beyond the power of man to believe that a
sane man would commit any murder at all in
broad daylight, where he might well be seen, by

a clumsy method and with an instrument that came out of the clouds. How then can it be believed that a sane man would commit, in those circumstances, a murder which — even if he had no conscience, no heart, no soul — could do him only harm, could only ruin him forever?

"You may ask yourself the question, 'If Packer did n't kill Rose, who did?' That, gentlemen, is not a fair question to ask yourselves. It is not the question which you are here to answer. And yet it is not altogether an unreasonable question. It is a question that must, I think, have already sprung up in your minds as it has in mine.

" If Harry Packer did not kill Amos Rose, who did? I do not know, you do not know, nobody knows; nor, I think, will any one ever know absolutely, finally, positively, beyond any mathematical doubt, beyond all physical possibility of error. And yet I believe that, beyond all *reasonable* doubt, it may be shown how Amos Rose died.

" Miracles happen: we call them miracles because we have no other word. If our Lord in heaven should prove to us that, on that Sunday morning last spring, a meteor, a fragment of a star, fell from the sky and, falling, struck Amos Rose and killed him, that indeed would be a miracle, and the defense asks you to accept no wild imaginings of an inventive mind. The de-

fense will lay before you a theory as to Rose's
death, a possibility which it believes to be a probability and a far greater probability than that
Harry Packer should take it into his head to kill
his lifelong friend, that he should have at hand
a weapon capable of inflicting the wound which
caused death, that he should so far lose his reason as to believe that Rose's death in such circumstances could in any way increase his chances
of winning the hand of the woman he loved, or
serve any useful purpose whatsoever.

"The physical evidence of the probability
which the defense asks you to consider lies before you." Mr. Lyle took the bottle from the
table and held it before the jury. "Where did
this bottle come from? It was found lying very
close to the spot where Rose was when he was
killed. Packer denies having taken it with him
or that Rose had it with him; innumerable witnesses have told you that neither Rose nor Packer
had such a bottle with him, or at least that they
did not see any such bottle or any article of
similar nature in their possession that morning.
Would one of those men have concealed a bottle
of this description about his person? It has been
stated by many witnesses that so far as they
knew neither of those men had ever taken a bottle
of any sort with him on their fishing-excursions;
neither drank intoxicating liquor; drinking-

water was close by. You may suggest that it had been left on the bridge pier by other persons, and I answer that that may be so, I do not know. And yet the witness for the state has told you that the instrument which killed Amos Rose was round and flat like an enormous hammer head. The bottom of this bottle is round and flat. The learned witness said that the diameter of the object causing death was about two and one-half inches; the diameter of this bottle is two and three-eighths inches, as nearly as I can determine it.

"The district attorney, performing his sworn duty, has not suggested to you that Harry Packer took this bottle in his hand and struck Rose with it. He and you and I know that that would be an absurd conjecture. If Packer had done so he would have grasped the bottle by its neck and struck with its side. The wound itself proves that the blow was not so struck. No man could grasp this bottle as I am grasping it now around its larger part or even about its neck and strike thus, straight down, with sufficient force to crush a man's skull. The prosecution admits by its silence that no such blow was or could have been struck.

"You have been told that the roadway over the Salt River bridge is wide, hard, and smooth; you know that the country is open all about, that

the road may be seen for long distances ahead
and you know that automobiles are driven fast
along that road and over that bridge, and you
know from your own experience that when a
heavy object is thrown from a swiftly moving
vehicle it takes on, undiminished in the air,
the speed of the vehicle. An automobile traveling at the rate of thirty miles per hour covers
forty-four feet in a second; an object thrown from
it perpendicularly moves forward at substantially that rate, and if it is thrown forward gains
in addition the acceleration lent it by the thrower's arm. Furthermore, as it falls gravity
gives it increased speed. If this bottle were
thrown from an automobile moving at thirty
miles per hour and fell thirty feet, as it must
have to strike Rose, then it was moving close to
seventy feet per second when it struck — a great
speed. A bottle traveling through the air at the
rate of seventy feet per second and striking on
its side or striking, in any position, against an
unyielding surface such as concrete, rock, or steel
would break into a thousand pieces; there can be
no doubt whatever of that. But if this bottle
killed Rose, as I believe it did, then it did not
strike a hard, immovable object. It struck his
cap, under which was his hair, and beneath his
hair was the bone of his head, which compared
with concrete, rock, or steel is a very soft, fragile

substance.   Furthermore, Rose was relaxed and his whole head and body gave to the impact: the shock was absorbed.   The glass of the bottle is thick and strong and the wound shows that it struck fairly on its end.

" Striking against concrete or steel, the bottle would leave no mark — a scratch perhaps, a bit of powdered glass, but no indentation. You know the depth of the indentation it made in Rose's head. Strike the firm, unyielding surface of a brick or concrete wall with your fist and the pain is great; yet you may strike the panel or a light door a hard blow with your fist with little if any discomfort, and the reason is that the door bends, gives, to the blow, a very small fraction of an inch, and yet enough to absorb the shock and save your fist. An egg held longitudinally between the palms of the hands cannot be crushed by any pressure a man may exert against it; yet its shell is broken by a slight tap with a spoon.

" You know from your own experience that if you wish to dispose of an empty bottle from an automobile you will refrain from throwing it to the side of the roadway but will make some attempt to throw it where, if it breaks, it can do no harm. What more natural place can be chosen for disposing of a bottle than over the side of a bridge?

" I do not know that this bottle was thrown

from an automobile, or that if it was so thrown
it struck and killed Amos Rose.   I do not know
those things absolutely, beyond all possibility of
error.   But I know that bottles are so thrown
and that if a bottle were thrown in this case he
who threw it expected it to fall harmlessly in the
river below, for, from an automobile, the men below, or even the pier itself, could not be seen.

"I am asking you not to believe in miracles,
but to weigh carefully in your minds whether
such an occurrence did not, in all probability, take
place and to compare this probability with the
probabilities presented to you by the prosecution.
If it did occur it was not a miracle, but simply a
fact that a man threw a bottle from an automobile over a bridge-rail — an ordinary, everyday
occurrence — and that the bottle struck and
killed a man below.   The probability that this
is what happened brings crashing down into
nothingness every scintilla of evidence, all argument, and every theory presented to you by the
State.

"I believe that in the jury room, when you
have freed your minds of all extraneous matters
and consider the two probabilities side by side,
you will conclude quickly and emphatically that
not only has it not been proven beyond a reasonable doubt that Harry Packer killed Amos Rose

but that beyond all reasonable doubt Harry Packer *did not* kill Amos Rose."

The jury was out less than an hour and returned a verdict of " not guilty."

Soleby, too, believed that it had been proved beyond all reasonable doubt that Harry Packer had not killed his friend; and it is reasonable to presume, in view of what happened shortly afterward, that Mary West had no doubt whatever as to Harry's innocence.

www.ingramcontent.com/pod-product-compliance
Lightning Source LLC
Chambersburg PA
CBHW011350010726
47494CB00008B/2246